P9-CAX-662

THE CRIME

A NOVEL BY

STEPHEN LONGSTREET

SIMON AND SCHUSTER • NEW YORK • 1959

LIBRARY OF CONGRESS CATALOG CARD NUMBER: 59–13146
MANUFACTURED IN THE UNITED STATES OF AMERICA
BY GEO. MCKIBBIN & SON, INC., NEW YORK, N. Y.

TO MY BROTHER AND SISTERS,

WHO WERE THERE IN THE FORMATIVE YEARS

BEFORE MERE WORLDLY WISDOM

GEORGE
MILDRED
HANNAH

Acts don't make murders, circumstances do. . . .

—CLARENCE DARROW

A WORD BEFORE

WHEN THE AUTHOR was a very young man in his late teens, he was involved, as a new and unimportant reporter, in an event that was labeled "The Crime of the Century." The murders are now forgotten, except by some burrowing student of the yellow files of old trials. The massive structure of law was baffled by the case. All the people involved are now dead. It shocked, and in a way invigorated, an entire community; the accused were from the top of the social pattern, members of a society that perhaps no longer has the value and importance it once held in the American scene.

It was a crime of passion, but not the ordinary matter of a country case of lewd and lascivious doings by mean, depraved people. The victims, as they are remembered, were charming and well-liked people. The crime was committed in a brutal manner and with a sadistic cruelty that made it almost impossible to believe that the accused could have committed it. It remains today unsolved, unexplained—though I have attempted to project a solution on these pages.

It is for these reasons that I have moved the story forward in time, so that it can be judged against our contemporary scene, changed its locale to the same kind of setting but in another state, and re-created its leading actors as fictional characters. The basic events and some of the trial strategies remain the same, but the emotions of both sides and their personal reactions are those of a novelist, not the actual lurid, and in many cases misleading, gossip of the town or the journalism of the period. It was assumed by the courts that the only three basic defenses in murder were (and are): that the crime hadn't happened, that the accused didn't do it, or that the actions were legally justified. In this crime there was added a strong factor to confuse the law—the social and political power of the defendants.

S. L.

Good and evil lie close together.
Seek no artistic unity in character. . . . .
                                    LORD ACTON

Give me a cup of sack to make mine eyes
look red that it may be thought I have
wept; for I must speak in passion. . . . .
                                    —FALSTAFF

The prosecutor is trying three people accused of murder; they are rich and influential and he is poor. Based on the Hall-Mills case.

BOOK ONE

MONDAY

CHAPTER I

THE DREAMER

THE MAN TOSSING on the big double bed begged mercy of his dream. He tore at the skin of sleep trying to come awake into a Monday morning. He climbed a long way up in the dark of the courthouse where he stood in the golden-oak trial room and glanced at the papers in his hand and said, "In the matter of the State of Maryland, County of King, this court sitting in the matter of Sarah Rodman, Mikel Hawley and William Hawley, indicted for murder . . ." The paneled walls of worn golden chestnut shook, the heavy tarnished silver lighting fixture rotated with the movement of the earth on its orbit, and a white plaster dust, bitter and choking, fell from the ceiling.

"Objection," said Roger Tindell, his red face flushed with

bourbon and fox-hunting weather, his portly football figure (Harvard '36, the year of a bad team) dressed in well-tailored hunting pink. "Objection is that it is irrelevant and immaterial to suggset a Hawley—three Hawleys—would, could, did commit murder in such a foul, mean, nasty manner and . . ."

The sleeper, eyes wide open, turned to the high bench of carved pearwood. "If counselor would only let me finish . . ."

Judge Wilmont Riggs accepted a frosted drink topped with a sprig of mint in a silver goblet, took it from Roger Tindell with one hand and with the other banged the handleless gavel he always used on the ancient historical wood in front of him. "Objection overruled. *What* damn fool has crushed the mint leaves instead of bruising them?"

The sleeper was suddenly awake. The dream had been one of the bad ones. Sarah Rodman. Sarah Rodman? He lay thinking and remembering. . . .

. . . When I was twelve years old I saw for the first time the gardens of Hawley House up on Barraclough Manor, where the best people lived. And I met Sarah Rodman. She was Sarah Hawley then, very beautiful, I thought, with the best of manners, who greeted a group of twenty schoolchildren invited, after careful screening—I never found out how I was included (unless I played The Game well)—to attend the birthday party for Sarah ("so democratic") in the Hawley gardens, to eat the special ice cream sent over from Baltimore, to stand later in paper hats while the photographer of *The Hawleytown Home News* lined us up for the picture to appear in the Sunday issue.

As we waited for The Game I remember Mikel Hawley, a year or two older than most of us, sneering in his good looks, his hands deep in the pockets of a prep-school suit, and Batty Billie, his brother, openmouthed and tearing petals off flowers and wiping his nose on the back of his hand.

"Now, The Game," said Miss Mortan, teacher of seventh-grade Self-Development. "We shall play The Game today as crossing the desert, the great American desert, a party of gold hunters. And some shall be the scouts, and some the wagon train, and some the attacking Indians. All within the boundaries of the rules of The Game."

We looked at each other glumly, itchy in our best clothes, shy at all the splendor of this house and grounds, and damn bored by The Game (which Miss Mortan made us play three times a month at school).

Miss Mortan held up a thin hand, brown and freckled. "We play The Game with our minds only, as you know. No toys, no costumes, no weapons. With the imagination alone. And seriously—always in character. Only The Game is real while it's played. Now appoint yourself characters, invent people. The scouts will move ahead and be cut off by Indians and driven into the desert, and almost die of thirst. Now, Hiram Ott, and you, Abe Pedlock, begin—as scouts, shall we say—through the pass, between those pine trees. Get going."

Miss Mortan waved us on. Hiram grinned and shaded his eyes, and said, "I'll just scout down that way, Kit. Yo' go yonder, see what's that way."

Feeling a fool, I went ahead, wary and careful, stepping with care. Then I went quickly, into the lower, wilder gardens, near the rocky edge that fell a hundred and fifty feet down to the Chichester River. Out of sight of the spreading Game, I lay on my back, staring at the blue sky, wondering when the ice cream and food would be served, knowing Miss Mortan would develop The Game a long time and demand that we suffer fully the pangs of thirst and hunger, desert winds, the pain of Indian arrow wounds, the bleeding feet of pioneers; Miss Mortan, inventor of The Game, was a fanatic on Self-Development.

I must have dozed off in the hot sun because suddenly I was staring into the dark eyes of Sarah Hawley, who was leaning over me. I wanted to say hello, but I saw she was gripped in The Game. "Friend," she said in a low husky voice, "me no bad Indian."

In the expected words of The Game I answered, "Me white friend."

Sarah fell down against me, her party dress grass-stained and torn. "No water. No water long time. White scout have water?"

"Have water," I said, not breaking any rules of The Game. "But must go long way. Have water only for one small drink every two days."

The girl rolled tighter against me; she smelled of sweat and bath powder. "Tongue black with thirst. No can move."

"We travel now. Must reach spring at Table Rock in four days. No water till moon come up." I looked into her open pink mouth, her licking tongue.

Her hand gripped my arm. "I show scout way, friend?"

"Friend."

Staggering to our feet, leaning against each other, we moved slowly down the gardens and their thick bush.

I felt we had lost contact with The Game. The sun was high over the river. I thought her long legs very attractive as we flopped ahead into a green hole in the bush.

She pulled me after her and sat cross-legged, showing, to my horror (and interest), brief lacy drawers. We sat deep in the bush; it grew half neglected here, heavy and old. It had been planted a long time ago to hold firmly the earth and rocks of the river-bank. Sarah scratched an armpit and put a hand down the front of her dress and pulled out a pack of crumpled Turkish cigarettes. "We smoke peace pipe till dark, white scout. Then move to avoid the enemy, toward spring Table Rock."

I didn't dare refuse. I took a bent cigarette and put it in my mouth. "Is sign of peace between us."

"Is sign." Sarah skillfully lighted my cigarette from a pack of matches, and her own, and inhaled and spit a bit of loose tobacco from her white, even teeth. "I am princess of my tribe. You too are not like others. Maybe we never get back to our people." She threw away the cigarette, put her arms around me and said in a new kind of voice, "Don't be such a stick. Kiss me."

I kissed her, holding my cigarette away from us. I had never seriously, intimately kissed a girl before. The cigarettes were discarded; they smoldered in the grass. Over us the spears of large flat green leaves, of some strange bush, cast shadows mottled and moving slowly in the river wind. I felt myself in a strange new mood, a fever of elation, fear and guilt. The girl smell was overpowering. We were suddenly flat on the grass. She was whispering to me. "You do like it, don't you? What is your name?"

"Abe. Abe Pedlock. Listen. The Game must be almost over by now. I'm going."

Sarah laughed and lifted her face and it was flushed and her eyes were larger and darker. She bent down and savagely bit my lip. She got up and said calmly with disdain, "You don't really know anything at all about girls, do you?"

I tasted the salt of the bite on my lower lip, and I stood up dusting my best and only party clothes. There was just a little blood in my mouth and it didn't hurt as yet. "I guess we really better get back."

"You want to go right back?"

Sarah looked at me closely, interested. She came over and put her hand inside my shirt and rubbed my chest with a steady, increasing pressure. One very red drop of blood fell on the ground.

"You like that, Abe?"

"I don't know."

She was almost as tall as I was and she looked at me and I was aware she already had breasts—small hard objects I could feel against me. I was frightened of Sarah, and confused because I did like it, and I did not know enough about what she expected and what my guilt would be if I displayed any boldness.

"You do know, don't you, Abe?"

"You're crazy," I said. "Real crazy."

"Nice and crazy."

I turned away, head down, and buttoned my shirt. Far off, Miss Mortan's voice called out over the landscaped gardens. "Everyone in. Everyone in."

"Don't go," Sarah said.

I broke away, sobbing, angry at myself, angry at Sarah Hawley, floundering in the bush. I didn't go up to the house to get the ice cream and food. I ran down toward the road, tripping over low stone walls and running across beds of flowers—red, pink and small blue ones. I ran through the big stone gates and down the road. I walked, breathing hard, till I came to the bridge that led across the river to Hawleytown, and it was a long way to walk as the sun set in the west. All the way across I tried to get the stains off my clothes and the dust out of my hair, and all I could feel was the bite of her teeth and the burn of the pain as my lower lip swelled from the first time I met Sarah Rodman. She was very young then, and still Sarah Hawley. . . .

Remembering, he fell back into sleep, but he had escaped nothing. The nightmare took over again, and the judge finished banging his desk and went on with his shouting.

The fragments of the sleeper's fears began to fall softly, like snow. The sleeper passed up confidential trial memoranda to the judge, to amend and supplement his requests for instructions to the court.

He heard himself say, "I, A. Lincoln Pedlock, State of Maryland, County of King, prosecuting attorney in and for the County of King, for and in behalf of the People of the State of Maryland, come into said court in the September term thereof and give the court to understand and be informed that Sarah Rodman, Mikel Hawley and William (Batty Billie) Hawley, late of the city of Hawleytown and in the county aforesaid, in the nighttime of the said day (Where are my papers? The date, the date?) with force and arms did commit murder there to wit, contrary to the form of the statute (Is it the right form?)." The judge spun faster than light in his swivel chair.

The sleeper was almost awake now. One more good push on it and he would be free of the night dream. He would rise, dress and hurry to court. There was a heavy, hot day ahead. He looked over at his sleeping wife.

CHAPTER II

AWAKING

ABE PEDLOCK LOOKED DOWN at Fran asleep—mouth slightly open —at his side, and he wondered how she could have slept through his nightmare. He sat very still, head down, arms locked across his knees, in the big bed, aware of the close smell of sleep in the room of two familiar bodies—shameless from long habit. Beyond the drawn drapes of the big double windows facing on the street there was a suggestion of dawn and the whistle of early birds in the elms. The freight engine in the Pennsylvania Railroad river yards was puffing and grunting; an early delivery truck passed, rattling a loose fender. The smell of cut grass, night dew and old house became strong.

Abe silently, as carefully as he could, got out of the big double bed. The rag rug under his naked feet was warm. It would be another very hot day. Fran's body, molded to the mattress, stirred in the semidarkness. "Abe, what is it?"

Her voice, feathered with sleep, made him turn, and when he wanted to answer he saw she was deep in sleep again. He let himself out into the hall and opened the screen door to the sleeping porch and sundeck. Grit and dust were under his feet on the canvas floor. He and Fran had planned to sleep here on warm nights, but somehow the dragging of bedding and other bed comforts seemed too much of a task. Abe, large and square and in his late thirties, looked off at the rim of the sunrise coming across the eastern shore and over the town. In a few minutes it would cover the rise behind Hawleytown and already it was silverplating the church steeples, the chimneys of the Hawley packing plants on the bay, and the swinging masts of the pleasure boats and yachts tied to the docks of the yacht club on the inlet of the Chichester River. In half an hour Hawleytown would be fully alive and complaining of a hot day ahead. At ten court would convene under a faulty air-conditioning system, and he had only a hazy idea of just how he had planned to call his witnesses. He turned and went indoors, stopping a moment, breathless, as the screen door got away from his grip and closed with a clatter. He walked down the hall under old deer antlers and yellowing photographs of Fran's family in Confederate gray, and opened a door. He looked in on the children. Deedee, aged seven, was asleep on her side, showing teeth that would need braces, and the red ribbon threaded through her soft, corn-tinted hair just taking on color as the day grew stronger. She had the determined, foxlike little face of a pert beauty and already a graceful body that gave promise of being in the style of her mother's family, the Ormsbees. ("Man, all them Ormsbee gals are sure stacked.") Davey was in his crib; even at five he refused to give it up. He was sleeping on his stomach, a wet thumb in his mouth, a damp chin pressed against the sheeted mattress. He disliked a pillow. A solid, questioning child with red-gold hair and some remains of baby fat.

Their father closed the door after removing a yellow metal toy truck from his son's ribs. He went quickly downstairs and into the kitchen. He measured the coffee into the glass coffee-maker, cut a large segment of cornbread from under its plastic hood and put it into the oven to dry out. Back in the lower hall, from the halltree, an ancient piece of dulled mirror and battered mid-Victorian mahogany—a valuable heirloom, Fran said—he took a stuffed briefcase of worn but good black leather and went back into the kitchen. He put cream cheese on the cornbread, poured coffee into the huge handleless blue cup called by the kids the Big Daddy Cup, and began to chew on the bread between great gulps of scalding coffee, which he drank black and without sugar.

Opening the briefcase, Abe spread out his private notebook, the case book, the transcript of the trial as far as it had been transcribed, some of the trial brief and the worn list of witnesses. Those already called were marked with a neat red star, and those he was prepared to call were as yet unstarred.

For a large man, given to thickness, with a face of oversized plain features, only the eyes, very dark, very large, could be called beautiful. His red-brown hair was balding at the temples, and he needed a haircut. He ate, swallowed and drank, his mind and fingers active in the words spread before him on the smooth top of the kitchen table. He heard the copy of *The Hawleytown Home News* go thudding against the front steps. (He had saved the newsboy—yes, Joe Fry—from reform school; matter of hub caps off a blue Cadillac.) The scratch of the cat Tom at the back screen door, the snort of the bus down by Central and Maple as it came swinging into the curb to take the early riders toward jobs that began at dawn—these were background noises he usually ignored.

He rose to let in the old cat. It stiffly avoided any attempts at friendship, and he offered it none. The cat was ancient and thin.

"All right, in a minute you'll get fed."

He reread in his notebook the court pathologist's report. "There were multiple penetrating and perforating wounds in the body of George Rodman caused by a bullet and twenty-eight shotgun pellets. The bullet entered from the left, the front of the left shoulder, and emerged at the posterior aspect at the posterior axillary line after going through the heart and left lung. Some buckshot perforated at the level of the umbilicus, and the peritoneum and abdominal cavity were penetrated. The woman had a massive hemorrhage in both pleural spaces and . . ."

He heard Fran's slippers in the front hall, and she came in wearing a pale-yellow nightdress showing what a big and wonderful girl she was. She wore her taffy-colored hair short, and it was still mussed into a head of ringlets. She held the morning paper under one arm as if keeping it locked there and away from him.

"You could have slept another hour, Abe."

"I had enough sleep. I wish the bond issue to modernize the courthouse had passed. The old air system is worse than nothing. I'll take two extra shirts."

"It's going to be a hot one." Fran opened the refrigerator door and placed Tom's cut-up horse meat is his special dish near the back door. "He's old. Very old."

"Have Doc Veemer put him away."

"No. I couldn't do that. He'll drink some milk."

Abe took the paper from under his wife's arm. As usual, the print came off on his fingers. He saw Al Muller was giving the trial four-column headlines, which was modest; the national press was giving it full banners, and the news magazines and picture magazines were in town with full staffs. The best people didn't commit—or stand accused of—murder very often. He chewed the last bit of bread.

> A. LINCOLN PEDLOCK MAY PRODUCE MYSTERIOUS EYEWIT-
> NESS TODAY
> Rumors That Assistant District Attorney Has Surprise
> Continues As Rodman-Hawley Trial Enters Second
> Week

Abe was aware that Fran was reading over his shoulder. He was very tired, and he inhaled the sleepy, personal smell of his wife and revived old familiar desires. He half turned and put his arms around her hips, looked up at her, and put his head between her breasts. Closing his eyes, he sensed how close to breaking, how taut, he was. He had a momentary memory of sweet lust, but he knew that when he lifted his head and released her the comfort, the desire, the sense of communion would go.

Fran leaned down and kissed his cheek. "I wish Butch Vogelhofer were handling this. Or old Ed Hightower. Damn it, they got up the indictments."

"Fat chance of them trying for murder anybody connected with the Hawleys. The indictment was forced on them by a coroner's jury. Besides, Ed doesn't try many cases, and Carl is preparing the Wudder arson case."

"You think the jury will convict, Abe?"

She sat down facing him, pushing her soft light hair from a tanned brow.

"I've a good case. I've prepared it properly. Damn it, Fran, you awed by the Hawleys too?"

"I just don't believe they could be guilty of such a brutal thing. Reverend Rodman and Mrs. Nash were mutilated, weren't they? I mean, sexually—with safety-razor blades."

"Police photographs don't lie. Or do you think Tindell is right hinting they were doctored?"

"A woman like Sarah Rodman and her brothers—of course, Batty Billie isn't all there, but he's harmless—doing such things. I'm a dopey country hick, raised to think—oh, well . . . Why don't you have a more filling breakfast? Let me make you some bacon and eggs."

"Not in this weather." Abe kissed her on the mouth and stood up. "I want to check some testimony, get shaved, pick up a freshly cleaned suit." He threw the paper aside onto a chair. "I wish Al Muller didn't act as if I were a black Jew witch-master pulling Hasidic secrets out of hats of the Cabala. Evidence is evidence."

Fran stood close to him. Her face was earnest and as pale as its tan permitted. "You're determined after all our talks to put Maman Celie on the stand?"

Angry, he picked up his briefcase and went upstairs to dress.

CHAPTER III

THE MORNING

THE EARLY-MORNING promise of a hot day had been fulfilled. When Abe Pedlock left his house on Ann Street, wearing an already wrinkling tan linen suit and a Panama hat that only looked like a genuine Panama and needed a new yellow band, he was already uncomfortable from the heat. The slight rash on his neck itched, but he did not scratch it. Under his arm Abe carried his overstuffed briefcase, into which, between legal papers, had been put two fresh white shirts to which he would change at noon and during some break before court adjourned in the late afternoon.

Abe Pedlock, his water-slicked-down hair already escaping into

disorder, did not look back at the house. He disliked leaving Fran
when he was angry, but he felt anger at the town that had put
him in this position with his own family. At the corner Abe took
out one of the thin little black cigars he smoked, and he lighted it
slowly, pivoting around to look back at the house under its
frayed and elderly elms that could come down in the next summer storm, for the beetles were present. The house was still called
"the Ormsbee place," after the old woman who had left it to
Fran, "my favorite niece". He and Fran, well—he made a quick
calculation in his mind as he inhaled the strong, cheap Virginia
leaves—he and Fran had lived in it for eleven years. It had been
built solidly of old bridge timbers in the seventies, it had been im-
proved, repaired, partly destroyed by fire the year the *Titanic*
sank, attacked by termites. It had survived, and its last coat of
paint, tan with green trim, had been three years ago. It was Abe's
first real home, and if he became D.A. and later state senator
("And from there, who knows?" Jake Barton had said), they
would have to move first to Lexington Avenue where the town's
solid people lived, and then across the Chichester River to the
landscaped ledge of stone and garden of Barraclough Park, where
important, very important, local people raised up their ideas of
colonial- and plantation-style houses mixed with a few daring
modern shapes out of California, Frank Lloyd Wright and
Gropius.

The first lungfuls of the little Virginia stogie cheered Abe up.
He saw Deedee's and Davey's faces at the side window of the
kitchen, noses pressed to the glass. He waved at them, and Fran's
head appeared between the children's. He waved again and
Fran waved back, smiling the pert tomboy smile he could not
resist. In the front garden under a scattering rose tree Tom the
cat dozed in the sun, a blot of impressionistic red-orange fur; he
was thinner than Abe had ever remembered him. Tom had come
from Fran's aunt—with the house—as a lusty two-year-old cat
stallion.

Abe felt better for having waved at Fran, at his family, and,
puffing strongly on his thin stogie, he went down Ann Street past
the BOARDING HOUSE and ROOMS signs stuck onto shabby-genteel

houses. (Yes, the neighborhood is not what it used to be, but we'll stay as long as we can.)

The last trolley line in town met Ann Street as it curved down toward Lee Street. (First open trolley I've seen this year—with the straw seats that once went out to the Sand City Amusement Park. Soon it will be gone, and with it will grow dimmer the pleasures of me as a small sticky boy who carried a wicker lunch basket and sat with the local ball team on the front trolley seat right behind Old Jack Hammond, the motorman with the large waxed mustache who is called Old Cock because of his Cockney accent and his boasted powers of seduction over the local factory girls. Three parentcy orders out against him right now.)

Abe kept the problem of putting his key witness on the stand in the back of his mind, refusing to let it take over his thoughts. Ann Street still had charm and fine old trees. Lee Street was busier. He turned into it, moving down under the great stone railroad arch that lifted the trains over the city at treetop level. The street was already opening its shops, lowering the awnings and sweeping its interior debris into the gutters (against the city ordinance). Early farmers in muddy cars were loading feedbags, and most of the parking meters were not yet in use.

He was near Walker House, the rebuilt colonial tavern that was now a hotel, bar and eating place.

(I wish I knew more about George Rodman, the kind of man he really was. Eddie Desmond, who drove for the Rodmans, he's holding something back. A lot, I'm sure. But how can I get what I want out of Eddie? He worshiped Sarah and George Rodman, the way an undersized little Irishman, with an old biddy of a mother who had overprotected him, would. I hope the fancy out-of-town reporters aren't waiting for me outside the Walker House.)

CHAPTER IV

THE TOWN

THE WALKER HOUSE was a town landmark, even written up in a small book sold at local newsstands, *Hawleytown Landmarks and History,* by Samuel Edward Hightower. The way to know a town (we hate being called a town; we think of it ourselves, with its forty thousand population, as a city), the way to know a place, was to be born there (I was), and grow up there and deliver newspapers, push bargain-offer folders under doors, walk home late at night from the Bijou movie theater with your head spinning with images of manly horse-aided adventure, and girls' bodies and the smell of Lysol and popcorn butter and theater rugs full of insects.

(The town boy remembers the big tree fallen after a storm, the heat haze dancing on the cobblestones on Lee Street, the wind rattling the tin signs over the shops on a busy Saturday in town, when the farm trucks are parked nose to the curbs and the root produce and the farm stock has been sold and it is time to have a soda with two straws; even offer one to a girl you know in your high-school English class. Banal stuff to remember, but powerful, like all things retained from simpler times.)

Hawleytown was like some other towns Abe knew—a lot like other cities its size. And not like other towns. It had its own local pride, veracity and directness. The town lay sprawled among good land—sepia-brown land, with not too much fat on it.

A blue-green river. Two big railroads ran through the town, bringing snow-covered cars and sun-baked freight from the far whistlestops.

A cement highway went spinning through the main streets. There were bridges and fishing boats, river boats gliding down on the bay. In the river shallows there was the hoarse thunder of bullfrogs.

There were parks, and very old houses in which had been bred heroes, and one that had bedded Washington—and wore holes made by British cannon. There were farms all around Hawley-town, green country acres and big pigs and prize cattle, and grain and rows of beans and tomatoes.

There were slums too—and red gullies, hills where the Negroes lived. And shacks and company houses for the hunkies and Polacks. (Poverty is as boring as anything else—if you have a lot of it.)

There were fancy houses. There were Yew Gardens, Barra-clough Park and Lexington Avenue. There were banks which made 6 per cent interest as deadly as machine guns.

There were two modern hospitals, and the ugly red stone pub-lic library given by an old steel pirate on his way to heaven.

There were the spires of the old Unitarian war gods, the domed heights of Catholics and Jews, a high school and a free-milk clinic. The town took pride in its paved streets and a college, its water system and all the modern safety of fire departments and garbage collecting.

It was even proud of its graveyards. On the rise past the big white church was the finest and oldest burying ground. Here the Barracloughs and Hawleys buried their dead. Here the good, the lustful, the great *and* the black sheep of the old families were given a green hillside to rest.

The Hawleys had a special corner under great elms, where the sun came through on the mounds, bright but cool, and stirred the blue-spired pickerel weed and the thistleballs.

("But the worms were just common worms," Ed Hightower said. "Not choosy.")

On clear days, when it was blue and warm, people sat on graves, remembered old joys, and were properly sad or grateful over the dead. They picked pebbles from the accumulated mold or caught a little shut-eye to sleep off a bender.

In a corner of the Hawley tract there was a grave on which stood a plain granite stone, a stone very simple and not at all in keeping with the Hawley importance. It had carved on it merely the two vital dates of birth and death, and the words GEORGE JUDSON RODMAN.

No matter how the man had died, he had to be buried properly. There were none of his own folks in town so his wife's family had thought it simpler just to bury him in an obscure corner of their private plot. As for Helen Nash's and her husband's families, neither had a plot in the old churchyard. Most likely Helen's remains were, Abe suspected, in the sandy ground of some new burial field on real estate at the edge of town that had risen so much in value.

Abe was aware of a young woman reporter coming into focus as he walked. She said something about love letters.

"No letters have been put in evidence." (She smells of New York City, an arty apartment in the Village, a charge account at Lord & Taylor, and her legs grow out of her shoulder blades.)

"I hear they were real hot stuff, Mr. Pedlock. Imagine a choir singer writing what I hear she wrote. Keats combined with Kinsey, Lawrence Hope and Henry Miller. You get what I mean, darling?"

"No comment, Miss Merton."

"What a fink town."

Two other reporters (men who had seen motion pictures of how reporters were supposed to act, and so never did; instead they wore horn-rimmed glasses and cut their hair very short) asked Abe several shrewd questions, but he shook his head and turned the corner into narrow, alleylike Greene Street and went up two wooden steps into Zimmer's Barbershop. *Birds Pet Foods*. The windows were full of large bird cages. Yam-yellow canaries and parakeets hopped on red legs, and cracked seeds. Near the door Napoleon, the moth-eaten old parrot, climbed up and down his white droppings-stained perch, the brass chain on his leg rattling. Overhead the shelves of pet food, cuttle bones, dog biscuits and mange cures overpowered the space given to now unused, individually initialed shaving mugs. Hair tonics and unguents that never seemed to be requested were reflected in several mirrors.

Old Zimmer, a pale German pink, his sparse white hair limply parted in the middle, was patting with his fingers a very hot towel into a face attached to a well-dressed body reclining in the first chair.

"Hello, Mr. Barton," said Abe, taking the second chair after shucking off his coat and letting Charlie, the colored boy, hang it up and put his briefcase on a chair.

From under the towel came the muffled answer. "Hello, Honest Abe. Going to be a pisser of a hot day."

Abe closed his eyes, inhaled bird dust, scented alcohol and the odor of shoe polish, and fell back as the barber chair was tilted into a reclining position.

"Shave," he said to Tommy Pagano, the second barber. "I need a haircut, but no time today."

"How she goin', Abe?" asked old Zimmer, chewing an upper lip that had no teeth behind it. "You think you set her for a verdict soon?"

"Nobody knows," said Abe, relaxing as the shaving lather was pushed into his chops and massaged around with Tommy's fingers.

Jake Barton, still under the hot towel, asked, "Fireworks today?"

"I don't know for sure who we'll put on the stand first."

"You convict a Hawley in this town, convict three of them, and the tombstones in the old cemetery will fall down in shock."

"You bet," said Tommy Pagano. "What for murder because people like to futz around. It's a natural, yes?"

The skilled scrape of the razor soothed Abe, and he didn't answer, only grunted a sound that could mean anything. (It's the first time I've ever run into Jake Barton this early in the barbershop. It could mean something, or it couldn't. Jake, the bright, alert local political powerhouse. There is talk he will take over the party machine if Big Ed Higgins' bad health doesn't get any better. And Jake was campaign manager for State Senator Paul Hawley Barraclough, of the high-nostriled first family of the Eastern Shore. Jake Barton doesn't come to lie under a hot towel at eight in the morning just to say to me, "It's going to be a pisser of a hot day.")

"Among us wops we just grab the bed rabbit, cut off the guy's nose. Know what I mean?"

"Once over, Tommy, is enough. I have a touch of heat rash."

Abe came back to a sitting position. Tommy slapped shaving lotion onto Abe's dark smooth skin. He never needed to tan; he was the dusky type. Jake Barton was standing at the big mirror looping his tie around his large neck while Charlie ran a whisk-broom over the politician's ample pants. Jake, born Polish Josef Kazimir Barinski and now spreading in middle age and losing his limp blond hair, turned half around and smiled. "Abe, wait, I'll walk you to the courthouse."

Old Zimmer said, "No woman worth gettin' killed for. I know."

Abe waved off the whiskbroom, slipped some coins into Tommy's hand, and got into his by now very wrinkled jacket. The handle of the briefcase was damp to his touch. He went out into the strong white sunlight, Jake Barton right alongside him.

It was already too warm to walk with comfort in the morning streets. The courthouse was two blocks away up slightly sloping Greene Street. Jake Barton wiped his brow. "It's amazing the way the whole country is excited by this trial. It's, I suppose, part of the sentimental Protestant ethos. A tradition that posits original sin. We Catholics don't take crimes of passion so big. Confess and forget isn't a bad way of life, if you can avoid thinking. I find there are times I can't."

Abe shifted the heavy briefcase to his left hand. "Even medieval society, Mr. Barton, didn't wait for punishment to come in the afterlife. Murder in our country is a frontier sport. There's no deep melancholy about it, only an attitude of resignation. Maybe too much pioneer thinking left around and everybody is able to handle a rifle."

Jake Barton laughed. The heat was making his big flabby body uncomfortable, Abe suspected. They waited for a traffic light to change. Jake said, "Abe, we Americans still admit only a few degrees of consciousness to our self-restraint, our toughness, in a world that kills us off impartially. Violence is the great impetus in our society, even if it's only driving a three-hundred-horse-

power car. We harden ourselves to bear the unbearable; even so
our controls slip sometimes. The case you're trying now is all out
of kilter."

"Why, Mr. Barton? People in fancy Barraclough Park get
drunk, hit their wives, fornicate, commit adultery, just as they
do at Polack Point. And when their sex patterns or emotional life
get tangled, they kill each other. They, too, I guess, end up by
knowing the big question of *this* world is how to live in it."

Two Negro kids licking ice-cream cones passed, each wearing
one roller skate.

"Mostly," said Jake Barton, watching the kids cross a rough
section of sidewalk, "I've found people want to live without
consequences. That's why there are politicians whom they can
blame. In love we say, There isn't any *me;* I'm *you.* In ambition—
maybe a poor substitute for loving—men come around to the
tragedy of realization that it is too late for achievement. All I ever
wanted to do was sit at home and read a lot of books I own so I
could finish off an education I never had. Abe, what are you
after?"

Ahead the cool green of the courthouse block—chestnut, oak,
hickory and elm trees—cast great blue shadows. Abe changed the
dragging briefcase back to his right hand. (Better watch myself.
This Jake Barton is a very bright man. He may yet make Senator
Paul Hawley Barraclough President of the United States. He's
the one who has the political ear of Big Ed Higgins, the state's
party boss. He's here because he wants to say something to you.
He has a kind of natural perception all "good" politicians have.
People, votes, are abstractions they use to gain power. What does
he want of me? Motives and illusions are everything they taught
me in college. And I've found out in law reality is not actually
a physical thing of just visible phenomena—that newsboy with
the brandy nose, the slender girl waggling her cute behind under
her summer dress, the color of the red and green glass in the sunny
traffic lights, the way the world is in a state of perpetual war in
a total estrangement of men and women—the reality of it all
isn't visible; only the surface colors.)

"Mr. Barton, I'm only out for winning this case. Victory

matters, of course, but I see the law as a tool. I use it in a combination of pride and craftsmanship. That seem too lousy a motto?"

The sound of car horns came from the courthouse parking lot.

"No. Even on this damn hot morning we all exist in a state of conflict, a contradiction between our underwear and our skins."

They crossed the street together, like brothers, to the trees on the front courthouse lawn. (He's going to get to the point now. Barton has finished the essential ritual of small personal talk—showing me he is a man well read and able to think on a good level. Now comes the soft sell. He'll ask me to call him Jake, not Mr. Barton.)

The sound of roller skates was back.

CHAPTER V

THE COURTHOUSE

HIS DAILY SIGHT of the courthouse grounds always gave Abe a lift. He thought it was the most beautiful part of the town. There were two square blocks of well-watered flower plots, shrubs and grass, and the trimmed trees were kept neat by jailhouse inmates working off drunk and wife-beating sentences. The old red brick city and county jailhouse on the grounds was two-storied, with bronze bars on the old keystone-topped windows, the bars smooth and patinaed, like Italian sculpture. There always seemed to be a Negro singing sad blues in his cell. Abe and Jake Barton passed the habitual drunks in overwashed jail denim stamped *King County,* the men smelling of tobacco, Lysol and old shoes, standing around with rakes and wheelbarrows under the scowl of Peg Leg Barnes, the sheriff's no-good brother-in-law, who ran the cockfights in the loft of the Walker House hotel.

"Hello, Peg Leg," said Jake Barton.

"Mornin', Mr. Barton, mornin', Judge Pedlock."

"Thanks for the promotion," said Abe.

The county building was of yellow brick, a product of the 1900s, undecided between being functional factory box or semi-Gothic library in style. Between the jail and the county building stood the great slate-roofed courthouse with its giant brick columns whitewashed and the dome of weathered green-blue copper with its weather vane of a running horse. (Ed Hightower said the horse was Dan Patch, who trotted the mile in record time.) The courthouse had been built in the 1840s, rebuilt after the Civil War, and enlarged during the period they set up the Spanish-American War bronze memorial in front of it (sailors loading shells into a nonexistent naval gun over old-fashioned letters reading: REMEMBER THE MAINE). The monuments were beginning to crowd the lawns, Abe noticed. The cement Civil War rifleman on his star-shaped platform with the names of the famous battles listed Southern style: Manassas for Bull Run, Pittsburgh Landing for Shiloh. But Gettysburg was still Gettysburg. The first World War was a drinking bubble and two rusting 75s set on a stone base, and World War II was represented by a large stainless-steel star with names of the local boys who died on jungle islands and on German plains.

Jake Barton stopped to mop his brow under his glazed straw hat as they reached the city and county jail building. The large man carefully wiped his jowls and thick neck with a clean silk handkerchief. "Abe, let's have lunch today at Chichester House."

"I don't know when Judge Riggs will break for noon. I think he's got a toothache. He keeps sucking one cheek and not sustaining my objections."

"He'll break early. He's going to pose for some magazine pictures for a story someone is running on him. Big Ed Higgins is joining us at lunch."

Abe felt the solid mocking punch Jake Barton gave him in the ribs, and said, "All right, Mr. Barton. Their air-conditioning works."

"Sure. Just ask for Big Ed's table. And call me Jake."

Jake Barton waved and went off down the wide, crushed-blue-stone path toward the side of the courthouse grounds that came out near his law office across the street. Abe frowned, returned someone's greeting, and shifted the briefcase to his other hand. (Damn. Big Ed doesn't get off his front porch with the river breeze blowing coolly on him to come to town on an extra-hot day to have lunch with me when he has a real sixteen-jewel French chef at home.)

Abe ran quickly up the steps, entered the jail building, and was hit in the face at once by a smell that stank like an animal house at a zoo. Mitch, the nine-fingered turnkey, was frisking a young half-breed Indian boy whose black ducktail haircut stuck up behind. Even in the heat he wore a heavy horsehide leather jacket, motorcycle boots, tight blue cord pants and a wide leather belt. The boy stood, face to the wall, his arms spread-eagled on the gray paint as the turnkey removed a switchblade knife, a tin of condoms, a balled-up tan handkerchief and two mashed cigarettes from the pockets of the boy.

The turnkey sniffed the cigarettes. "Tea. All right, into the tank. Our tip was you were blasting with H. Hello, Mr. Ped-lock."

"Mitch, I want to talk to Vargis."

"Sure. Hot enough for you?" The turnkey pushed the boy hard in the neck with his open four-fingered hand and kicked at the lean, hard buttocks with a wide shoe. "Get goin', reefer man."

The boy moved ahead of them, face down, long hair in his eyes.

(The jail smell is always like this no matter when I come in, no matter how the jail is scrubbed. Vomit, cold hamburger grease, armpits and lavatory smells smothered only partly by Lysol.)

Not so restful, clean and neat as the sheriff's living quarters attached to the jail on the east side, where the three people being tried for murder were lodged. Sarah Rodman's housekeeper was with her. And her brothers Mikel and Batty Billie had their cigars and bourbon-and-branch-water at every meal—meals brought in on heated trays with silver covers from the Walker House. The only time Abe had walked past the sheriff's iron deer and under the porte-cochere to see the three prisoners was the first day of the trial. He had walked on the clean yellow linoleum still damp with the footprints of the hag from the women's section of the jail who did the sheriff's floors, and he had gone up the stairs covered with the melodius red carpeting to the room where Sarah Rodman sat against the bronze-grated windows, the sun behind her; so Abe saw no details of her face, or what this catastrophe had done to her.

Roger Tindell, chief defense lawyer, stood by the door smoking a cigarette in a jade holder and smiling, as if he thought Abe were acting foolish, but what could you expect.

He said, "Mrs. Rodman has permitted you to talk to her, Mr. Prosecutor, because, as you so delicately put it, Abe, you'd rather not say this in court. A. Lincoln Pedlock of the D.A.'s staff, Mrs. Rodman."

"Mrs. Rodman, are you comfortable here?"

Her voice was clear, firm; Abe wished he could see her face. "It was considerate of you to permit the sheriff to house us here privately."

"I would not be doing my duty if your brothers were not handcuffed until they get to the courtroom from here. But no matter what you have heard, the escorting of you to the courtroom will be just by the matron and the sheriff's wife, with . . . with no restricting devices."

"Thank you."

That was all. Abe had gone out, not bothering the brothers, feeling he had been granted an audience rather than having conferred a favor. Now, walking in the stink of the jail, he resented his visit to the special three inmates of the sheriff's house. (Why does it reek so in the jail?)

It had been a difficult case to prepare, to complete the dossiers of the prospective jurors for "The People vs. Sarah Rodman, Mikel Hawley and William Hawley. Charge: Murder." Now that a week of the trial had passed, he had to wind up the state's case and let the defense have their whack at bat. The defense was smart and wily. Tindell had calmly opened by saying, "Your Honor, the defendants waive the reading of the information and stand mute." Judge Riggs had looked down like a hairy jack-in-

the-box and answered, "A plea of not guilty will accordingly
be entered by the court." Abe had opened with the full bill, the
contention of what he would prove, and a quoting of section
28.1043 of the annotated statutes on the entering of a not-guilty
plea by the court. There was a fourteen-man jury (four of them
women), with two spares in case someone became sick, and so far
no one had. Stipulated copies of all photographs and charts had
caused no trouble; the defense was not pressing just yet.

The defense had asked for a continuance to the December
term, but Abe had fought it off; Tindell's tentative trial strategies
were all based on delay upon delay and trying to get as many
errors into the court records as he could as bases for appeals for
new trials if there was a verdict of guilty. Abe had made it plain
to the jury he wanted a first-degree murder verdict. "There is
no 'unwritten law' in Anglo-American jurisprudence."

Abe was aware of the notorious undependability of juries.
That was why his total involvement in the case made his sleep
so haunted, and his relationship with the rest of the world almost one of a cataleptic trance. The jail smell brought him back
to reality from his somnambulist's walk. (The women's section,
the fish tank, is even worse.)

The male tank was just a big square in the middle of the
jail cellar made by enclosing the area with heavy iron bars. The
turnkey opened a steel door and pushed the Indian boy into a
population of hobos, drunks, small domestic tragedies, and
several unprotected bookies picked up as a result of a reform
editorial in the local paper. The turnkey relocked the cell, spat
thickly on the cement floor, rubbed the results with a wide shoe,
and motioned Abe toward a bank of single cells under naked
yellow light bulbs. "Had to put Vargis in one of the small cells.
Some fiesty nigger tried to steal his smoke fixings and damn
near got himself killed. Vargis is tough; don't rile him."

The turnkey unlocked a cell door, and Abe went in. A large-
muscled man with a big broken nose sat on the sagging wire
netting that passed for a bed and smoked a short handmade
cigarette stub. The man looked liverish from indoor confine-

ment, and fat was beginning to form on a body that was kept trim by hard outdoor work.

"Oh, you," said the man, after one quick lift of his head.

Abe sat down on a backless kitchen chair—the only furniture —and held out a stogie.

"Eff you," said the prisoner, refusing the smoke.

"Vargis, you're really held as a material witness. The other charge is just to make it legal. I don't want to force you onto the stand. But I'm a sworn officer of the county."

"It won't do much good if I don't co-operate, check?"

"Check." Abe lighted the stogie and puffed it aglow and handed it to Vargis. The turnkey said through the bars, "Varg, you show some respect for the assistant D.A. or I'll see you get a good roust sometime late at night with a rubber hose."

"Go fill your hat, turnkey."

The prisoner took the stogie and smoked it with pleasure. He closed his eyes and inhaled deeply the pungent, strong tobacco. "Christ, all I want to do is mind my own business and get the hell out of this clink."

"Vargis, all I want to know is when you last went duck hunting with Mikel Hawley. Which of his shotguns he used, its gauge? And when he used it last time and where is it now? You are his caretaker, favorite boatman. You cleaned his shotguns, even had the key to his gun cabinets."

The prisoner opened his big brown eyes. "Look, as a muskrat hunter—meaning no offense—look, Mac, you and me, we'd be crazy to go up against the Hawleys. I'm squatter stock, river shanty boat trash, and me and mine we've et because the Hawleys let us squat where we don't belong, or own. We fetch and carry for 'em and it's not a bad life boatin' and huntin' for 'em with a few varmint pelts added. I'm not puttin' my ass in no sling for you. Besides, like I said—" the prisoner sucked deeply on the stogie— "I don't particularly recollect no special shotgun, or how many guns Mr. Hawley had. I never counted 'em. Want your cheroot back?"

"Keep puffing."

Abe shook his head and stood up. The courthouse bell was

ringing nine. He still had to get to his office and see the D.A., Ed Hightower, and tell him what he planned for the day in court.

"Vargis, the Hawleys—your friends—haven't made any attempt to get you out of jail."

"Oh, I don't think this thing you figured out for keeping me here—nettin' fish illegal with a wrong-sized mesh—is goin' to stick when it comes up before a judge that takes deer out of season. A twenty-buck fine. The Hawleys trust me. Hell, you can't bring back the dead. And it wasn't as if they—Mr. Mikel and Mr. Billie—were real criminals."

"Vargis, I may put you on the stand under oath. Perjury can get you five to seven in this state. Think of that time away from the river and the duck blinds, the muskrat runs and the deer paths. And your wife, alone when you're gone, eh?"

Vargis looked up, grim-faced. "I could kill you for hinting she'd become a shack job—kill you and walk out of court a free man. But you wouldn't know that, not being one of us."

"I was born here, Vargis. And it's *you* who worry about your wife becoming a shack job." Abe held back from finishing the sentence with "again."

Vargis, also thinking of his wife's past, scowled at the end of the stogie; he almost decided to toss it to the dirty cement floor of the cell but changed his mind. He stuck it into his thin-lipped mouth, rolled over, first on his back, then on his side, and turned his face to the wall. The turnkey held the door open for Abe.

"These peckerwoods got no manners."

Free of the jail smell, Abe walked slowly toward the county building. Civil-service employees were moving past him, taking their time. Citizens with a sure job, a pension and only a certain number of years of boredom ahead on the public payroll. Their only problem, Abe felt, was the coffee break. (Vargis touched me on a sore spot. Even being born in Hawleytown isn't enough. I've not had any other world except for some semesters at the University of Maryland, where everything seemed covered with the greasy dish water from the dishes I washed and the oilcloth-covered tables I cleaned up working as a campus waiter.)

Someone passed and asked, "Goin' to surprise us today in court, Abe?"

(Hell, my great-grandfather was Major Joseph Pedlock, C.S.A., who fought four years for the Confederacy and almost lost a leg at Chancellorsville. And invented a copper smelter in Butte, Montana, and fought the Copper Combine for years. He died an old, old man—I've got the clipping someplace. His grandson Harry, my father, died before I was born, choking and spitting with the Spanish flu in an Army camp in 1919. And if he actually married my mother we never found the records anyplace. He died after a three-day honeymoon pass, and my mother died when I was born, right here in Hawleytown in the house her family had on Belden Street, by the old dock the vegetable barges use. The relatives moved me around, from one bundle of rags to another, taking turns raising me the best they could. So they can't say I don't belong here, and my name is as good a one as any here. It should have been a sad childhood, but it wasn't. The sky was always blue, the river gulls geeking overhead, and Jacob Yuron letting me watch him develop wet glass plates in his darkroom and paying me a dime a trip to deliver the wedding group photographs or the high-school graduating classes, so glassy-eyed and earnest. . . . That goddamn swamp rat; wait till I get him on the stand. Trying to withhold evidence.)

The offices of the District Attorney and his staff took over the whole second floor of the county building. Abe, as he mounted the stairs, always got a bang out of the gold letters as they came in view, outlined in black on the two big frosted glass doors:

COUNTY OF KING
District Attorney
Samuel E. Hightower
Assistant District Attorneys
A. Lincoln Pedlock
Carl Vogelhofer

Miss Munday, gray hair rigidly set, gold-rimmed glasses polished, stiffly aware of being the oldest secretary in the building, sat outside Ed Hightower's office. Abe always had the impression her two dark-blue eyes in pools of pure salt water operated independently of each other as their owner typed and watched the people in the waiting room.

Abe said to her, "Hello, Munday, the chief in?"

"Carl's with him. Go right in."

"Thanks."

He watched her eyes; it was only an impression they roved independently. He opened the plain oak door into the chief's office. The big room fronting on the white tall flagpole had large ceiling-reaching windows, a worn red rug and historic furniture —even a fumed-oak roll-top desk—in need of replacement. Ed Hightower and Carl Vogelhofer were seated on their spines, legs on the window sills, smoking corncob pipes full of a strong burley tobacco. Corncob-pipe smoking was the latest male fad in the county service at the moment. Before that, Abe remembered, it had been colored socks, jalopies with lowered floorboards and the wearing of red knitted vests. On the walls hung F.B.I. portraits of the ten most wanted criminals, institutional ads for leg irons and bail bonds that amused Ed.

Ed Hightower turned his aged head as Abe came in and spit into a polished cuspidor. His voice was thin and ironic. "How fares our knight in his shiny drawers this morning?"

Ed (hard to believe he had been Skull and Bones at Yale once) had been District Attorney too long, and he had no special plans beyond moving upward to an appointed position on a judge's bench. He was a handsome man, hair gun-metal gray, the handsomest district attorney since Sockless Joe Desmond held office in 1910. Ed had aged like well-rubbed furniture into a bourbon-toned specimen of an ironic, wise public officer who did his job well, and nothing beyond that. (He drinks too much, loses a little in poker sessions, owns a red setter hunting dog, has been faithful to his small, barking shrew of a wife for forty years, and knows his law. That's all I know about him. And I think I amuse him.)

Abe sat down on the littered desk and smiled. "Somebody open a window or send out for some air."

Ed shook his head and fingered some state supreme court reports, ruled legal pads and brown Manila envelopes. "And let the heat in? Hell, no. This tanbark we're smoking bother you?"

"Tell me something, chief. You see Jake Barton lately?"

Ed looked wisely at Carl Vogelhofer and knocked out his pipe on a huge seashell used as an ashtray. Carl grinned, the heavy Pennsylvania Dutch smile of a fat boy with wavy blond hair, a good brain in a lazy body wearing clothes tailored for Princeton. Carl was the spoiled only son of a brewery family; he had been forced on Ed as part of a political deal for the brewery interests to change party affiliations. Carl had turned out very well interpreting abstracts, had legal infallibility. He puffed his pipe and said, "This office is free of party pressure and bribery, within reason. We do take a gift turkey now and then and we don't let pretty girls pay traffic fines or permit the probate court to loot decadent estates."

Abe wiped his face with his first reserve handkerchief.

"Eddie Desmond call in? He used to drive the Rodmans. I want a stronger statement from him."

"He didn't call."

"I'm having a Chichester House lunch with Jake Barton and Big Ed Higgins. Mr. Barton asked me to call him Jake."

Ed began to refill his corncob pipe with loose yellow tobacco from a bowl on his desk. "The food is damn good at the Chichester. Wish I could afford it." Ed looked up, and his cold blue eyes were noncommittal. "Abe, there haven't been any promises made here. This office is free of deals. You want to make a Yahoo of yourself in court, you go ahead. I'll back you. It's a case I was sorry to hand you."

"We didn't ask for the indictment, Chief, but when you handed it to me I had to follow through all the way. As prosecutor, I collected what I think is proof of guilt."

Ed held a large kitchen match to his pipe and sucked flame into the bowl as he moved in a half circle in his swivel chair. Carl pursed his fat lips together and said, "It hasn't looked so good legally so far. Maybe Sarah Rodman had grounds for murdering a guilty husband. But have we proof? Not that adultery is so rare in marriage. Yet somehow it shakes the foundations of our genteel country society here to see her and her two brothers tried for settling a private matter. I am speaking ironically, Chief."

Abe picked up his briefcase. "Where have I failed to make out the state's case since putting the case on the trial docket?"

Ed coughed into the blue pipe smoke, got up and turned on an old-fashioned brass electric fan, which began to buzz and hum. "You haven't failed to present a good case, have complied with the letter and intent of the law. Abe, I've been around a long time, too long a time. I've had no ambition to be Senator or Governor. It's my nature to accept life on easy terms, with honor, a backwoods honor that doesn't always face the modern facts of life fully but has a code that seems to most a little old-fashioned. Abe, sometimes we can pull society down by defending it. I mean, the town feels a crime was committed and two sinful people were murdered. Fine people, actually—we all knew George Rodman, the public figure, even if we didn't attend his church. A hell of a sweet guy, I hear. And I once courted Helen Nash's mother. She was the most beautiful redhead in three counties. And Helen—I remember her as a cute baby riding on a pinto pony getting her picture taken at Jacob Yuron's Photo Gallery. A better-built, sweeter girl didn't exist."

Abe didn't interrupt; he was staring impassively at his hands. He sat on the corner of the desk earnestly listening to the old man who could have been Attorney General but preferred bourbon.

"Abe, it comes down to this. The coroner's jury came in with a certain verdict—death by violence, by parties unknown—and we had to follow it up with an investigation. *You* came in with what you thought was enough for an indictment of three people. I let you go ahead. That's law. I'm too easygoing. We've made a circus of this town. We've begun things here that will take a generation to forget. We're breaking a lot of fairly good families' hearts. And now, Abe, I'm beginning to think we haven't the evidence we need to convict, and the dirt will still remain. It just was wrong from the minute the swearing in of the jurors for examination on the *voir dire* began."

Carl said softly, "The chief means he's not so sure your theory of how and who is right."

Abe swallowed hard and banged his first on the desk. "Damn it, you think I'd go into court on a hunch alone? I've got—as you know—an eyewitness to the crime, to the corpus delicti!"

Ed said softly, looking out at the lawn below, "I know what you've got. Maman Celie. An old voodoo witch who doesn't know truth from fantasy, can't walk, I hear, and who will make some kind of a fantastic appearance on the stand that nobody—but nobody—can predict."

"I've got more. I'm building slowly. But I'm sure Maman Celie can convince the jury she didn't imagine anything. She saw it."

Carl began to ream his corncob with a large fluffy pipe cleaner. "The chief is pretty sure now you can't convict with what you have and—"

"And so," said Ed Hightower, slapping a paper at a persistent buzzing fly, "I think it better we don't make too big a stink before we wind up the state's case. Now don't stare at me as if I were a helot, Abe. If you had a solid case and sure evidence I'd say roar ahead no matter whom it drives off the rails. And I'd back you to thumb your nose even at the President of the United States if he said go easy. *But* can any counsel concede any merit in developments so far?"

Abe stood up. He felt he was swimming damply in sweat and rage. He tried to show no emotion on his damp face. "*But* what, Chief?"

"Never mind. I've just made my pitch and you've got it. And nobody made me do this. A murder trial isn't as easy as notarizing a quit-claim deed."

"You've said a lot this morning, Chief," Abe said. "A real lot."

"No more of Carl's destructive irony, Abe. The law in a small town like ours doesn't stand self-condemned by intellectuals the way it is in big cities. We have our own sense of sin, doubt, the limits of human goodness, but in the main we get a good kind of rough justice here."

"Chief, you depress me."

"We have a little of the feeling of decay, death and hopelessness that hangs over all courtrooms but we don't strip ourselves down to as full an absurd set of bleeding hearts, self-conscious clichés, as some fancier courts do. Hell, Abe, let's get the case over with, and we'll all go fishing and take a couple of cases of beer along. That is, if I can get the old woman to buy the idea."

Carl grinned. "How does the poet put it?

> "Who drags the fiery artist down?
> Who keeps the pioneer in town?
> Who hates to let the seaman roam?
> It is the wife. It is the home.

> "Beer, beer, glorious beer,
> Fill yourself up to here, here, here.
> Up—with the sale of it,
> Down—with a pail of it,
> Glorious, glorious beer."

"All right, you two kids, so we old men are unsophisticated here, gawky, but our sensibility, temperament, is an essence that isn't alien to you two either. This case has become world-famous. Why, I don't really know. Damn the invention of the printing press and newsprint."

Ed was looking into his pipe, carried away by some abstraction he was trying to bring closer for his own inspection. "I don't know where we're going on this case. Lawyers exist to ask questions, philosophers to answer them. Abe, you'll learn the appearance of life is fragmentary and contradictory. Time is unreal; no calendar has ever trapped it. I mean, let's not think this is the *only* case we'll ever have, and the most important one. Cheer up."

Carl looked at Abe and shrugged his fat shoulders, as if to say, "Old Ed is like this when he's gotten started on the process of law as more than mere procedure to punish the destroyer of the

morals of society." Ed caught the look between the two younger
men and grinned.

Abe said, "You'll back me up?"

"I'll pull Carl off the firebug case to help you if you want me
to."

"No, thanks. Unless I get up shatcreek."

Carl said, "The missing shotgun—anything on that?"

"Get out a search warrant, Carl, and go to the Hawley farm
and Martin Vargis' cottage. Pull it all apart. Then have one of
his kids show you his favorite duck blinds, dredge around, see if
that shotgun or the rifle haven't been tossed overboard."

Ed was again standing at the window looking down at the people moving toward the courthouse. He didn't turn around. "Abe,
you don't have to promise Big Ed anything at lunch today. He
can stop me getting that judge's appointment. But I wouldn't
want it on those terms. And if he does retire me, well, I've had
my nose in the public feedbag long enough to earn a pension."

Abe said, "Come in and watch the lion act."

The corncob pipes made moist sucking sounds.

Abe went out and crossed the hall to his own smaller office.
Mary Durant, his secretary, stood at a mirror in the outer office
brushing her long red hair into place, showing a lot of nylon-clad
leg and a very fashionable shoe. Mary was in her thirties, her
regular, classic features shopworn and promising soon to thicken
and grow bitter. But she was still in many ways the town's hotshot
party girl. (I remember her in high school in pleated skirt and
well-filled sweater, with bold red lips and a kind of sticky adoles-
cent sensuality that attracted the bolder boys and gave rise to
many startling details about her in our male bull sessions, most
of which, I found out later, were romantic lies.)

"Morning," Mary said, putting away her comb. "The tests and
report came in from Doctor Wymer on Maman Celie."

"Does he testify as to her ability to tell fantasy from reality?"

"Sure, if you can make sense of his Freudian doubletalk. It's
in on your desk. I got the extra copy of trial memorandum to the
judge—also our amends to the supplement requests. Hot day."

"We could try this case best in a nudist camp."

"That's an idea. Judge Riggs in a G-string."

Abe went into his own office and wondered how Mary ever found anything in his habitually disordered desk. He'd get the office repainted after the trial and frame some of the pictures of Fran and the kids, and get a bigger filing system put in. (I wish Mary would stop keeping her tampons behind the F.B.I. file.)

Abe picked up Doctor Sidney Wymer's report and began to riff through it quickly. Mary Durant came in and leaned in the doorway of his office, legs crossed, one hand on her hip. Her father was the court clerk, Snooky Durant, and the Durants had always managed to get on the public payroll. Funny about Mary. It had been expected that she would marry one of the rich young men in the town who rushed her in her twenties. But somehow she hadn't, even if there had been rumors of some violent and passionate courting and two fist fights at the country club. Abe looked at Mary over the top of the report. There was something about her that was always unsettling. She was too consciously a woman, had too flaunting an awareness of her sensuality. Perhaps, Abe thought as he turned a page, her directness had frightened off the few desirable small-town bachelors after a hasty taste of honey. (I can't say she doesn't do her job well, and she covers for me in the many ways a good secretary has to cover. But after ten years she still makes me uneasy.)

"I'll take this with me, Mary. How is Judge Riggs this morning?"

"Pappy says the Judge's tooth is worse. He'll have to adjourn court some morning when it gets him suddenly to get it pulled. Impacted wisdom tooth. They're murder."

Rod Miller, Abe's law clerk, came in and put his heavy football arms around Mary's waist and said into her ear, "How's the most beautiful civil servant today?"

"Stop clowning. It's too hot." Mary pushed him off. "Why aren't you in court seeing to the witnesses for Mr. Pedlock?"

Rod kissed the back of her neck, casually released Mary, and turned toward Abe. "I've at last got the hotel registers from Atlantic City. And the witness, Murad. George Rodman, as we

know, was there last June twelfth at the Braymore, and Mrs.
Rodman and brother Mikel were at the St. Charles at the same
time. It's all in writing. Helen Nash was also registered at the
Braymore—connecting door."

The courthouse bell began to chime ten o'clock.

CHAPTER VI

THE TRIAL

EVERY BRICK of the courthouse building gave Abe confidence,
gave him a feeling that in its marble and polished red stone and
mahogany corridors he was the representative of the state, the
people and the law. He liked its many high-ceilinged rooms
(slightly water-stained). The law library, with its decaying paper
and rotting calf bindings and strong canvas-covered books, had
for Abe the odor of the temple. The attorneys' conference room
had wide pigeon-stained window ledges, and the brass cuspidors
seemed to make it a room for putting on armor. Even the court
stenographers' room, when he went there to pick up copies of
the official testimony, was cheerful with some home-grown flowers in pint milk bottles. He respected the mahogany and walnut
of the judge's chamber, not spoiled by its dark lighting and oil
paintings of dead legal minds, the electric ring on which the
judge's coffee was made and his toasted cheese sandwiches
browned.

The prosecuting attorneys' offices were smaller—a battleship
gray, with piles of old plans of the original courthouse forgotten
in a pine cabinet. There were very worn leather chairs; everything smelled of old cigars slowly smoked to frayed wet ends. Abe
preferred his own office in the county building next door.

Stone, slate, marble, green copper roof, bird lime, old brick, great white columns—the courthouse never failed to please Abe.

The courtroom itself was a stage on which he felt a ritual was held that was part country circus, part pagan blood ritual and torture chamber used for the good of the community. The judge's bench was of good rubbed wood; the enclosed chairs of shorthand clerk, bailiff and the court clerk stood in a railed cubicle across the front. The green leather tops of the counsels' tables were faded a bit. There were bigger brass cuspidors on rubber mats, benches for the expectant jurors, litigants, the press, witnesses, the shifting herd of spectators. Abe tried to drive out the idea it was all a platform for a continual play that made itself up as it went along yet was set in grooves that followed something called evidence, and quoted authorities that were sustained when you cited them ("70 *American Law Reports,* page 792, Your Honor . . .").

("You do solemnly swear that you will tell the truth, the whole truth and nothing but the truth, so help you God?"

("I do.")

The bright yellow interior of the big courtroom was still fairly cool when Abe motioned Rod Miller to put their first witness of the day, Mrs. Ott, on the stand. The out-of-date air-circulating system would function for another half hour and then fall behind and the bone-white heat beating on the tall window curtains of the courtroom would by some process of osmosis come in and melt tempers and sag collars into soggy broadcloth.

Abe sat back on the well-polished court chair, at the table of his group—Rod Miller and Mary making notes—while Mrs. Ott slowly blinked at the clerk, Snooky Durant, and repeated the oath in a polite low voice. On the bench Judge Wilmont Riggs looked down, expressionless, as if half asleep, his wide, puffy face with the thin, clever mouth in repose, the gray tufts of eyebrows looking unreal, as if stuck on carelessly in a poorly dressed stage play. Over the judge were hung dusty reproductions, under flawed glass, of Washington and Jefferson, faded national and state flags, and on the vaulted ceiling were old bronze chandeliers that seemed to Abe to stir slowly with the rotating movement of the earth in its orbit, stir only slightly but stir they did. They had been lamps once created to burn whale oil, then Pennsylvania distilled coal oil and, in the early years of the century, gas. For three generations they had been wired for electric bulbs that never gave enough light in the late afternoon sessions in the fall.

"Your witness, Mr. Pedlock," Abe rose to his feet. "Please get comfortable, Mrs. Ott."

Abe walked from the table where Rod Miller was piling papers and past the table where the defense lawyers were grouped, ready, alert and a little overgroomed in tan and ivory Palm Beach suits. Roger Tindell, leading the defense, gave Abe a small, indirect smile. His two assistants tried to appear busier than they were. Only a large fat man with a fringe of low-comedy red hair (must be dyed) around a great bald egg of a head showed any interest in Abe and his witness.

"Keep it sweet, Abie," the big bald man whispered, sounding very friendly. "Keep it fragrant, and keep it short." He added a small, deep laugh of almost two full tones. He was Denis Cavanagh, better known as "Devil" Cavanagh. He had been imported from New York City to assist and advise the defense. He was a fantastically successful criminal lawyer, mostly a defender of rich hoodlums and top-ranking gangster figures. Devil Cavanagh's record of not-guilty verdicts was amazing, and his fees huge.

Abe turned to face the seated Mrs. Ott on the witness chair. "You are the Mrs. Martha Ott of Rodman Manor?"

"Yes, I am." She was a small woman with a wide head of pale, almost pink hair and very washed-out robin's-blue eyes. She held her head to one side as if she had difficulty in hearing.

"You were employed as housekeeper by the late Reverend George Rodman?"

"Mrs. Rodman hired me. When they moved into the Rodman Manor place in Barraclough Park."

"Mr. Rodman, however, approved of your being hired. Let's get all the facts on record."

"I wouldn't know, I'm sure. You see—"

"He paid you your salary."

"Will you talk please a little louder—I'm a mite—"

Roger Tindell's Boston accent rose behind Abe. "I don't see that it matters much, Your Honor, who hired or who paid the salary of the housekeeper. It's pretty plain and we all accept that she was and is the housekeeper."

Judge Riggs seemed to have his tongue in his cheek, probing for something. Without uttering a word, he waved to Abe with a square hand of short fingers to go on.

"Mrs. Ott, you were housekeeper at the Rodman residence for all the eight years of the marriage?"

"I was with Mrs. Rodman's mother, Mrs. Hawley—Mrs. John Dremain Hawley—for six years before that."

"Was the Rodman marriage, as you observed it, a happy one?"

"Well, now."

"Objection, Your Honor. The witness is not testifying as, and is not, an expert on marriage."

"Sustained. The clerk will strike out question and answer."

Abe turned half around to face the defense table and for the first time fully saw in sharp focus the three defendants. He had been aware of them so far this morning as only vague shapes, but now they were alive and in detail. He carefully framed his questions to the witness. "In your eight years as housekeeper at the Rodmans', did you see or hear anything that might lead you to believe that the marriage was not a successful one?"

Sarah Rodman—sitting stiffly at the defense table—was wearing a blue dress with dull, dark-navy buttons. Her hair, a heavy load of it, was of a reddish brown, growing dull but skillfully treated to preserve it. There was a kind of classical beauty in the oval face, a cool beauty held under control and not pampered. Her eyes were very dark, the nose long and delicate, the result, no doubt—Abe thought—of generations of patrician breeding. The mouth was a puzzle to him, being fuller than one would expect of such a cool face. It was a sensual, wet mouth, a disconcerting detail. Sarah Rodman's skin was too pale to be fashionable in an outdoor age.

"No more than most marriages," said the witness, and Abe pulled himself away from brooding over Mrs. Rodman.

"Did they ever shout at each other, Mrs. Ott, when you were housekeeper?"

"No. Oh, no. The Reverend was a gentleman, and Mrs. Rodman was a Hawley."

"Yes, that is true. No slammed doors? No signs of temper?"

"None at all. He didn't like glasses—wet ones—left on the furniture. And Mrs. Rodman liked the maids to take their baths after clearing at night, twice a week."

This had been casual and easy, setting the witness at ease. Mikel Hawley looked like Ernest Hemingway, Abe decided, as he turned and phrased the next question in his mind before asking it. He was tweedy, florid, a pattern of very black, thick mustache, stained yellow teeth of a heavy cigar smoker, graying hair, still thick and low, parted in the middle, and big fists, very hairy (somehow they looked naked without gauntlets and a hunting hawk on them).

"It was a well-run house?"

"Very well run."

Batty Billie Hawley sat on his spine, eyes closed, half asleep, looking like a Rowlandson caricature, a parody of his brother Mikel. His mustache too was shaggy and tinged with red hair, the face foolish instead of hard, cruel, proud, the mouth open and like a wet carp's. The hands were restless and misformed and obscenely hairless.

Abe had the next question to the witness shaped the way he wanted it.

"Mrs. Ott, on June twelfth last did Mrs. Rodman go to Atlantic City and spend a weekend there at the St. Charles Hotel?"

"June twelfth? Yes, she went to Atlantic City in June."

"Had Mrs. Rodman ever gone to Atlantic City in June before this?"

"I wouldn't know."

"I mean, during the time you were housekeeper there."

"I couldn't be sure."

"Yes, you could, Mrs. Ott. You keep a housekeeping book, don't you? In which you list, as a good housekeeper, the guests, family events, visits, trips, all such information? As part of your job, of course."

The little woman on the stand folded her hands on her lap. "If he knows this much," the gesture seemed to say, "he must have been through the book somehow very carefully." "I don't remember Mrs. Rodman going to Atlantic City in June before. She usually went to Newport summers, to the family summer house."

Abe looked over at the defense table. Tindell was fingering the small golden football on his watch chain. Devil Cavanagh was folding a bit of silver gum paper into some intricate shape. The defense wasn't going to object and make this trip a major issue for the jury if they could avoid it.

"Did Mrs. Rodman leave suddenly or just pack a bag and call a cab and leave for the station?"

"She called me to her private study at ten and said she was taking the train to Atlantic City." The little woman smiled. "And she didn't give me any reason for going and I didn't expect it."

There was a loud laugh, and the jury joined in. Abe put back his head and joined in the merriment. He had learned early: if you provoke a laugh in court by your questioning, join it, *never* fight it.

"I'm sure, Mrs. Ott, you knew your duties and were not a Nosy Parker. You were of course aware that Mr. Rodman on that day was already in Atlantic City."

Tindell stirred as if to object, but the little woman was too fast for him. "Oh, yes, Mr. Rodman had left a hotel number in Atlantic City with his Philadelphia club in case anyone called him there; he had had to go to a charity group meeting in Atlantic City."

"Can you name the charity group?"

"Oh, no. Some church group he was connected with was all the message said."

"Mrs. Rodman that morning called his Philadelphia club to speak to him and was given the Atlantic City number and the message. Correct, Mrs. Ott?"

"Yes."

Abe looked over at Devil Cavanagh. He expected a challenge that didn't come. His back to the witness, Abe asked her, "How do you know?"

"I put through the call for Mrs. Rodman."

"Did Mrs. Rodman go to Atlantic City alone?"

"No, Mr. Mikel, her brother, was in the cab that came to pick her up."

"He had a bag, a piece of luggage, with him too?"

"Yes, he did."

"Were you aware that Mr. Rodman at this time was at the Braymore Hotel in Atlantic City with Mrs. Nash?"

"Objection. The witness has no way of—"

"Sustained. Mr. Pedlock, you know what is proper questioning and what is not."

Rod Miller handed Abe a folder. "Your Honor," Abe said, "I would like to place in evidence, as the state's exhibit B-22, a photostat of a hotel register, of cards for Mrs. Rodman and Mikel Hawley at the St. Charles Hotel in Atlantic City for the dates indicated on the cards. And Exhibit B-23, the register cards from the Braymore Hotel, same dates, for Mr. George Rodman and Mrs. Thomas Nash. His for Room 234, hers for room 236. And this check, signed by George Rodman, made out to the Braymore Hotel, paying for both of these rooms."

Judge Riggs looked over the forms Abe handed him in the folder. "The defense care to examine the exhibits before the clerk marks them as exhibits for the state?"

Tindell shook his head.

Abe turned back to Mrs. Ott. "Mr. and Mrs. Rodman returned to their home from Atlantic City together, didn't they?"

"Yes, they did."

"Was there any indication that they had had a quarrel, a major domestic disagreement?"

"I never poke my nose in my people's business."

Abe joined in the laugh again. "I know, Mrs. Ott. You are a respectable, God-fearing, kindly person. But answer my questions. Did they speak to each other?"

"Of course they spoke."

"A great deal? More than a few words? More than 'It's good to be home,' 'Is the cat in?,' 'Did it rain?' "

"They weren't a talky couple."

The judge pounded for order.

"What did Mrs. Rodman do when they were inside the house? Tell me in detail anything you want. But give the court details."

"She went up to her room."

"Walk or run up the stairs? Did Mr. Rodman carry her? How did she get upstairs?"

"She, she—I'm sorry I'm so slow—she hurried. Didn't run."

"Hurried, didn't run. And Mr. Rodman?"

"He went into his library."

"Walked, didn't hurry, closed the door quietly, or slammed it?"

"He always closed doors briskly."

"He slammed the door hard?"

"No. He had hurt his hand, his right hand, and the doorknob was hard to reach with his left hand. He didn't slam the door."

Abe wiped his face with the palm of his hand. The point had come up better than he had expected. "*Hurt* his hand?"

"It was wrapped in a thick bandage. He couldn't pay off the station cab. Mrs. Rodman had to do it for him."

"Did Mr. Rodman hurt his hand *before* he went to Atlantic City?"

"No, it was properly all right when he left home. He told me he had hurt it in Atlantic City."

Tindell was on his feet. "This court is being mocked. Mr. Pedlock is well aware people do cut their hands, catch their fingers in a door."

(So Sarah Rodman had given the injury no importance and had not informed her lawyers fully of it.)

Abe acted out injured rage. "Does the defense declare I am inventing this hand injury?"

"You have a good, fancy imagination, Mr. Prosecutor. The whole case so far is something out of scientific fiction."

"This evidence isn't going to fly out the window to the moon via a rocket." Abe felt like a very bad actor, but he had to get Tindell angry.

The judge looked from one lawyer to the other. One more exchange and he would rap for respect to the court. Abe turned back to Tindell, wanting that last sharp exchange that would bring the last bit of testimony into sharper detail. "Mr. Tindell and his legal house guest, Mr. Cavanagh—all the way from New York City—have managed so far to treat the state's case as if the brief were written by a ten-year-old moron."

Devil Cavanagh said, "You still overestimate its skill, perhaps its value. Eight-year-old idiot would be closer."

Judge Riggs was rapping for order. "The attorneys will stop this exchange at once. It's no credit to their profession. Mr. Tindell, what is your objection to this testimony of a hurt hand?"

"Immaterial, irrelevant, of no value to the case, and if this piling up of debris keeps up, we'll have the minutes of the Lady Birdwatchers Society, and the scores of the Polack Point Bowling Team on record in this case."

"Your Honor," Abe said, "I do not intend to call either the Lady Birdwatchers or the Polack Point Bowling Team."

Judge Riggs, wiser than Tindell, sensed something. "Objection overruled. *If* the hurt hand is of no value, Mr. Tindell, it can stand."

Tindell was aware now that the point might be important. (Mrs. Rodman had only told him part of the story.) "I see no reason for it. However—"

Abe turned briskly to Mrs. Ott. "Tell Mr. Tindell how Mr. Rodman hurt his hand."

"He had, he said, been shot by accident."

Abe was pleased at the effect this had on the court. The judge covered up a grin.

"And by whom?"

"That is all he said."

"Your witness, Mr. Tindell."

Roger Tindell (it had jarred him) stood up and faced the jury, adjusting the two Roman gold coins set in cuff links in his fine broadcloth shirt. Abe glanced at the jury. The pistol wound had startled them too. They were moving around more than usual, and the bald man in the back row was whispering to the elderly woman who obviously cut her own hair and peered suspiciously at the world from under ragged inky bangs. It was the usual jury; Abe couldn't call it an average jury—he had long ago learned there is no average jury. They were honest enough, moderately literate, and he hoped not too neurotic or cluttered with intellectual grudges against the world; he rather suspected the registered nurse, juror six, with the thick glasses, of an interest in the occult. She jotted down dates and numbers like a believer in horoscopes.

Roger Tindell, covering whatever emotions he felt at this turn in the witness's story, said simply, "No questions."

Clerk Snooky Durant said softly, "The witness will step down."

Abe said, "I call witness John Boles Murad."

A young man with acne scars and varnished brown hair, stooped shoulders under a hound's-tooth jacket with extra-padded shoulders, came forward and was sworn in. Murad had a bovine expression, was a mouth breather, and had a habit of turning his head like an owl on a pivot about once a minute—or like a lighthouse lamp revolving, Abe decided, to take in every corner of the courtroom.

"What is your full name?"

"John M. Boles Murad. The M doesn't stand for nothin'."

"What is your address?"

"606 Arctic Avenue, Atlantic City, New Jersey."

"What is your present employment?"

"I drive a jitney there on Atlantic Avenue that my brother and me own—that is, the two of us."

"On June twelfth of this year what was your employment?"

"I was a bellboy at the Braymore Hotel, on the boardwalk in Atlantic City."

The witness's eyes pivoted from the jury to the three defendants to the table of the prosecutor, enjoyed Mary, and stopped. His long fingers terminated in heavy yellow fingernails curved like small seashells.

"Where were you at eleven o'clock on June twelfth last—that is, at eleven A.M.?"

"I get you." The eyes came back to Abe. "In the mornin'. I was on the second floor havin' just taken up a set of matched pigskin bags for a travelin' salesman named Mitch Condon who often stays at the hotel. He tipped me two bits and I was walkin' toward the east bank of elevators when I heard a small poppin' noise, and—"

"What kind of a popping noise?" Abe broke in. "What did it sound like?"

Tindell said, "Leading the witness, Your Honor."

Abe turned around. "I see no ring in his nose. I am trying to define for the court the exact type of sound this witness heard. Now, Mr. Murad, go on, in your own words, to describe this popping noise. Don't let me suggest it to you. I'll just stand here silently. Go ahead."

"Well, it was the kinda noise a paper bag makes when you fill it fulla air and bang it, and you don't hit it dead center and get a real loud bang. You know what I mean? If I wasn't passin' I wouldna heard it. I mean, it didn't carry far. Then the door of 234 smacks open and a big guy comes out and yells to me, 'Come in here!' I walk in and there are four people in this room. A single—double bed and bath, like all rooms on the wing."

"I want you to describe the people as you remember them, Mr. Murad, and how they were dressed and what they were doing."

The witness half closed his eyes and fingered a healed face scar. He looked cunning and earnest and aware of his importance. "Well, there is this beefy guy who called me in from the hall. He's dressed good, neat but not sharp or zoot, you know. His button-down collar is open and his tie is pulled loose. Then there is this da—, this lady, she is also dressed neat, but not flashy. And standin' by the bathroom door is the guy, the gentleman, whose room it is. I took up his bags that mornin' so I know. He's wearing swimmin' trunks. He's holdin' one hand over the other hand, which is bleedin'. Like *this*—" Murad held his own hand.

"Yes, we understand. Show Mr. Tindell and Mr. Cavanagh just how he was holding his hand. Go on."

"Sittin' on the double bed is the woman from room 236, which is a connectin' room with a door latched on both sides. Which is now open, I see. She is cryin' and her bathin' suit, one of them strapless ones, doesn't fit right, like it had been pulled around or somethin'."

"What do you mean 'somethin' '?"

"Well, the truth is she's trying to get all of her into . . . inside the suit in a hurry when I come in. Or has been and it's tight and torn, and she's havin' trouble. She's cryin'. You know, tears. Nice-lookin' girl. The man in the swimmin' trunks, holdin' his bloody hand, he says, 'It's nothin', just a scratch, I tell you.' The other man says to me, 'Is there a house doctor in the hotel?' I say, 'Yes, Doctor Rolland, but he's makin' a speech at an advertising convention in town.' The man with the hurt hand says, 'It just cut the skin on the back of my hand. We don't need to bring in a doctor.' The cryin' girl she puts her torn suit in place and she puts her face down in her hands and keeps cryin'. I smell something funny in the room."

"An odd atmosphere, Mr. Murad? Describe it in your own way."

"I mean a firecracker kind of smell. And then on the floor I see a shiny revolver. About *this* big. One of them twenty-two kind. Silver-plated, or chrome, I guess, that some broads—women— carry in their handbags. I pick it up. But nobody puts out a hand to take it."

Abe frowned. (The witness is too good. He has a sense of the drama of the scene and he is telling it in order.)

"Didn't you think all this pretty odd? Oops, sorry, Mr. Tindell. Mustn't lead the witness. Go on, Mr. Murad."

"If you've worked in a hotel as long as I have, the things you see, nuttin' is very oddball."

"Anyone take the revolver from you?"

"No."

"What did you do?"

"I put it on the night table. The woman, the standing one, she said, 'Next time I'll bring somethin' bigger and not miss. And tear every stitch off you, you no-good bitch.' "

Abe said, "You sure of the words?"

"Well, maybe she said filthy bitch. Yes, filthy bitch, not no-good bitch."

It was very still in the courtroom. The hiss of the air conduits overhead was heard and the beating of some large bluebottle flies against the windowpanes. Someone coughed and someone shuffled his shoes. Abe glanced at Sarah Rodman; she was expressionless.

"Mr. Murad, to whom did the woman address these words: 'Next time I'll bring something bigger and not miss. And tear every stitch off you, you filthy bitch'?"

"She just said it."

"Whom was she facing?"

"All of them characters."

"Did she address it at one particular person?"

"It was a small room. Nine dollars a day. She just stood near the window and said it."

Abe rubbed his chin. (Better let it go. He's getting too cocky.) "What else did she say?"

"Nuttin'. The big guy said somethin' about not makin' a side-show out of it, and to laugh the whole thing off."

"What were his exact words?"

"That's the gist of them. I was getting a towel from the bathroom and helpin' the man with the hurt hand sop up the blood. It didn't look deep, the wound, but it was bleedin' bad. I saw that. Then the woman on the bed kind of keeled over, and the big man he said to me, 'I think you've been of great help. It was just an accident with a target pistol. Went off by itself. You're a real smart boy. I can see that.'"

"He said that?"

"They always tell you you're real smart and not to report it to the cops. Mostly we don't. Respectable hotels don't, you see, like to make trouble for guests, unless it's somethin' serious like murder or a miscarriage or under the age of consent, doin' the deep six, you know, suicide. Stuff like that we gotta report."

Someone giggled, and the judge beat his handleless gavel hard.

"Bailiff, throw that spectator out of the court."

"Mr. Murad, you told no one about this scene until our investigator interviewed you?"

"No, sir, I didn't."

"Why not? The defense will ask you that."

"Like I said, lots of crazy things happen in hotels that don't get reported, unless somebody gets—"

"Yes, you did explain good hotel practice. Will you look around the courtroom. Do you see the well-dressed large man and the woman who were in the hotel room with the two people in the bathing suits?"

Tindell was quickly on his feet. "I object, Your Honor, to an identification so positive being asked from a witness who only saw some people once in a hotel room."

Abe didn't wait for the judge to rule. "I'll change the question. Do you see any people here who resemble the two people I asked you about in the hotel room?"

The witness nodded, wet his lips, and nervously rubbed the back of his two hands together. "Sure. The man seated at that table and the lady next to him. It's them all right."

"You make a positive identification of them being the two people in the hotel on June twelfth?"

"Sure. Besides, as soon as I saw their pictures in the newspapers a couple of weeks ago I knew it was them."

Devil Cavanagh at the defense table began to laugh, and then to cough and choke. Someone handed him a glass of water. Abe tried to look blandly at his too talkative witness. "And what about the two people in bathing suits? Can you identify them?"

"Sure. Mr. Rodman and Mrs. Nash."

Tindell, without rising from his chair, said, "I gather you can read—so also from the newspapers, Mr. Murad?"

Abe said in a second burst of anger, "Wait your turn, Mr. Tindell. There will be enough meat to get your teeth in." Then, recovering, "Your witness."

Devil Cavanagh stood up, rubbing at some freshly made water stain on his canary-yellow vest. He advanced cheerfully to the stand and faced the witness, hands on hips.

Abe said, "You're honored, Mr. Murad. Mr. Cavanagh will cross-examine."

Devil Cavanagh said, "Your Honor, will the prosecutor please go cool his head."

Cavanagh was a skilled and dramatic cross-examiner, a brutal man when he got a witness to lose his confidence and his limited sureness. Devil Cavanagh was tricky and often ended up in contempt of court, but he was usually victorious for his client.

"Now, Murad, tell this court the last time you were in trouble with the police."

Abe saw the trap at once; Cavanagh was guessing, springing a tricky question on the chance the witness would think the opposition knew everything about him. Before Abe could speak, the witness said from between twisted lips, "It was a bum rap. I didn't know the tires was hot, and they got 'em back."

Cavanagh smiled over his shoulder at Abe as if chiding him for bringing this kind of criminal witness into court. "Just how much time have you served in prisons? A rough guess will do."

"When I was a kid in the gang I got in reform school. A guy I was with just borrowed a car, not tellin' me—"

"Just give us time served, not details, please."

"I was three years in reform. And then I had a two-year stretch in Trenton at the state prison. This gas station was knocked off and—"

"When were you dismissed from the hotel, and for what?"

"I quit. The bell captain was holding out tips on us. He and the doorman had a racket, and we got sore. So when we beefed, the house detective ordered us to—"

Devil Cavanagh turned away. "The witness can stand down."

The witness, now ashamed of himself, his past exposed, started off the stand. Cavanagh turned around as if in afterthought. "Murad, how much—you're under oath—were you slipped by Mr. Rodman in that room, to keep your mouth shut about all that really went on?"

The witness lowered his head. "Twenty bucks."

Abe wondered if enough credibility remained in the witness

to show Sarah Rodman had once fired a pistol and wounded her husband.

In the taxi, driving in the noon heat to the Chichester House, Abe thought of Sarah and the wounding of her husband in the hotel room. How very like her; how he had hidden away the images of Sarah he remembered, the few times they had met in this town, and how far apart they really were and had remained. Except for that one time . . . That one time . . . No, not The Game in the garden. The night of the country club. Had it really happened? Yes, just as she had shot George Rodman in that hotel room. Sarah was always in character no matter what she did. The night of the country club . . .

. . . I didn't see Sarah Rodman after The Game (she was still Sarah Hawley then) until she was seventeen. I was parking cars nights at the country club that summer, taking the cars at the front doors of the club and driving them down past the ivy-covered pump house and onto the gravel parking space, then running quickly back to take another car Old Man McMurtry, the doorman, would wave me to. It wasn't work that was too hard, but I used to get pretty breathless when the cars began to arrive, gleaming, whitewall-tired, in groups just before dinner. Some of the parties—friends or business associates—were already loaded, but the rest would almost all catch up at the bar, and at a table overlooking the river; the colored waiters sliding the trays of martinis, old-fashioneds, Tom Collinses and bourbon-on-the-rocks into place. These were the best town people, and I was impressed by them, while Hal Palattzo's local Dixieland boys played Cole Porter in swing. The elderly folks were a little overweight and given to gray hair rinsed in a blue tinge. "The younger set," as Mary Neely Blair, society editor of *The Hawleytown Home News* called them, were in better shape, but working hard to catch up with their elders drink by drink, meal by meal.

Sarah Hawley drove up this Saturday night in one of those wonderful Packards they used to have in those days; powder-blue, a solid car with powerful lines, disk wheels and power, lots of it, under the hood. She was wearing a tan fur cape over her silver lamé evening gown. I saw she had filled out a bit at Sarah Lawrence, where she was being educated. Freddy Mitchner, in evening clothes, was with her. Freddie was a soft blond boy with lazy eyes and the Amherst look about him; it can't be explained, but certain colleges give some people a look you recognize.

Old Man McMurtry opened the door of the Packard, and Freddie slid out and held a hand to Sarah. Old Man McMurtry waved me forward. "Boy, park Miss Hawley's car. Fine night for dancin', Miss Hawley."

The Dixieland combo was timidly trying out "Yellow Dog Blues" (later when most everybody was properly fried, the club's usual Saturday-night brawl, the boys would begin to jam and improvise around something stronger). I stepped to the car and Sarah passed me. I didn't expect her to remember me from our one meeting years before in the family garden, and she didn't. She had developed her legs, and her breasts were pear-shaped, half out of the silver lamé gown, which fitted her well. Her dark hair smelled of something exotic I couldn't name.

"Damn it, Abe," said Old Man McMurtry, "drag-tail out of here with that Packard. The mayor is just behind."

I leaped into the baby-blue leather seat, still warm from her body, and clashed gears and went off down to the parking area. I had never before envied the country club crowd and their fancy life; I was very young, callow and earnest and overworked and had a goal. Now suddenly running back up the rise to the country club porch, I wondered why there couldn't be a girl like Sarah Hawley for me—warm, clean, perfumed, sure of herself, and able to arrive casually in several thousand dollars' worth of mobile machinery.

Old Man McMurtry spoke over his shoulder as he opened a door. "Abe, take the mayor's car down and run back. Here come the Tumiltys, and Doc Wymer, and he's goin' to hit the porch post—he's oiled already."

I drove the mayor's car off. Behind me I heard Doctor Wymer's auto crunch into a porch post. In half an hour the dinner rush was over, and Old Man McMurtry went around to the side porch where the bar kept its empty beer cases, and he came back, stepping the way a Spanish-American war hero should, wiping his mouth, and he said, "Go snag yourself some dinner. It's a long night. And don't go flashin' yer searchlight into the parked cars and don't ask who's with who. Ah, the quality they live it up nice and soft, don't they now, lad?"

I had a steak and half an apple pie in the lean-to behind the kitchen and shot the breeze with Ollie Hansen, the salad cook who smoked a thin cigar and lied about his life in the Navy. After that I helped Old Man McMurtry and a driver get Mrs. Seeder into her green Lincoln; she was a fine old lady, and two drinks did for her and she was no bother and always sent Old Man McMurtry a five-dollar bill Monday, and he often gave me a dollar of it.

"Well, lad, you keep the watch. I'm goin' unofficially to test some brew for the liquor committee of the club."

It was cool alone under the club porch, the moon tarnishing the river below, and the band playing free and easy now, swinging a few licks into "Melancholy Baby." There was a scuffle in the club entrance, and Mikel Hawley came out shaking off somebody's arm. He had just been bounced out of Princeton and had grown into a young man large and full of muscles. He hadn't raised the Hemingway mustache yet, but you could see he would be a big, ornate member of the country gentry, in a too solid way.

"You see my sister Sarah?" he asked, not looking at me.

"No, I haven't."

"She's out here—I know it—someplace with that trumpet player, that character Welton. You know about trumpet players? Anybody ever tell you they're all cocksmen?"

"I hadn't heard," I said. Mikel wasn't dangerously drunk—not for a Saturday night at the country club—but a few more and he could turn mean, as the college boys from the better families sometimes did. Old Man McMurtry, the waiters and myself had learned how to handle them. But I never liked it, and I didn't think it would be easy to pull Mikel Hawley's arms around behind his back and walk him toward the car-parking area while telling him, "Sure, sure, sir, you just need a little air, sir, that's all, a little sniff of air."

Mikel Hawley looked down at his patent-leather shoes. "Where does she think she is? Weekending out at Hampton with the usual cruds in her group?" He leaned toward me, the snappy young college man, democratically inclined, while in liquor, to share his problems with a fellow townsman. "The sooner we marry Sarah off the better. Always off on a psycho kick. Need a drink." He frowned and turned and went back inside.

I looked down toward the parking area. Two or three dash-board lights were on. I could hear the low, tinny growl of some car radios, a fragment of Bing Crosby in voice.

"Well, that's what country club parkin' spaces are for," Mc-Murtry said at my shoulder, smelling of the club's private stock. He was smoking a large cigar and handed me one. "Uncomfortable way of makin' love. But that may be half the fun—standin' on yer ear."

I got out the hose and watered down the black-top drive, coiled the hose, and went back to the kitchen and had a cup of coffee. There was yelling from the parking area, and I ran out, pulling my flashlight out of my back pocket, and the only impression I had was that the night had turned very cool, and the band was *not* playing, just the piano player with a good left hand fingering Noel Coward's "Someday I'll Find You."

I remembered—I don't know why I expected the trouble there—where I had parked the blue Packard and I ran for it. Sarah, slim legs hanging out of the car, was seated there, and Mikel Hawley was battering at a long thin man with the indoor pallor of a reefer-smoking jazzman. The trumpet man was not defending himself, just getting up with dignity and saying, "Listen, cat, listen, don't be a lousy square. I mean, man, the chick suggested it."

Sarah, her shoes off, her hair hanging in her face, was laughing. "Break his jaw, Jimmie, break his goddamn jaw. Don't let him hit you again."

I grabbed Mikel, who threw me off and swung, and the jazzman went down again, his mouth a fearful mess. (I wondered how he'd ever lip a trumpet again.) I had hold of Mikel's left arm and was twisting. Ollie Hansen, the salad chef, was there suddenly, and he had the other arm, but it wasn't until Old Man McMurtry came up and put his long arms around Mikel's shoulders that we had him helpless.

"Now, there, Mr. Hawley, it's not worth brawlin' like this at the club, and yer folks charter members and all. You just come on back to the locker room and calm down."

"Take your goddamn bog-trotter hands off me."

We didn't relax our hold. Old Man McMurtry said, "Now, Mr. Hawley, you just come along. Abe, get Welton back to the dressing room."

Old Man McMurtry and the salad chef walked a muttering, tightly held Mikel off. I leaned over the trumpet player, who was pushing a dirty handkerchief at his torn mouth. I got him to his feet and asked, "How are you?"

"How the eff do you think I am? I won't be able to take a gig for a couple of weeks with this swollen lip."

Sarah shook her shoulders and grinned. "Come here, Jimmie, and I'll kiss it."

The jazzman looked at her with a cold eye, said a string of obscenities and walked off slowly, shaking his head.

Sarah, expressionless, moved over to the driver's seat and stepped on the starter. It grated, clashed, but the motor remained dead. I went around and pushed Sarah by the naked shoulder to the other seat and got behind the wheel. "You've flooded it."

"What are you waiting for?"

"The gasoline to evaporate." I put the fur cape around her. "It's getting cold."

"You better drive. I've had a hatful of drink."

"All right."

"You know where I live?"

"Up at Barraclough Manor."

She leaned against me, wet mouth open. "I know you. Don't I know you?"

"No, you don't know me."

"No, I guess not. I don't know what happened here. That hill-billy was all right—didn't mean any real harm, I mean. I mean, Mikel is a prude, a real solid jackass about these things. Just a little making out with a nice guy, I mean. You like jazz?"

"Some of it."

"Mikel is going to kill somebody someday. Violent temper."

I started the car and swung it up the drive and gave Old Man McMurtry the old club sign—a gesture of swallowing a drink—that I was helping a country club member home and would take a taxi back. There was an empty road along the river, and Sarah stared ahead of her as if in a trance. Then she began to cry. I didn't do anything but watch the night road and the insects bumping noses around the high yellow globes of the road lights; some of the houseboats on the river had lanterns out, and I could hear voices in unseen canoes. I swung the car up the climbing road to Barraclough Manor.

Sarah went on crying. As we came to the gates she said, "Wait a minute."

She wiped her eyes, blew her nose, pulled her silver lamé dress around and shook her head. "*Why* do I do these things?"

"Shall I drive up to the house?"

She grabbed my arm. "Don't be so starchy and formal, fella. Be friendly."

She hunted in a small pearl-studded handbag and held up an open, thin, gold cigarette case. This time she had American tobacco. I lighted her smoke and the one I took, and we sat puffing.

She looked at me, trying to shake cigarette smoke out of her eyes. "Look at me."

She put an arm on the back of the seat and around my neck. "You know, you think I don't remember you, but I do."

"You better go in, Miss Hawley."

"Sarah to you." She leaned over and kissed me, smelling of alcohol and Virginia tobacco (what a foolish detail to remember) and young-girl odor and excited flesh, and her mouth was warm

and wet, the way it was always described in very bad novels. I
didn't bother to have any literary thoughts beyond that one, and
she pulled me over and for a desperate moment I ached and gave
way and she began to open my shirt and then my belt buckle.

I wanted to resist, but I didn't. I watched her lower her
evening dress and expose her breasts, and she pulled my head
down between them, and the rest of it was quick and cruel, done
in great haste but with fine feeling. I drifted and twisted and I
held her. When it was all over I had gained a kind of pride in
being. I had crossed over the line that marked off a poor, dull,
plodding young man with no background and no money. This
lusty girl had accepted my manhood, here, on the top of the
world where the Hawleys lived in their great lion house, lording
over the town and the county and the state. I thought I loved
her. Loved her then, not protectively—she was too much for
that—but as an equal. She broke the dream suddenly by pushing
me off.

"Stop looking at me that way. It's only a crazy mistake."

"You better go in now."

Her fingers gripped mine. I saw her shake off a tear.

"Be real friendly. I've had a horrible holiday time home from
school. Everybody asking me how is school. Well, let's face it.
It's dull and the girls are dull and when I get away weekends
I drink too much and I get sick. I can't really drink—you know
what I mean? But what else is there to do with these college boys?
You don't drink, or let them know you crack a book once in a
while, and you're Miss Back Row and you might as well get a
roommate with short hair and go dyke. Light a cigarette, fella."

I lighted one, and she closed her eyes. I drove the Packard up
the drive, went around and opened the door. Sarah put her arms
around my neck and hung on. "I can walk. I can walk fine. Just
start me in the right direction."

I leaned her against the door and pressed the bell button.

She said, "It's all mixed up. Mikel is a fool. Mikel spoiled his
lip. That trumpet player wanted to marry me."

A servant opened the door and I asked, "Will you please phone
for a cab for me?"

Abe in the taxi rubbed his damp face. In a small town like this it's odd how you know almost everyone and meet them every few months—even years—and you think nothing of it until something like murder happens. Then some things fall into place, and some don't. In a daffy calf-love way he had been in love with Sarah Hawley, the one big moment, the few images of her he could recapture. Until he met Fran. Then full reality was stronger, and desire in one's arms was so much better than something once possessed and respected from far off; what the hell kind of thinking was this on *this* Monday? . . .

. . . But I can't stop thinking about Sarah this morning. I don't know why. Hell, yes I do. In the car with her that night I changed from a frightened boy into a man. And now we're both older and both trapped in different ways. Everything was simple then, and now it's not.

I loved her then, or I thought I did. And now I don't feel anything much. It's a case. And I want to win it. And if I do?

But there's no turning back to the past. I couldn't throw the case even if I wanted to, just because I remember what it was like all those years ago.

And what does *she* think of it? Does she remember that night? Probably not. For her I was just another boy, and not a very suitable one. Not a very experienced one either.

And she's a Hawley. If she does remember, she won't show it and she won't expect me to. It's The Game. . . .

I remember the next time I spoke to Sarah Hawley, then already Sarah Rodman, and murder done. I was deep in sleep that night, when the phone began to ring downstairs in the hall. I got out of bed to avoid waking Fran—making another mental note to have an upstairs phone put in while I was with the D.A.'s office.

"Hello? Don't you know it's one o'clock in the morning?"

A dignified old voice on the line answered. "This is Eli Chaucer talking, Mr. Pedlock."

"Yes, Mr. Chaucer. What can I do for you?" The head of the old Maryland law firm that represented the Hawley family in-

terests didn't usually call anyone late at night; and most likely
he never had in his long, successful legal life.

"I'm picking you up in half an hour. I want you to come with
me to the old Hawley house at Barraclough Manor."

"What's this all about, Mr. Chaucer?"

"If you want, arrange to have two detectives from the county
staff with you. I guarantee everything is legal and aboveboard. I
have, you know, a certain reputation for integrity and conduct in
this state, and—"

"Certainly, Mr. Chaucer. I don't question your motives at all."

"Good. In half an hour, then."

The phone clicked off and I stood wondering, then called the
night desk at the county station and asked for two plain-clothes
men to be detailed to me. I went slowly upstairs to dress, wondering if I could do it without waking Fran. (I couldn't.)

Mr. Chaucer, in his car, shook hands but said nothing beyond
the usual banal greetings. He nodded to the two beefy detectives,
and we all got into the huge black car, ten years out of date, and
drove to the Hawley house in Barraclough Manor. The gate
lights were on and the house itself had many lighted windows. I
told the plain-clothes men to wait outside, and Mr. Chaucer rang
the bell hidden in the wall ivy. Mikel Hawley let us in. There
were no servants about.

Mikel was wearing a neat tweed suit—English-tailored, I
suspected—a striped blue shirt and a thin black knit tie. He
looked ready for a long trip. Mr. Chaucer and I followed him into
a large paneled room with old framed maps and a great many
leather-bound books that looked rubbed down with saddle soap.
There were some watercolors that I remembered from an old
college Art II class as being Turners. Sarah Rodman was standing
by an unlighted fireplace; she was wearing a fitted knit-wool
dress of a deep blue, and her dark heavy head of hair was pulled
back and pinned behind her neck. Batty Billie was seated on a
chair, his arms folded, staring with interest at the bearskin rug
under his feet.

Sarah turned her head toward us as we came in. There was
little left now in her of the teen-ager in the garden or the country

club flapper. She was a tall, mature woman, with smooth, solid planes on her pale face, and only the eyes and the curl of the mouth suggested those things I had witnessed or experienced with her. Perhaps she was not really beautiful; she was certainly impressive.

"Thank you, Eli," she said.

The old lawyer nodded. "Mr. Pedlock, it has seemed best that—"

Sarah shook her head and placed an arm on the lawyer's broad-cloth shoulder. "Let me talk. Mr. Pedlock, you represent the District Attorney?"

"Yes I do. I'm an assistant, or deputy, district attorney. I have been appointed by the office to proceed with—with this case."

"The murder of my husband and a woman?"

"That's right."

She nodded. "We have been informed that indictments are to be served on us tomorrow morning. That we are to be arrested."

"I didn't come here to explain anything, Mrs. Rodman."

"No. Of course not. However, to avoid an arrest in public, with its cameramen and pushing crowds, my brothers and I are ready to surrender to your indictments tonight. Right now."

Mr. Chaucer said softly, "Much against my advice, I might add."

"Yes, Eli," said Sarah Rodman. "That can be part of the record. Well, Mr. Pedlock, shall we go?"

"No arrangements have been made tonight for receiving you. But I think the sheriff can house you all tonight in his apartment. Of course you know that because of the nature of the indictments there can be no bail."

The old lawyer said, "Let's make no firm ruling tonight, Mr. Pedlock. The people in your indictment just want to surrender themselves tonight. You don't, I hope, object?"

I thought of the newspapermen, the cameramen from out of town, the TV groups, and I shook my head. "No. This avoids a lot of shoving and pushing."

Sarah nodded. "I'll take my own car, if it's all right, and you, Mr. Pedlock, can ride with me, and one of your officers."

She seemed to take command naturally, and I nodded. However, I sent both detectives back with Mikel and Batty Billie and Eli Chaucer. I asked Sarah Rodman if she minded if I drove her car.

"If you want to. You ever arrest a woman before?"

"Oh, yes, Mrs. Rodman. I used to draw the late raids down near the ferry station when the cat houses were raided."

She laughed, and hunted in a handbag. "I forgot my cigarettes."

"I'm sorry. I only smoke stogies."

I drove carefully. Sarah Rodman, a tan coat over her shoulders, sat by my side. "Ever drive a woman accused of murdering her husband?"

"Yes. Twice."

"What happened to them? I have a purely clinical interest."

I shook my head. "No comment, Mrs. Rodman."

I felt her shiver slightly. "You haven't changed much since my birthday party. You know, you never really played The Game properly that day."

"I didn't think you'd remember, Mrs. Rodman," I said.

"Oh, yes, I did."

She was thoughtful and silent the rest of the trip to the sheriff's office. Had she forgotten the night of the country club fight? . . .

The taxi pulled up in front of the club.

CHAPTER VII

AROUND THE TABLE

THE CHICHESTER HOUSE, "the town's oldest and most exclusive dining club," was set high up on a grassy cliff on the rim of Barraclough Park, facing the blue bay on one side and the green river on the other. Abe got out of the cab into the lime-white sunlight and gave the driver two dollars. He could not afford to take taxis like this; Fran, however, needed the one car they had for the kids' school and for shopping. Unlike the rest of the D.A.'s staff, he could not bring himself to add the taxi to his expense account. But—what the hell—he wasn't invited to the Chichester House every day. In fact, it was only the second time he had ever been there. The other visit was to the testimonial dinner for Ed Hightower.

Touching the collar band of his just-changed-into shirt, Abe walked into the marble hallway through the solid plate-glass doors the Negro doorman held open for him. A sweet stream of air, well cooled and slightly scented, greeted him. Under mounted game heads of dangerous animals Abe hadn't thought about since his childhood storybook days he stood, while the club steward searched a list, bowed to him, and said, "This way, Mr. Pedlock."

Two dozen people lunched in various rooms with leisure and ease, in surroundings of pale-green and pastel-colored covered furniture too comfortable for any modern designer. There was no smell of cooking, and the waxed furniture proclaimed its age discreetly on Queen Anne legs. In one shaded corner of the small turquoise dining room, under indifferent paintings of the Hudson River school that were turning brown, Big Ed Higgins and Jake Barton were seated at a table watching a mulatto waiter set down old-fashioneds. The political chief was solid where Jake Barton was soft. He was tanned, large-fisted, with prominent knuckles on well-muscled hands (as Abe discovered when the introductions were over). Big Ed shook hands till the bones protested, and Abe wondered how this would fit into a psychologist's frame of reference.

"I know, Pedlock, you belong in court setting off legal land mines. But it's my one free lunch date this week."

"It's all right, Mr. Higgins; Judge Riggs has recessed till three this afternoon. He has to pose for some photographs on a magazine story about Hawleytown. This trial has attracted national attention, I regret to say."

Barton unfolded his napkin. "I arranged it, Ed. This damn picture magazine is usually so full of the opposition party's propaganda, I couldn't resist shoving this at them. An old-fashioned, Abe?"

"No, I have a key witness to put on this afternoon. I'll take a beer."

"They have fine draught beer here," said Big Ed as he turned to the very light waiter. "Dudley, bring Mr. Pedlock a pitcher of beer. And get the steak off the fire. I don't like it too well done."

Dudley bowed and walked off; the club never hired white help, Abe had heard. They preferred Negroes who acted the part of old family retainers, types called Uncle Toms and handkerchief-heads by other Negroes.

It was good beer. They talked of the weather and the view of the bay and river, and the real-estate values of twenty years ago, when "great bargains could still be gotten in the neighborhood." The steak came on a hissing platter, a sizzling, savory side of beef, and it was sliced at the table. The three men ate, helped themselves to a tossed salad, and sipped iced coffee. Abe found he was hungry and, for the first time in a week, comfortable and cool. His shirt dried.

Big Ed cut sharply into the thick slice of meat on his plate. "Pedlock, the party takes an interest in bright young men. Our party is the party of the people, and it's a political party, which means it's called dirty, a machine to turn out the votes, and tricky to win elections. All true. We haven't got the big-business money like the opposition, but we play the same kind of politics they do. But I don't have to tell a smart lawyer all this."

"I'm a loyal Sixth Ward man myself. Started there in justice court fender-and-wreck cases."

"They say I'm an honest party boss, and I've found that to be a smart policy. We have a good, well-run state. We try to do better."

Jake Barton took out a large pipe, filled it carefully with the aid of a wide thumb and an oilskin bag of aromatic tobacco. He said, "We have our crooks, grafters, freeloaders, Abe, the same as all party machines. We play footsie with labor unions and corporations. But in people like Senator Barraclough we have a pretty great man for the country. Governor Dooley is the best man in the capitol in fifty years."

"No speeches, Jake," said Big Ed Higgins, throwing down his napkin and letting Dudley set fire to his cigar. He held out the leather cigar case to Abe. "Montecristos. Try them."

"No, thanks. I can't afford to get to like them. I'll smoke these stogies. I get them mail order, a hundred for three dollars."

They sat digesting, enjoying the full effects of their tobacco. With a stiff finger, Big Ed drew a square on the tablecloth. "Pedlock, we're thinking of running a young man for District Attorney, making him District Attorney. Dooley likes your record. Jake likes it. And you look like an eager beaver to me. With brains. And no smart-aleck. You could become a power in the party, and if you're thinking of going that way, you could become a high-court judge before you're fifty. You're a Jew, I'm a Catholic; that makes us outsiders. But the party doesn't worry too much about a man's genes if he's got the ability to get off his duff and use his head for more than a hat rack. Or do you want lucrative criminal defenses?"

Abe carefully shook the long ash off his stogie into the silver club ashtray. "Something is bothering you about me, Mr. Higgins."

Barton said, "What'd I say about him, Ed? Aware, *very* aware."

"I let the courts run the processes of law. If I don't like the way it's done, I change it. But when it's the law I obey it. This trial, now . . ."

(I knew it was something like this. The two of them, powerful, successful, but worried, like some prospective client in a jam. Always worried about their positions. Their faces half the time are turned back to see where they came from. And always worried about how high they've come. Bright men, both of them. And they want something from me. About the trial.)

"If my political future, Mr. Higgins, depends on winning this case, I wouldn't take any heavy bets on me. It's a very involved case. And I don't know how much relevant admissible evidence I can get by Judge Riggs."

"No, no, the way you're handling it is more important than putting Mrs. Rodman and the two Hawleys into prison. Naturally we don't hang Hawleys in this state. Not all frailty is evil, Father O'Mara says."

Jake Barton smiled and sipped his iced coffee. "They may not be the important original Hawleys that intermarried with the Barracloughs, but they're country cousins who came to town barefooted and hungry and managed to grab up about everything, including a social position."

(I still don't get it. The Hawleys are big important leaders of the opposition party. They hate Big Ed, and even their distant relative Senator Paul Hawley Barraclough for being a turncoat and Big Ed's friend.)

"You may think what the hell are the Hawleys to me. I'm no evasive witness. And I tell you, Pedlock, they're not a small wind making a bad smell in a paper bag to me. I'm big-gummed shanty Irish and my grandfather was a redheaded potato-famine ape who pounded stone ballast as a gandy dancer on the Panhandle, Southern and Great Gulf right-of-ways. But I'm a citizen with a place of my own in this community and it's a beautiful place. This trial can destroy a lot here I don't want destroyed. Tell me, have you a real case? Or are you grandstanding?"

"I have a very solid case, Mr. Higgins. Up to a point."

"Maman Celie your eyewitness?"

"That's right. Will she be believed in court, you want to ask? I don't know. I believe her."

"Do you?" Big Ed looked at him directly, assured and taciturn. Abe stared back, using an old lawyer's trick, looking not into Big Ed's eyes but at a point just between them where the powerful nose began its jutting shape. No man could stand that stare long. Big Ed laughed. "Don't give me the Big-Chief-Stare-in-the-Face. Do you fully believe your eyewitness?"

"I'm going to put her on the stand."

"You believe? It's not just courtroom histrionics?"

"She's an odd old gal. The defense might make her so ridiculous in court she'll do more harm than good. Or she might lose her temper and raise up a storm and curse them all out, rattling her magic omens."

Big Ed killed his cigar by breaking its neck in the club ashtray. He touched his thin lips with the corner of his napkin. "Pedlock, that D.A. talk for a good young man was no soft soap. But I'm not interfering in this trial. I don't work that way. But if you think I'm too soft worrying about the Hawleys' position in local society, just remember you're worth less to the party if you become the laughingstock by using a witness that isn't going to impress the court; and maybe with this testimony your whole case can be made to look like a pipe dream."

"I've been thinking it over for several days. I've just about decided not to call her today. But maybe tomorrow."

"Jake here is a lawyer. He'll tell you to save your best witness for the last. Law, I once heard, is the putting of an accepted pattern on experiences. Eh, Jake?"

Jake Barton, devious, complicated, wise, looked at his wristwatch. "I was never much of a trial lawyer. I did my best, but I knew I couldn't win them all. It's the process of the law we lawyers protect, Abe—the code of society, the individual. I'm not good at giving advice at a trade I was never much good at myself."

Big Ed looked sourly at Barton and with a wild hentrack scrawl signed the club check.

They parted cheerfully, with firm hand grips of solid citizens

too full of lunch, and Jake Barton said, "I'll be seeing you, Abe."
And he answered, "Sure, Jake."

Back at the courthouse the judge was still out at two-thirty,
and Abe went to the attorneys' room and called Fran on the
phone. Her voice sounded loud and worried. "Oh, Abe, we've
had a dreadful morning."

"One of the kids, something happen?" Images of domestic
tragedies filled his mind.

"No, the cat, Tom. He just seemed so sick. I took him down
to Doc Cathers', the vet, and he said he's just a very old cat."

"Why don't you have Doc put him away? It's kinder."

"No, I couldn't do that. Tom's old, but he's still something
alive. I can't."

"But Tom will only suffer in this weather with his heavy coat
and his asthma."

"Doc gave him a shot and some pills. It's pitiful to look at
Tom. His eyes stare at me as if I've let him down."

"Better let him be put away. He at Doc's?"

"No, Doc said Tom would feel better at home, in surroundings
he knows. What kind of morning have you had?"

"It's hard to tell." The room smelled of old tennis shoes and
was painted a bilious green. Abe heard Fran inhale hard, a habit
she had when she wanted a little extra courage.

"Abe, you'll think things out. I mean—" she inhaled again—
"oh, do what you think best, honey. See you for supper."

Fran still said the country word *supper*. He blew her a kiss
over the phone. "All right. And don't worry over Tom. He's a
very, very old character. Hot on Ann Street?"

"Steaming out here. How's court?"

"Boiling. I'm going to get into my last dry shirt right now."

Abe hung up, feeling happy at talking to Fran, wondering what
his life would have been if he hadn't met and married her. He
hurried off to change his shirt again.

He let his thoughts wander as he buttoned on the crisp broad-
cloth. Courting Fran—marrying Fran—in spite of her sisters' disapproval. Abe reflected as he smoked. He remembered their first

room on Sumter Street and his first breaks as a young lawyer. He sweated delicately in memory. Wonderful times. He and Fran camping out on the beach, sailing in Ed Hightower's ketch around the bay and down to Annapolis, or packing in on horseback at Lone Mountain up in the Blue Ridge country, and eating rainbow trout and drinking black coffee from tin cups. Sleeping and loving on pine boughs, and brushing the dew of morning off their faces before swimming in the ice-cold stream under blowsy storm skies. Such plain and simple happiness.

Fran had a good voice, and they used to sing: *"O Tannenbaum, O Tannenbaum, wie grün sind deine Blätter."*

Abe knocked out his stogie butt and put it into a ceramic ashtray that Deedee had made in a summer camp. Deedee had Fran's serene, reflective stare, the deft charm, enormously sure of itself, self-contained like an egg.

Deedee's birth had changed the settled mold of their life. It was the year the D.A. had asked if he liked politics, and the year Fran's aunt died; the year they moved into the house, while Abe worked in the D.A.'s office and Ed Hightower said he might do. Fran at first had gone odd on producing a child, had locked him out of her life after the birth of the soft, pretty baby. A fear of germs and local help seemed to enter into her; she locked herself and the baby into the nursery and the front bedroom. They wore gauze masks over mouth and nose, they bought fancy sterilizing machines. Doc Ringel came and went the moment the baby sneezed or rashed. The informal poker and beer parties that began in the house Friday night and lasted till Monday morning were done away with. But Fran grew calmer, her old self. At three years of age Deedee had an infected ear. Fran lost weight, but both recovered. Deedee was a big, spoiled, healthy baby. Then Davey was born. They were a family.

Very ordinary and very satisfactory, Abe decided. (Now, how am I going to get some relevant evidence out of my next witness?)

The courtroom was uncomfortable in the muggy afternoon. Court had readjourned at 3:10, with the judge looking serious, poker-faced, but not apparently in pain. Abe felt waterlogged, he had drunk too much beer and eaten too much food at the Chichester and had a tendency to yawn in the damp heat of the courtroom. It would be fine to get into a soft bed of cool linen, lower the shades and go to sleep.

Chief of Detectives Jasper Smith was being sworn in. Abe had changed into his third shirt of the day and stood near the stand holding a damp handkerchief between his fingers, watching the big bulk of the new witness indifferently take the oath. Chief Smith had an astonishingly high voice for such a large, lumpy man, and his close-cropped black hair showed a great deal of red scalp. He had been in the law-enforcement office for six years, and before that he had been important in the police department of St. Louis. Local courthouse rumor was that he had been forced to resign after a gang-killing witness died while undergoing examination by the chief. No one knew very much about Chief Smith except that he didn't smoke or drink, wasn't married, and lived on a small farm two miles beyond town. Hospital bills for hoodlums injured in the county jail while "falling downstairs," or "out of chairs," were interesting items on the yearly budget. Abe was aware of a devious, complicated ego.

He moved toward his witness, balling up the handkerchief between the palms of his hands.

"You are Jasper Smith, chief of detectives of this county?"

"Yes."

"You were at your office on duty on the night of July eighteenth last?"

"I was."

"Will you tell the court what happened after you left your office in the county jail that night."

The big man clasped his hands together on his stomach, as if he were still a boy in school. "I'm not given to regular hours of duty off or on. I'm always on call. That night I left my office at ten o'clock and went over to Peter Blue's bar, where I had heard through a connection that somebody was using loaded dice in the back room. I got home at eleven-thirty or thereabouts. I heard the twelve o'clock news on the radio, and on the short-wave police circuit that a hamburger stand had been knocked over, robbed, in the next county. After which—"

Judge Riggs leaned forward. "Chief Smith, it's a very warm day so it's all right to skip details not related to this case."

"Yes, Your Honor. At two-twenty-eight my direct line rang. This is now the morning of July nineteenth."

"We understand."

The girl at the shorthand machine nodded in agreement.

The chief of detectives took a small notebook from a pocket. "This is my personal notebook that I keep for jotting down things as they happen."

Abe said, "I'm sure the court will permit you to document your memory. The defense object?"

Tindell waved a no.

"It was officer Harve Fugate, on duty on Leap Road, calling in direct. I have orders that in any major development I get called the same time they call in to H.Q. Harve Fugate, said, 'Chief, there's something pretty terrible has happened out here on the lane.' The chief looked up. "Fugate is a rookie and he was being broken in by patrolling Leap Road. It's about the usual kind of lovers' lane, where people go in cars to pet and make out, and the police feel it's better to have these sort of things under constant patrol than to have people go just anyplace and get held up or molested."

Judge Riggs said, "Yes, we understand, Chief Smith. Don't digress so much."

"Harve Fugate said there had been a double murder right across from the apple orchard, about half a mile off the main highway. I got dressed, got my car, and was there in twenty-two minutes. The apple orchard forms a kind of bend in the road, and across from it there is a half acre of low bush and some pine trees. There's a wire gate lettered *No Trespassing* and the sign *The River Boat Club*. The club burned down ten years ago and the place is all wild growth now. Past the gate I found two prowl cars, their headlights and spots turned on two bodies layin' on a blanket on the ground under a big pine. White squares of paper later identified as letters were scattered over the bodies."

Abe asked, "Officer Fugate told you on the phone who they were?"

"No. He said he didn't know either of them. As I got out of my car, I heard the department ambulance make the turn into the place past the wire gate, and then the medical examiner's car. Fugate and Troopers Redman and Cahn of the State Police were standing over the bodies. I asked, 'Has anything been touched?' Fugate said nothing had. The moon had come up. There was a small breeze, and the spots and headlights of the prowl cars gave us all the illumination we needed."

"Give us the exact positions and conditions of the bodies, Chief Smith, as you first saw them."

The big man turned a page in his notebook. "The body later identified by Medical Examiner Cook as George Rodman was lying on his back. My actual notes read: 'Age late thirties, by appearances, tall, six feet two, about one hundred eighty in weight, dressed in gray tweet suit, buttoned-down white Oxford shirt, tie off, found later in his own car parked behind the burned-out clubhouse. No vest, English imported brown leather shoes, pale-blue socks, no garters. Wearing black belt. An Engar Swiss wrist-watch; no other jewels. Wallet—personal contents listed. Two hundred six dollars not removed. A key chain, three keys, a cigar cutter, twenty-six cents in silver. A tin of contraceptives. Body not yet cold or stiff. Had been shot through the left chest. A forty-five rifle slug emerged two inches from back and was found in soil under blanket and body.' "

Judge Riggs asked, "Isn't this all covered in the medical examiner's and county pathologist's report? Mr. Pedlock, I hope we're not to hear all this over and over again from witness after witness."

Abe turned to face the judge. "Your Honor, we have placed the medical examiner and pathologist on the stand. But I want to include all this now as being a first impression, just after the crime was discovered. Before the doctors went to work."

Judge Riggs waved Abe back to his witness. "Just remember not to repeat testimony. Go on, Chief Smith."

"Touching the body of the dead man was the body of the dead

woman, identified in the morning by her husband, Mr. Thomas Nash, as his wife Helen Nash. Again from my notes made at the time: 'She was in her late twenties, weight about a hundred and thirty pounds. Dark, thick hair—loose. Wearing a green knit dress, a garter belt attached to flesh-colored nylon stockings. Nearby on the ground were a brassière, white lace-trimmed panties, a pair of blue leather women's I. Miller shoes, open-toed. She had been hit full in the face with a blast of a .410-gauge shotgun load. Very close. Estimate at the range of about six feet. The condition of her head made identification difficult. Her husband identified her by a small diamond-set wristwatch, an anniversary gift, a wide gold wedding ring. The pair of ruby earrings her husband said he never saw before. Later her dentist identified certain inlays and dental work for positive identity.' "

"Did the shotgun blast kill her?"

"The medical examiner found a bullet hole in her heart and a slug was recovered—from the same rifle that killed the man, our lab reports."

"Which was fired first, the rifle or the shotgun?"

"There is no way of telling. It could be assumed the shotgun blast was first, and then she was finished off with the bullet shot to put her out of her misery, if she was still twitching."

Abe waited for the objection he knew was coming. Tindell's voice remained level but crisp. "Objection to the witness deviating into details of this sort to tickle the morons who read the newspapers. We never denied there have been two deaths."

"Thank you," said Abe simply, facing the jury with a grin. "It's nice to know the defense admits there have been two murders."

"We said deaths," repeated Roger Tindell.

"The bullet holes and the shotgun blasts make it murder."

Devil Cavanagh stood up, serious-faced, hands deep in pockets. "Your Honor, the prosecutor is a young man making his way up in the world, and of course from our viewpoint the worse he conducts this case the better we like it. But in fairness to the local bar association, among whom I have many friends—"

Abe asked in a low voice, "Would the imported gentleman from big, sophisticated New York City like a soapbox?"

Judge Riggs shook his head in disapproval. "This is all time-consuming. Just what is the defense objection?"

Devil Cavanagh went on. "We object to the details of the dismal scene, a gory one, as we have heard now from two witnesses on opening day of this trial, being dragged around like butchered Christians in a Roman arena to entertain the slobbering newspaper mob. I belong to a religion that thinks the human body, in life or death, is sacred."

Abe said crisply, "I believe, with Mr. Cavanagh standing at attention, we shall now get Old Glory waved next, and a statement that Mr. Cavanagh, a solid family man and a power in Tammany Hall, is for home, mother and the five-day week. I am perfectly willing to turn Chief Smith over to the defense to prove through what they can ask him that the murders never took place, that no one was shotgunned and rifled to death. And that how dare an ordinary court try people for murder."

Judge Riggs rapped for order. "No more talk from anyone. We'll all calm down. And take a fifteen-minute recess. The clerk will strike out all this bickering, and see if the cake of ice has been delivered in my chambers. The defense and the state are invited into my chambers for a drink of lemonade. And *no* shop talk."

When Snooky Durant called the court back to proceed, Tindell rose to face the judge. "Your Honor, we do not want to drag out this hot day, as you so well put it, in bickering. We again object, however, to Chief Smith's being asked, from his police report, to guess at theories, at conjectures there are no ways of proving."

Abe shook his head as if shocked at what he was hearing. "We hope to prove this is no conjecture. Chief Smith is an expert on both weapons and crime procedures."

Judge Riggs spoke up with a fierce urgency. "Objection sustained. The witness will stick to only what he saw and observed."

The witness was turkey red and twisting his notebook in big, clumsy-looking hands. Abe moved close to his witness. "Have you now told the court all you observed about the condition of the bodies?"

"Pretty much."

"In a court, pretty much isn't enough." Abe motioned to Rod Miller, who handed him two enlarged photographs. "Chief Smith, are these official police photographs taken within an hour of the discovery of the crime?"

"They look like them."

"Take them, examine them. Are these the police serial numbers and code marks?"

"Yes. These are the police photos."

"Taken at direct eyeview from above, in good strong light. Your Honor, I enter these as exhibits for the state, and I would like to pass them up to you, and then to the jury."

The judge, his petulant mouth tight, looked at the photographs and then peered at the defense table. "The defense have any objections to the jury seeing these? Bailiff, pass these to the defense."

Tindell didn't bother to look at the photos. "We have seen them, and have no objection, unless anyone on the jury is sensitive and is already aware there has been a double murder. Exhibiting the cadavers proves nothing except they are dead."

Abe said, "Mr. Tindell, please don't make speeches to the jury just yet. Any real objections?"

"No objections."

Abe looked down at the photos again back in his hand. "George Rodman is shown in this photograph, lying on his back, his hands twisted as in protest, his expression one of horror, eyes wide, mouth open, a section of his tongue out. I'm sorry if I must itemize these things in court. His trousers are unzipped and pulled to his knees. Is that how you found him, Chief Smith?"

Abe passed a photograph to the jury to study.

"That is the way we found him."

"There are some signs of mutilation visible on both bodies. Will you describe it as you and your men saw it."

Tindell's protest was overruled.

Chief Smith looked at his hands, lowered his head, looked

around the courtroom with eyes in which the lights never went up. He got no comfort from the look the judge gave him. "Well . . . it's all in the pathological report."

"We know that. We want you as an expert witness to corroborate the medical report."

"Well, Mr. Rodman had been mutilated. Or, rather, somebody had made a good start."

Abe glanced at Sarah Rodman; she sat encased as if with folded wings in the protective chrysalis of her breeding.

"How was he mutilated?"

"With a razor blade."

"In what way?"

"Cutting."

"Cutting how?"

"Him."

"You mean Mr. Rodman? George Rodman?" Abe leaned forward toward the witness.

Sarah Rodman's face had remained perfectly controlled.

"Yes. Mr. Rodman."

"How was he mutilated. Speak louder."

"His genital organs."

"What was done?"

"Well, hacked like—the condition being what it was." The man was not testifying like a professional law-enforcement officer. More like a shy schoolboy.

Judge Riggs rapped his gavel. "I have before me the medical report already filed as an exhibit. It says here—I quote—'An attempt had been made to amputate the penis with a small, sharp instrument, most likely a razor blade.' Is *that* what you want to say, Chief Smith?"

There was a titter in the courtroom. Judge Riggs turned a stern face toward the people facing him. "Legal language is meant to convey a precise image and give direct information. I've so far kept this court free of people under eighteen. If there are here any fools, birdbrains or perverts who find any of this delightful or amusing, make your presence known by your laughter and I'll see you get thrown out of here. Answer the question, Chief Smith."

"The condition was as you—as stated in the medical report."

Abe said, "In what condition did you find the body of Mrs. Nash?"

The witness kept his head low, not looking at the judge. "We had to remove some of the letters—and there had been mutilation attempts there too."

Abe wondered at this big man on the stand—did he get his kicks, his satisfaction, in just beating prisoners, sublimating his own drives into that sadistic direction rather than into normal emotional channels? His stare suggested insanity in the latent stage. But this was no time to think of that.

"In what way was Mrs. Nash mutilated?"

"She was on her back, her dress was pulled up over her hips and there were razor blade slashes around her thighs. However, not deep. Little slashes about two and three inches long."

"Would you say the murderers had done a bad mutilation job?"

Tindell's voice said, "Or murderer."

"They, or he, or her, or it, were unskilled?"

"It looked as if mutilation was tried and given up."

"Is this common in crimes of passion?"

Abe waited for an objection, but none came.

"Yes—not too often, but it happens. Among the foreign-born."

"Your opinion was not asked as to racial guesses. How many letters were found scattered on the bodies or close by?"

"Twenty-eight."

"Just the letters, no envelopes?"

"Just the letters. No envelopes."

Abe turned to the judge. "Your Honor, we have these letters and we would like to enter the letters in evidence as an exhibit in this case."

"You may do so when you are through with this witness. I would like to adjourn court for the day soon. The heat is very bad. Will you be questioning the witness much longer?"

"I think I can come to a conclusion of my part of the examination within the half hour. This is my last extra shirt, and it's stuck to my hide."

"Go ahead. Go ahead."

"Chief Smith. You found direct evidence of the presence of the murderers."

"Objection. We have no knowledge if there was one murderer, five murderers, twenty murderers."

"You've made your point. Sustained. Strike the question."

"You found evidence of the murderer, or murderers, near the bodies?"

"The ground is very hard and stony and the brush is wild and the pine needles were piled up. But we did establish certain shoelike tracks, not clear, impressions, marks, that showed us there was more than one person there."

"How many?"

"We have no way of knowing for sure. There were no actual detailed footprints we could record."

"Could you tell if the marks showed if they were man or woman or men and women?"

"No. We did find tire marks—still untraced—about a half mile down the road, marks leading from them to the old club. But there were no clear woman's footmarks even there. At least none we could use."

The objection was loud now, and it all ended in an admission there was no evidence these tire marks were from the murder party or parties. Abe suddenly decided he had all he needed from Chief Smith. "Your witness."

Tindell rose "Chief Smith, you have faithfully done your duty in this case in following all clues and all evidence available, no matter how small?"

"I have, and my office has."

"You have no direct evidence as to who, or how many people, murdered Mr. Rodman and Mrs. Nash? Or if they were men and/or women?"

"They were one or the other."

This brought a laugh.

Tindell said, "Thank you, Chief Smith. That's all."

The judge ended the day of trial. Abe felt tired and aware he had a long way to go.

In his office Abe sat damply uncomfortable staring at his notebook. The image of Sarah Rodman still was printed on his eyeballs. He should never have thought of their intimate moment in such detail in that taxi at noon. Yet he knew why, knew for two reasons why he had remembered it. It had, in a way, promoted him from being an outsider, a barbarian from beyond Hawleytown (even if he had been born there); it made him a full citizen, even if in secret. In possessing for a few fumbled moments the body of Sarah he had become part of the town, the culture of the surrounding fields full of old local history. And the other thing? He had created a love image, never satisfied again until he met Fran, and in Fran the close, wonderful life had chipped the perfect romantic gloss that is only on things held high over head, things which we desire and never fully get. Would Sarah have become domestic, accepted? A daily event of sleepy yawns, household tasks, small bickerings, settled pleasures and tiny grins and amused looks? He never found out. In the few women in his life he knew always there had been this image of Sarah that he tried to find again. How disloyal one's mind can become—disloyal to one as fine and real as Fran. He shook his head and mopped his face. Good thing he hadn't seen much of Sarah in those years. . . .

. . . I saw her again in my first law case. Joel Whitney on River Road raised Cornish game hens for the market. It never paid very well, and just when he seemed to have the prospects of a good season some disease ran through the flocks, or someone amused himself by firing into his breeding pens. Once the someone turned out to be Batty Billie Hawley, who killed thirty-seven Cornish game hens one afternoon with a boy's slingshot and large truck ball bearings shot from behind a clump of huckleberry bushes on the Whitney farm.

I was newly admitted to the bar, and Joel Whitney had no

money to pay an experienced lawyer, so he came to me. Batty Billie had been arrested, fined twenty-five dollars and set free. I promised Joel Whitney I'd take the case for damages, and he figured out that the Cornish game hens that had died were worth a dollar-twenty-seven each, that his nervous system had been shattered three hundred dollars' worth, and that the trespassing violations of posted land were worth something too. I took the case with the stipulation that if we got anything I'd get 20 per cent for my fees.

I served the papers of the lawsuit myself (to save three dollars). The Hawleytown Yacht Club had been taken over for a private party. Mikel Hawley was home from the hunt, and I knew Batty Billie always hung around the punchbowl smiling at everyone in his silly way. Batty Billie had been away for some years to a special school where the misfits of good families were taught table and bathroom manners, how to tie their shoelaces, and not to belch or unbutton in public. He was a cheerful, fat young man, already growing his large, red, patchy mustache, and he was considered harmless.

I parked my unpaid-for secondhand car across the road from the yacht club and walked down the smooth lawn and along the bluestone path to the big two-story houseboat permanently moored on steel and cement piles. The breeze swayed the lights strung on outdoor wires and swayed the few plants in an anchor-shaped flower bed that had managed to survive the summer. I went around on the loose outside walk to the kitchen and waved to Ollie Hansen, who used to be at the country club but had taken over the catering at the yacht club.

Ollie was helping two Negro waiters knock off the soft wood tops of cases of champagne labeled Bollinger, Piper-Heidsieck and Moët and Chandon. "Hello, Abe, what's on your mind?" Ollie poured two kitchen glasses full from an opened bottle and handed me one. "Here, try this. The Hawleys are howling tonight."

I sipped the bubbly wine, wondering how one got to like it. "I have to serve a paper on William Hawley."

"Batty Billie? Sure, if you want to, but where's your sense of

honor?" Ollie refilled his glass. "There's goin' to be an engagement announcement tonight. Miss Sarah Hawley and the Reverend George Rodman are going to run in double harness.
Drink up. There's plenty more. Or you rather have a Château
d'Yquem?"

I said no, put down my glass and went past the swinging doors
to the dining porch where the party was finishing dinner. I
didn't see Batty Billie, but I did see Mrs. Hawley, who had a
fallen eyelid and a desperately worked-over aged face; also a
very loud laugh. But she must have been a striking woman in
her youth. The family had the big center table under the large
oil painting of the yacht *Atlantic* winning the famous Trans-At-
lantic race in 1905. Sarah, her ink-black hair long and crisp and
wavy, was looking up at a very handsome man who was seriously
explaining something to her. She kept nodding and rolling her
head as if very ardent and interested. It was the first time I'd seen
George Rodman, and he was not in clerical garb but wearing
evening colthes. The colored waiters were filling large wine-
glasses.

I went out to the bar, and Solly Webber, who was yacht club
steward (I later sent him up for embezzlement), said to me, "I
don't think you're a guest."

"I've got to deliver something to Mr. William Hawley."

"Not here you don't. You're serving a paper, aren't you? I
can smell them."

Solly grabbed my jacket collar, and I made a motion as if to
backhand him across the chops, at the same time looking for an
exit in case he should call some of the hired hands to roust me.
But Solly just stood rubbing his nose. I walked back into the
dining porch while he made up his mind. Batty Billie was standing, like game in open country, by a dessert table, feeding himself salted nuts as fast as he could toss them into his mouth. I
went up to him, smiled, put the paper in his hand and said, "I
serve you in the matter of William Hawley versus the Whitney
Game Hen Company."

Batty Billie stared at the paper, and someone laid a hand on
my arm. It was Mikel Hawley, very tanned, with his full-grown

mustache, just back from Alaska and grizzly-bear killing. "What did you give my brother?"

Solly Webber was standing behind Mikel, and I wondered if they'd rush me. I moved back toward the family table. Old Eli Chaucer, the family lawyer, was standing there with a filled glass of wine and saying, ". . . at this time to announce for Mrs. Townsend Hawley the engagement of her daughter Sarah Elizabeth to the Reverend George Rodman."

I was handed a filled glass by one of the waiters, and I stood there and listened and watched Mikel and Solly as I drank a toast to the engaged couple. Sarah was a little glassy-eyed and clinging to the engaged man, who was pale and dignified but nervous. All the people in the room were applauding and lifting their glasses. The waiters began to pour from new bottles.

Mikel said, "Don't go away."

Solly kept his eye on me, and Mikel went over to the table and talked to old Eli Chaucer, who looked at me as if I were a defendant. Mikel came back. "Billie's guardian is now responsible for his actions. Mr. Chaucer will settle all this later if you'll withdraw your paper."

"No."

"All right. Solly, show Mr.——? Have you a card?"

"Pedlock. A. Lincoln Pedlock. I haven't a card with me."

"Show Mr. Pedlock into your office. Mr. Chaucer will talk to you in a few minutes. This is a private party."

I followed Solly to the door of his office and went in to battered fumed oak and dusty ship models in glass cases. The door in the room on the left next to Solly's office opened and shut, and I heard the sound of a kind of amorous struggle and of rejected kissing. A man began to speak; after a while I could make out words and the controlled anger of the speaker.

". . . would have been proper, it seems to me, to find out what my church thinks of announcing this thing in these surroundings. You have no sense of the decency of the proper place, Sarah. Oh, stop smiling and grabbing at me. You've had too much to drink. . . . Yes, of course I'm very angry. Well, not just angry but trapped. I'm in no position to marry, at least not someone like yourself, Sarah. I've no income but my salary, and there is my work."

I couldn't help listening the way I was sitting in Solly's office, and if I walked out they'd hear me—the floors were very noisy. Sarah said something rapidly and earnestly, but her voice was low and muzzly and I got no sense out of it. The man's voice tried a new tone. "Look, Sarah, of course I like you. You're a wonderful girl and your interest in me, and the church, was something, well, I suppose, a young, lonely man, I was carried away by your presence. I'm as human as the next man. I'm not yet in my work free of pride and a liking of little flattery. My sin is a kind of vanity, in being admired, and—please, Sarah, listen seriously. This thing tonight, this announcement of our coming marriage—it was ill advised on your family's part. I'm new to the church, the town. And I'm not interested in accepting money from your family or your money. I must make it clear to you . . . that . . ."

I walked softly to the windows and looked out at the bay. It was growing darker.

Sarah's voice came clearly through the wall. She was suddenly loud and crisp. "You think this town will let you stay if you break our engagement? And what will your blasted church heads say when suddenly they lose, because of you, the best families and the support for the building of the new wing? Don't be a damn fool, George. This is all for the best and don't stiffen with pride and glare. There's no way out but this way, and you love me, and what does it matter whose money we live on? As long as we live together. So don't make me get mean about this, darling."

I tiptoed out, deciding I'd call old Eli Chaucer in the morning.

Joel Whitney got a hundred-and-fifty-dollar settlement for his slaughtered Cornish game hens. He tried to pay me off with ten dollars and two cleaned and plucked hens, which I refused. The Reverend George Rodman left town for several months. I heard he had had a nervous breakdown and was out in Kansas at the Menninger Clinic. In the spring of the following year George Rodman and Sarah Hawley were married by the bishop in the big church on King Street. The couple went to live in the new house the bride's mother, Mrs. Townsend Hawley, had given them in Barraclough Manor, and the Reverend Rodman announced that building funds for the new church were nearly oversubscribed. . . .

CHAPTER VIII

IN THE NIGHT

IN THE PALLID glow of dusk the stored heat of the day still steamed in Abe's office. He sat with an electric fan blowing on his head and back, his shirt drying. The county help had long since drifted out, and now at six-thirty few people were left in the building. Mary Durant, changed into a voluminous white pleated skirt, was putting ice cubes into coffee on the corner table. Rod Miller stood stapling together the transcripts of the morning's testimony that had just come off the mimeograph machines.

Rod said to Mary, "How do you think it went today, Duchess?"

Mary, hands bent outward at the wrists, shook her head. "I'm no lawyer."

Abe leaned his head on his arms and let the fan blow through his dark, damp hair. "Don't kid us, Mary. You think they made some big point today."

Rod looked up, gave a twisted smile, and grabbed Mary's arm. "Come on, give. What are you holding out?"

Mary struggled free, the flaring skirt moving in graceful slow time. "It's too hot for pawing, Rod. They got Chief Smith to say there was no evidence that a woman had been at the murder scene."

"Damn clumsy testifying Smith did, too," said Rod, pushing a set of manuscripts at Abe. "Anything else tonight?"

"No, you and Mary run along. I want to see the chief."

Mary got a towel from her desk, put it over her shoulder, and picked up her plastic soup container. "Go home, Mr. P. And watch some TV and forget this case till tomorrow."

"Maybe I will."

She went off to the washroom, in that soft, shaking walk that Abe remembered first from his high-school days. Rod crumpled an empty cigarette package and with it made a hard basketball shot off the wall into the wastepaper basket. "You have any plan or order for the witnesses to be called tomorrow?"

"I will have in the morning. Goodnight, Rod."

Rod nodded and went to the door. He turned there and like a little boy smiling (with his fist in the jam) asked, "Do you think I'm going to make any time with Mary, the Body Beautiful?"

Abe looked up, his eyes out of focus. "That's your problem. Her private life is her own."

"She looks and acts pants crazy. But so far all I've gotten is a little polite push at the front steps."

"What do you want, Rod, stipulated briefs, with detailed clauses?"

Rod smiled again. "The calm advice of an older man."

"No comment."

The washroom door banged open, and Rod left quickly to meet Mary Durant. Abe drove his thoughts from the blond people, the golden athletes, back to the case. He put the new transcripts into his already bulging briefcase and crossed to Ed Hightower's office. Below on the lawns the locust trees were seeding, and men from the jail were wetting the black macadam. Everybody had gone but Miss Munday and Ed, who was signing a batch of letters.

"You didn't have to hurry these, Miss Mundy. They could have gone next week."

Miss Munday, shiny with duty done, picked up the letters and went out. Ed looked up at Abe. "Fifty-fifty today, Abe. You got some evidence of atmosphere and intent and threat into the records, I hear, but your witness got riddled a bit. What the hell was the matter with Chief Smith? He acted like a kid pulling down his first pair of long silk stockings."

"He's afraid of sexual details; most likely he's an oddball of some kind who gets his kicks scientifically beating hoodlums in the cellar of the jail."

Ed rolled down his shirtsleeves and began to snap shut cuff links made of some polished bits of local stone. "How was lunch?"

"Too much lunch. Ed Higgins bothers me. The Hawleys are members of the opposition party. But Big Ed wouldn't feel too bad, I gather, if we just let this case slide along without trying too hard for a conviction. He was as clear as a twelve-sheet circus poster."

Ed picked up his tan alpaca jacket, folded it neatly and put it over one arm. "My pappy said, 'Avoid platitudes, respect money.' You want to be D.A., don't you?"

"Not for any deal."

"It's no deal. Maybe they honestly don't think you can prove anything. Abe, suppose—just suppose—George Rodman and Helen Nash were murdered by someone else, not the three people on trial."

Abe leaned forward, mouth open, hurt, pierced with panic. "What do you mean?"

"I'm not saying it's so. But Helen Nash was a very delicious dish. And her husband is an old man and not much of a lover, it would seem. His alibi is air-tight, so don't think I'm saying he committed the murders. But—I'm guessing now—suppose Helen had strayed before, with somebody else, who maybe didn't like losing her. Opens up new ideas, doesn't it?"

"What do you *know*, Chief? You've been around a long time. You know Mr. Nash from the Masonic Rites, don't you?"

"I know nothing that will help your case, Abe. Only be more sure of your witnesses. And remember, it's better *not* to put on a witness that can be used by the defense than to put on a witness to make a point for them. I'm for getting this case honestly tried and off the calendar."

Ed pulled out the light over his desk and went out, a lean, tall old man looking forward to his before-dinner cocktails.

Abe sat looking irrevocably deprived, sat staring at Ed's thin, departing back, feeling marooned in shadows. He picked up the phone and called the jail and asked for Chief Smith.

"Hello. Chief Smith? Pedlock. Just called to say you did a fine, real great job on the stand today."

"You're not that bad a lawyer, Mr. Pedlock. I did nothing for you. I was all thumbs."

"You don't always have to spell them out in black and white. Chief, you've reorganized our crime files. Would it be easy for you to reach in and get me a list of lovers' lane items? You know —fights, holdups, molestings. Also wives and husbands and odd partners—the strangers breaking up homes. That sort of thing."

"Can do. How far back do you want to go? A hell of a lot of data. Most of it in crummy condition. They never heard of modern office machines in this H.Q. before I come here."

"Five to six years back. Ten if you could. I've heard you've done miracles in scientific cross-filing."

"Easier if you tell me what you really want."

"Names of anyone involved with anybody in the case."

"When you want it?"

"The minute you find anything. Call me at home tonight if you snag anything."

"Tonight?"

"Come on, Chief Smith, I know you hang out at H.Q. till one and two in the morning. Let's see your scientific cross-filing at work."

"I'll call you if I come across anything. I've got to run up to Perth Corner tomorrow, pick up a knifing suspect. You don't want me on the stand?"

"No. I think we're through with you. Unless I need some rebuttal witness."

"Be seeing you, Mr. Pedlock."

Abe hung up. He called the General Hospital and asked for Doctor Wymer. The heat of the day was not diminishing an iota, it seemed. As dusk darkened, it seemed to take on the power of all the reflected heat from the stones, walls and walks. A moon

rode deeply imbedded in a mottled sky. The wet-grass odor cam
up to Abe.

"Sidney Wymer speaking." A crisp, ironic voice, amused bu
not happy.

"Hello, Sidney. Abe Pedlock. You're very busy, I know."

"You know damn well I am. Just took out the biggest set o
gallstones in town. Beauties. And I'm talking tomorrow—nee
to prepare—to the Country Medical Society at eight on encap
sulated subcutaneous tissue."

"I want to go talk to Maman Celie, to see if she's ready fo
the stand tomorrow. In case I should decide to use her, put he
on."

"You have my report."

"I have. But do me this favor, Sidney. Come with me. Thing
aren't going well."

There was silence on the wire; then, "When?"

Abe's call to Fran on the phone to say he would be late wa
not as easy. Her voice was first hurt and then sharply angry whei
he got her on the phone. "But I've got supper ready to eat ii
half an hour, Abe. In this weather it spoils."

"I'll only be an hour at most. I must see a witness."

"Oh, damn, double damn, I have strawberry shortcake, too
You know I have to make it now, for Deedee and Davey, and i
will be soggy and sour by the time you get home."

"Just cut off a section for me, and don't put the cream and
strawberries on it. Look, tomorrow night we'll all go, kids and
all, to the Spare Rib and have a real fancy dinner. I'll buy you
two coffee grogs with rum and lemon."

Fran didn't answer for a moment. "Abe, I've been crying
Everything seems wrong. The weather, I had a fight with m
sister, Tom is lying on the porch not moving. I think the cat i
dead."

"If his ribs move he's alive. Now, Fran, I'm having a hell of a
time with the trial, so please, only a few more days and the de
fense takes over. Be patient, darling. I know I'm a lousy hus
band."

"Yes, dear, you certainly are. Here is Deedee; she wants to talk to you."

"Hello, Deedee. How's my girl?"

"We saw you in the newsreel this afternoon. You looked super, and . . ." After which it was Davey's turn to talk. There was, he said earnestly, a bear who climbed the tree outside his window every night when he was just falling asleep and made faces at him. But he wasn't scared. Fran came back on the phone, sounding happier and the way he liked her, suggesting blond sunshine and tanned limbs. "I suppose when you're really D.A. it will be even worse. Darling, did you have enough shirts? And do eat something if you're very late. Remember, Doctor Wymer thought last spring you might get an ulcer."

"Sure. Love you."

"Love you too, you big goon."

Abe was down in the lobby of the county building smoking a stogie when Doctor Sidney Wymer honked the horn of his black Cadillac. The doctor had a lean, fish-belly-white face on a bean-pole body, a large nose (a size too big), thin, receding blue-black hair and very thin, bone-white fingers that looked parboiled and suggested at once he was a good doctor and surgeon. His wife had left him years ago, he said, for Zen Buddhism, and he often went to Europe for months at a time. He collected Cambodian bronzes, Picasso prints, and had a reputation at the hospital of being a seducer of nurses (which amused the nurses, who adored Doctor Wymer for his skill and his hard gemlike charm).

Abe got into the car beside Sidney Wymer, who shot the Cadillac away from the curb with skill and grace. Abe sighed. "An air-conditioned Caddy. Now I've lived."

"Except for air-conditioning and surgery, I detest the entire twentieth century and its toys. The goddamn telephone, the rocket and plane and the fast printing press will make us the lowest-reaching century since the crusades. The only bright spot is it may be the last century."

The scent of good Scotch filled the air-conditioned interior of the car. (Sidney has had a few. I hope he doesn't have to operate

tonight. Why do wise men like Sidney and the chief booze s
much)?

"I'm not sure any more, Sidney, about anything my eyewitnes
says."

"I told you to go easy. She's sharp, and bright, and her reflexe
—except in her legs—mostly aren't bad. I myself believe any
thing she'd say against the quality. But that may be because no
one of them would help me through college, medical school an
interning. Well, what good will it do to see the old bat again
Her legs are bad. But her red-blood count, hemoglobin estimate
is good."

"I want to hear her tell it again."

They had crossed town and were mounting toward a row c
shabby hills. Dark Town had once been called Darky Town, an
originally Nigger Heaven. With the years its name had yielde
to certain pressures to refine itself into merely a stinking mino
ity slum and end up as Dark Town. It was the powerful Secon
Ward politically—a ward that often decided a close local electio
Jim Caesar and his three wives lived with Maman Celie, wh
was his mother. He was a party barman, extra butler, valet an
pants presser to the town.

The car pulled up to a clapboard shack. Dark Town's gullie
of red clay, the mean, paint-daubed shanties, the junk, tin-canne
goat meadows—all were motionless in the warm night.

Clinker, Jim Caesar's boy by his wife Goldskin, pulled hi
frayed red shirt closer and hoisted the burlap bag of stolen apple
on his back. He was dirty, and he had torn the seat of his pant
on a coal car skipping past a railroad guard. "Come on in," h
told Abe and Doctor Wymer.

He pushed open the door to the yellow-painted shanty an
dumped his load by the dead fireplace. An oil lamp hung, turne
low, from the ceiling. It gave the pasted newspapers on the wall
the illusion of décor.

As usual his grandma sat asleep in her chair, an enormou
chair, made by sawing part of a big barrel apart and stuffing i
with old rags.

"Gran, we got company."

Maman Celie was huge, very old. She herself in gin-happy moments claimed to be a hundred and ten. No one said her no, for she was known to be a great sorceress—a queen of the Legba Voodoo, a maker of deadly ouanga packets and bags. She rested—asleep, serpentine, majestic, full of solemnity. Long ago she had given up much walking and spent her life in her barrel chair—eating, sleeping, casting spells and making charms. A terror to all the blacks and off-colors of Dark Town. She glared them all into silent importunity. She weighed over three hundred pounds and had a wide, flat face, slit eyes and a great, powerful mouth from which a short clay pipe of strong, rank tobacco was never removed. She was as nonmalleable as her big, yellow stone teeth. She blinked awake as Clinker threw the bag down, and her long-lawed fingers struck a match and held it to her clay pipe. She became at once wide-awake; elation, life, sprang into her eyes; her mouth twitched open.

"*Servir de deux mains,* boy!" she howled in her Haiti French. "I'll tear your lights out, making all that noise. Make a light!"

"I was just going to, Maman Celie," said Clinker. "The old nanny goat chipper as ever. Drunk or sober."

There was a stirring in the next room, where Jim Caesar's three wives, Tess, Big Mag and Goldskin, slept. Bare feet pattered on the plank floor, and Goldskin, half nude, pretty and yawning, her smooth bronze skin glowing, appeared in the doorway. She was the most impudent of the wives and the youngest.

"That you, Clinker?"

"That's me," said her son, grinning and lighting two oil lamps. "I've got apples and they got the back of my pants. We got company."

"That's more'n your damn father brings. He thinks only of his white folk. I've a mind to pack up and move out on him. Sit down, folks."

Maman Celie turned her huge bulk. Her black-and-white cat, Loup-Garou, leaped into her lap and purred madly in his throat. The Voodoo queen said, "Keep your mouth buttoned, you slut. Men got other things to do than think of yellow wenches thet h'ain't any better than they should be. Lemme hear no more sass. Mr. Pedlock, Doctor. Good to see you again."

"We want to talk to you," said Abe.

"Get chairs."

Goldskin wrinkled her small, well-shaped nose, cupped her firm breasts and rubbed. Then she yawned and showed her pink tongue at the unseeing back of the giantess. "Yes, Maman Celie."

Loup-Garou, the tomcat, leered at her with fruit-green eyes. He was a ferocious cat.

Silent convulsions of laughter shook Clinker when he saw his mother make faces at Maman Celie.

Maman Celie said, "Caesar might have some gin at that."

Loup-Garou curled himself into a ball and hissed himself to sleep, to dream, Abe suspected, of tortured mice.

"Gin," said the old sorceress to the leaping flames.

Jim Caesar, shoeless, came in from the bedroom. He was coal black, large, powerful and red-eyed.

"Glad to see you all again." He had a strong British accent and claimed to have been butler to the Crown in British West Indies colonies.

Two small black children, dressed only in short shirts, stood around, prominent abdomens well forward, the umbilicus protruding like a melon stem. Big Mag and Tess and Goldskin stood very proud, nostrils flaring. The gin was poured into kitchen glasses.

Maman Celie sat in her barrel chair, her cat Loup-Garou on her wide lap. Near her stood Jim Caesar. Maman Celie puffed on her black clay pipe and glared at her son, then stared again into the fireplace. "Tovodown will see me through."

Doctor Wymer drank his gin with pleasure. Abe's was drunk by Clinker.

Doctor Wymer winked, said, "Some folk say Maman Celie can no more walk than the statue on the courthouse roof. Her leg muscles are useless. Say she hasn't taken a step for thirty years. All the nerves in her legs are dead, they say."

Maman Celie scowled, mildly facetious. "When I walk, I walk. I have but to will it."

"Sure," said Abe, mopping his brow. Reassured, persuaded, then doubting again. "You ever seen her walk, Caesar?"

Jim Caesar shook his head with melancholy dignity. "A bit. But she's a powerful friend of Gouede Oussou."

"Who's he?"

"A spirit, a friend of all sorceresses."

Maman Celie said, "When I will it, I walk."

"So walk now! Walk across the room," said Abe in anguish. "Come on!"

"I don't will it," said the black woman in a benevolent voice.

Doctor Wymer shrugged his shoulders.

Abe put away his handkerchief and went over and spoke softly to Maman Celie. "Is it true, Maman Celie, that you told your son Jim that you were out picking herbs in the hills on the night of the slaying of Mr. Rodman and Mrs. Nash, and that you saw the murderers arrive and enter the old boat club grounds?"

Loup-Garou yawned, showing his teeth. Maman Celie patted him and then said with a grimace of pleasure at all this excitement, "It is so. Every month I go to the hills. I go to gather herbs for my ouanga bags. When the moon is high, I will my feet to walk and I rise from the chair and go into the hills."

Abe said in a voice full of precautions, "You can't walk all the time? Only when the moon is high, and only to pick herbs in the hills?"

Maman Celie nodded, making the concession.

Doctor Wymer had another gin.

Maman Celie went on. "The night I was out in the hills I am one who *servir de deux mains*. It was a dull night, but there was a moon. There was a storm brewin'. I could smell the sulphur in the air. Goldskin wheeled me to the hills. Then I walked alone —away. I was pickin' catkin roots when I heard a car stop near the club. Three people got out. A woman and two men. They went up to the old boat club. Then I heard many shots. Boom. Boom. I went up, creeping, still like, toward the old building. I heard voices talking. Then they came back. A woman and two men. One man he had a gun in his hands, a shotgun. The woman she was shaking like in a fit. The other, he was holding her up. I saw it."

Abe balled his handkerchief between his hands; his palms were sweating.

Her son said, "Now, Maman Celie, you got to be sure, you got to be very sure."

"I is sure. Very sure. I saw that the man with the gun was Mikel Hawley, and the man holding up the lady was his brother Batty Billie. And the lady—I'd know her anyplace—she was Mrs. Rodman."

"But how would you know these people, tied to this chair for years, or most of the time?" Abe asked.

Maman Celie laughed. "Mrs. Rodman was here for voodoo help. At first veiled; then just like other folk."

"Nonsense!" said Doctor Wymer.

"She want the power of love over her husband, to keep him from other women's beds."

"Mrs. Rodman came here?"

"Ask Goldskin. She was here in the back room most times. She saw her. She remember. Oh, I know how bad white women are in bed. *Tous trois ont le pouvoir* . . ."

Abe turned to Doctor Wymer. "Well, am I nuts or her?"

"Don't ask me. Are you going to convict those three for murder with this witness?"

"How do I know how much of this dream is true—if any?" Abe shook his head in a jumbled, puzzled manner. "Still," he went on, "if this is the truth . . . Oh, hell! Have her sign that statement I brought, Caesar, and witness it."

Caesar patted his mother's shoulder with excessive familiarity. "You are a great woman, Maman."

Maman Celie said, sucking her pipe, "You, Jim, was always a showy fool. A flash nigger."

Abe showed Maman Celie where to sign. She took the pen in her long claws and made a ragged cross. The witness signed. Abe had his handkerchief out again. "I'll get a statement out of

Goldskin also; and all of you keep this under your hats. I wonder if she really can walk?"

The huge black woman said with unwonted liveliness, "When I will it, I walk."

Doctor Wymer shook his head. "Show us."

The voodoo queen turned toward the doctor. Her eyes burned at him with a look of derision. Her hands gripped the barrel edge. The cat leaped off her lap, hissing. Her powerful arms lifted her to her feet. Her eyes were shut and she was muttering in Haiti French. Sweat beaded her brow and her breath hissed in between her tight lips. A tremendous enthusiasm shook her. Huge, black, menacing, she took a step, trembled, took another; then, shaking with great effort, she took a third step and fell forward panting onto her knees, contemplating the floor.

Her son caught her and lowered her to the floor. She lay there, still panting, her eyes closed, a jubilant smile on her face.

Abe snapped his fingers. "You all saw that! Well, Doctor, so she *couldn't* take a step—not even *one?*"

Doctor Wymer frowned. "But could she walk across the street, let alone climb the hills back of here?"

"Sure, sure," said Jim Caesar. "That's what you said before, and that she couldn't even take one step. But she did, didn't she!"

From the dark heap on the floor came a labored voice raised in bellicosity. "I willed . . . it."

Jim Caesar grinned, patted the big hulk, and reset her in her chair. "You sure did, Maman!"

Doctor Wymer said, "It would make a great courtroom scene when the defense says she can't walk, and she does."

Abe said, "It's a hot night."

"Not for doctors."

Abe began to reword two statements.

Maman Celie's pipe glowed red, and her sharp eyes looked around the room. Clinker now slept rolled ingeniously in some old rugs in the corner, and from the darkness of the next room, the limbs of the three wives could be made out faintly. Loup-

Garou dreamed of some dreadful event and moaned in his depraved tomcat's sleep. The voodoo queen relaxed. Her shadow salaamed to the flickering light. The bright eye of her short clay pipe went out. She said, "Gin."

Caesar took Abe aside. He whispered, "Maman Celie serving a great many white folks these days. Folks one does not associate with voodoo. They come to her shack in Nigger Heaven, and leave clutching some charm of love, hate, passion. And not all are Polack women, or farm wives, hunting a charm against sour milk. The quality is coming too.

"Roots, herbs, strange messes, powders, pastes, leaves, chicken feathers—all has a meaning to Maman Celie. Voodoo is great. Big John the Conqueror is a root shaped like a foot and sure to get results. There is also Little John, Black Evil, Tiger Tears, Drops of the Devil, Expanding Good Thomas, garlic and leek and semen-contra seed, Milan Wood and scrolls addressed to Saint Agrippa, Toby the Traveler, Magnus, Anima, Dolor. Oh, yes, Mr. Pedlock."

"Tell me, Caesar, about Mrs. Rodman coming here."

He told them that one night Maman Celie had two important white visitors. Big Mag, just home from three months in the workhouse for a razor-slashing brawl, was stirring the fire under a smelly brew, and Maman Celie was watching the flames. Loup-Garou was on her lap when the visitors came. One was a tall man, his companion a veiled woman.

Big Mag put down the poker and took herself away to the bedroom. Maman Celie knocked her pipe out into her palm and threw the tobacco ash into the fire. It flared up, and a sweet, biting smell filled the shack. The veiled woman sobbed, perhaps at the disgraceful expedient that had brought her here. "It was Mrs. Rodman. I know her. I am in corner playing on drum."

"Go on," Abe said.

Maman Celie, Caesar said, recited, *"Pas lacher plui sou nous.* You have come, madame, for an ouanga bag. A bag to bring back a man's love." The veiled woman gasped and reached for the man's hand and held it. Panic communicated itself to the tall man.

"How . . . how did you know?" asked Mrs. Rodman.

"*Pas bruler caille moin*. But I am one who knows."

The veiled woman asked, with a gesture, "Can you really work charms? I'm not a believer in such things, but Mikel, here, has seen strange things done in Africa by . . . by witch doctors, and—"

Maman Celie sat firmly on her barrel chair. "And even if you don't believe, you would still try?"

The veiled woman nodded. She bowed her head. "I will try anything. *Anything*."

Maman Celie put down her cat. The cat spit, leaped onto the fireplace, and glared down on the company. Maman Celie reached down into her skirt for a small skin bag. She held it toward the leaping fire. The flames seem to reach for it.

"This, madame, is a rare ouanga bag," she said. "It has worked wonders in bringing back the love of men who have grown tired of old passions. It has created much licentiousness. I will tell you what is in it, for it is in believing that it can help you, not its contents alone that will bring back your man. You will believe?"

"I will try. I will!" the woman said, trembling.

"Of herbs, *immortelle, bois lait, feuilles* and *sequine*. The dried meat of the salt-water conch called *lambie,* which is esteemed as an aphrodisiac. Mud, sulphur and alum. Human semen, three drops, and . . . and . . . what else I cannot tell you. Wear it between your warm breasts. Heat it with your flesh, and it will heat another. This ouanga bag has helped many; and before going to bed repeat this: *Exurgent mortui et acmo venuient*. I require of you that you come to me."

The veiled woman took the bag and asked, "And he will come?"

Maman Celie picked up her pipe and said, "If you believe in voodoo."

The man held out a bill to Maman Celie. She hid it without looking at it. "You have been overgenerous."

The veiled woman trembled and the man had to help her through the door.

"That was the only time Mrs. Rodman was here," Caesar ended.

Abe said, "The ouanga bag didn't seem to work."

"Mrs. Rodman," said Jim Caesar, "did not believe enough."

Doctor Wymer said, "It's all in the believing. Let's go get a drink, Abe."

Maman Celie sat by the fireplace, not moving.

"I must call Fran first. Just one round."

Doctor Wymer nodded.

CHAPTER IX

AT THE DESMONDS'

STANDING OUTSIDE Jim Caesar's house, Doctor Wymer asked Abe, "You ever talk to Eddie Desmond, the Rodman chauffeur?"

"Just for a glib statement. It wasn't very enlightening. He's been avoiding me. I don't want to arrest him. But he's got to tell me more."

"Mrs. Rodman was very fond of Eddie. Come on, I'm treating him for boils on his buttocks. I know he didn't tell you everything. He's a very loyal little mick. Lives with his folks down by the railroad station."

Eddie himself let them in. Small, neat, skinny, with a long, sad face and a thin, curling lip.

"How are the boils, Eddie?"

"Doc, I can't sit long. Hello, Mr. Pedlock. We're having a bit of a party."

The Desmonds lived in an old brick house in the middle of the Fourth Ward, a house loved by ivy. Here, as Eddie told it, the first Desmond had carried his bride across the scrubbed brick

teps, and here they stayed on—even when Eddie hinted they
night move to a better neighborhood, to a place with new plumb-
ng and a bathroom on the first floor.

"Sure now," Ma Desmond said, "and what for would I be
wantin' to go in among the stuck-up snobs on Standish Avenue?
Here I was born, here I stay. It's near to St. Mary's for mornin'
mass—and you might go to confession yourself, Eddie; Father
Flanegan was askin' for you—and here I stay among the neighbors."

"If it's a party," said Doctor Wymer, "I'm sorry we bothered
you, Eddie."

"Ma's birthday," said Eddie.

"Why didn't you come to see me, Eddie?" Abe asked.

"I've been thinking about it, Mr. Pedlock."

The house was full of Desmonds, music and the odor of three
great turkeys cooking. Abe and the doctor were introduced to
Uncle Desmond and Eddie's two brothers, their wives ("girls
of great fecundity") and six children. And Aunt Mary ("she,
poor soul, who had been disappointed in love") and Mrs. Desmond's brother, Neil, a yellowish, bilious man who was "poorly,
thank you, since I lost an eye in Dublin during the Trouble,"
and Fluter, who was no relative but came from County Limerick
("wasn't so good in the head since a horse kicked him"). Abe enjoyed it while Doctor Wymer went upstairs to look at Eddie's
boils.

The children ran about shouting, and in the dining room Ma
sat at the head of the table feeding a few of the guests. The table
held six people, and they ate in turn, so there was an apparent
contradiction in courses. Eating, serving, some dancing, some
clattering at the piano or twittering the radio knobs, the folks
were poignantly alive.

Eddie and Doctor Wymer came down, and Eddie kissed his
mother, waved to his brothers, pinched a little niece and took
the place Fluter made for him with a sad, crooked smile.

"Too much rich blood brings boils," said Fluter.

The table was full of turkey and potatoes, nuts, fruits and
sauces, many whisky bottles and a local spring water called

Delmar's Delight (with a colored picture of Saint Delmar, glass in hand). Abe said it tasted fine.

Fluter took an old hat down from the piano and began to dance and sing "The Hat Me Father Wore." Ma beamed, hummed the tune and handed a huge plate of giblets and drumsticks to Eddie. Panting, she said, "Isn't it dreadful about poor Reverend Rodman, Mr. Pedlock? And you trying to find the murderers. God rest his Protestant soul."

Brother Tom slapped a child and picked his teeth at the same time. "It's a strange case." He pointed his toothpick at Eddie. "I was just talking this morning to State Trooper Malin. And he made a penetrating remark to me—strictly under your hat. All ain't what it seems in this case, is it, Mr. Pedlock?"

Abe blinked his eyes.

"They say," said Tom's wife, eating corn on the cob, "that the poor girl's been cut—all jagged it was, like someone had been tormentin' her."

Ma shook her head and watched Fluter dance. "Who could have done that, now, in the good Saint's name?"

Tom said slowly, deliberately, "State Trooper Malin told me, on the q.t., that it looked to him as if someone tried to hack her legs off after the shooting."

Neil opened his mouth.

"Oh, no," said Ma in horror. "Can such things be? Holy Mary preserve us!"

Eddie patted her hand. "It was mice, Ma, I'm sure."

Ma said, "Mice, huh, Mr. Pedlock?"

Abe shrugged.

Joe's wife swallowed nuts with an undulation of her body, and said, "Play Uncle Eddie your new piece, Alice Mae."

Alice Mae stuck out her tongue.

Abe said to Eddie, "I hear you were very fond of both Mr. and Mrs. Rodman."

"Yes. It was sad to see it coming, in a way."

"I wish you'd fill me in, Eddie. You were with Mrs. Rodman a lot."

"I don't know anything about the killing. I've already told you that."

"No, no. I just want to know them better. What they were like, when it came to a crisis. I feel I don't know them. It confuses me."

"After Alice Mae plays her new piece, we'll go to my room."

Abe eyed the child with distaste.

"Don't wanna," said Alice Mae.

Her mother slapped her and dragged her to the piano. Neil shook his head. Aunt Mary clattered dishes in the kitchen.

Tom lifted the breastbone of turkey and said, "Mind you, now, Eddie me boy, I shouldn't tell this, but they found the poor Reverend Rodman mutil—"

"Doctor, Mr. Pedlock, listen to Alice Mae," shouted Alice Mae's mother. " 'The Lakes of Killarney.' "

Alice Mae played loudly. Tom waved his turkey bone and told more details sworn to him by State Trooper Malin. Fluter had stopped dancing and was drinking Delmar's Delight, with whisky. Uncle Desmond came in from the kitchen with a plate of pan-browned potatoes and began to eat very fast.

Ma cut the pie and said, "The mice, huh?"

Eddie nodded and cut his meat with care. He sat on tender buttocks, favoring his boils.

Uncle Desmond said, "It's a pickle the police find themselves in. My guess is it's not herself did them in; it's one of them neurosis fiends, Mr. Pedlock."

Eddie pushed back his plate, half finished.

Ma said, "Eddie, you ain't eatin' any of my good cookin'?"

"Sure I am. What's this story about having an eyewitness?"

"State Trooper Malin told me—"

Uncle Desmond winked and wolfed some pan-browned. "A blackleg, that man Malin, or I'm no English-hating Dubliner."

"Poor young people," said Ma, pulling a child on her lap. The walls were hung with long-faced, dark-brown portraits of peasant dead and, kittens and puppies tangled in colored yarns and daisy chains. Ma was pouring Delmar's Delight down a baby's throat.

"Dead them two so young. They're only Black Protestants, but I had a prayer said for their souls. Drink it down, darlin'."

Tom got up and reached for a cigar in a tray on the piano.

Fluter took Tom's empty seat and filled his plate again. "Livin' in sin, it ends in no good. A good wife now wouldn't be out there cavortin' around like the great war of Babylon with a married man."

Ma went "Shush" and pointed to Alice Mae.

Alice Mae asked, "What's cavortin'?"

Tom held his cigar like a hammer in his fist and said, from the maturity of his weight and experience, "Mr. Pedlock, it's as plain as the nose on me face it was a fiend. Don't tell me no. Old Nick himself in human form. The fiend's marks are all there. I was saying to Fuzzy Kertz only this morning at mass, take them marks on the—"

A child choked, and Ma punched it on the back. She held the child and shook her head in a lamentable gesture. "I don't believe it was mice, Eddie."

Uncle Desmond grinned and eyed a disheveled drumstick. "Eyewitness! More eyewitnesses in a case than there are black eyes in Dublin on a Saturday night!"

Eddie motioned Abe to precede him up the narrow stairs. Doctor Wymer was building the kids a table statue out of turkey bones and mashed potatoes and drinking Jameson's whisky.

Eddie Desmond's room was plain to the point of resembling the cell of a monk of some strict order. The walls were a flat, dull gray. There was a narrow Army store cot, made up with a brown blanket and one pillow, a kitchen chair, unpainted, and a small table that held a lamp with a pale-green cloth shade. On the wall was a sentimental reproduction of a Christ painted by some overrealistic German artist of the last century. On the one window sill was a sprouting sweet-potato plant half submerged in a dish of water. Green vines were creeping from it to hug the window screen as if begging for sun. There was nothing else in the room but a pair of polished shoes under the cot and a hook on the door from which hung a faded tan raincoat.

Eddie Desmond pointed to the one chair and then sat down on the narrow cot, lowering himself slowly to one side to protect his boils. "I guess you may think I'm a bit goofy over the Rodmans, but if I am it's because they were good to me. I'm kinda the shrimp of the family, a big family, and the Rodmans they treated me like a son. Mrs. Rodman never had any kids, and at first she seemed a hard type, the bones in her face on top of her skin, you might say. But when I got to know her we used to talk a mile a minute when I drove her on long trips. She'd unbend to me." Eddie's face was now the face of a man in a trance. He was reliving it all, re-enacting, with some total recall, a wonderful time in his life.

Abe, careful not to break the mood, asked, "What did you talk about?"

"We'd talk about almost everything. For instance, now, witchcraft. I bet you wouldn't believe anybody that had been to college like her, to Smith or Vassar, would believe in that kind of mumbo-jumbo stuff, would you now, Mr. Pedlock?"

"You drove her to Maman Celie a lot?"

"Oh, you know about that. Proves what I said, doesn't it? About three times we went there, I guess." Eddie looked at the sweet-potato vine, got up and began to pick off some yellow leaves. "I know what you want to know. How they got along. Well, Doc says I should help you. You can say I saw a lot. They liked me and after a while I was kinda one of the family—easy and familiar as an old glove—and they couldn't cut down their bickering in front of me. Yes, I guess I saw something coming. About a week before the murders I was in Mrs. Rodman's room —oh, they didn't sleep in the same room; hadn't for a couple of years. I was watering the window plants—fancy modern jungle stuff, man-eating-looking leaves they had. I have a green finger and I sort of took over the house plants. The new drapes were up. I tied them back. Mr. Rodman came into herself's room. It was about one o'clock, after lunch. Mrs. Rodman was sorting out her summer dresses in her big closet. We had been talking of wakes; she'd never been to one. Irish feasts for the just departed.

"The windows were all open and a breeze ruffled the drapes.

The coverings had been removed from the furniture; coming out of the closet, Mrs. Rodman stopped when she saw him and slowly put some clothes hangers onto the bed. She looked thin, her face almost lean, making her eyes larger, burning. 'Hello, George. You've come home,' she said."

Abe was aware how carried away Eddie was. He was either a natural actor or gripped in a passion that possessed him; he couldn't stop talking now. Yes, Eddie in his own way had been in love with Sarah Rodman too.

Eddie made a gesture with his hands. "She went up to him."

Abe was translating Eddie's words into personal images. He saw Sarah facing her husband. He saw her move. She kissed him on the cheek. He kissed her too, on the cheek—a gesture that was done before he could withdraw it. "Yes, I'm home," he said. "Hello, Eddie."

Eddie started to leave, and Mrs. Rodman said, "No, I want Eddie to stay. I may need a witness." She sat down on the sofa, smiling that strange, slanting smile of hers.

"You've won, George," she said. "I've fought myself. It was no good. My pride is cracked; my intentions mixed."

He sat down facing her, then got up. "Frankly," he said, "you puzzle me, Sarah."

"Are you happy?" she asked him. She watched him closely.

"A lot of things have happened," he said.

She took a long, gold-tipped cigarette from a silver tray and lighted it with a small gilt lighter. She spoke in intimate tones, but not with anger. "I know you've been unfaithful to me for some time, George," she said. "I forgive you. It's natural for husbands to run after village wenches. Don't look so solemn. I should thank you for being so discreet about it. Eddie, don't leave."

"I love her," said Rodman, "and whatever was between you and me is cold and finished; it was long ago. Oh, for some good persuasive phrases to make you understand that!"

Sarah shot to her feet, her temper up; then she caught control of herself, smiled and watched her cigarette burn. When she spoke there was entreaty in her voice. Eddie felt terrible watching. He tried to leave again. She waved him back.

"You're my husband," she said, "and have always been so. Don't have illusions about me doing the sporting thing and saying, 'God bless you both; now go and be happy.'" Her tone changed, and she said, "You don't know me if you think that! I'd see you both in hell first! Yes, melodramatic as it sounds, I'd destroy you both before I'd set you free! I'll be damned first. Have your mistress, I accept her, but I remain your wife, you my husband."

There was a smile on her face for what she must have thought about the affair her husband had gotten into. But she was fire inside.

He said, "I'm going away; going to have her even if you rave like a thousand tigers."

"You have my terms, George," she said.

"No, I can't live two lives," he told her. "This one had to end."

"Don't be a romantic fool," she told him. "You're too old for this cheap gallantry."

"There is no use making threats, Sarah," he said. "I'm giving up my pulpit, I'm going away . . . without you. You must understand that. We're not for each other."

She looked at him. She was calmer now, holding herself under control. She said, "No, George. Nothing between us will ever be over. You don't know the hell I've lived in since you told me. You've broken my pride. You've smashed what character I thought I had. I wanted you to be big in our world, at the head of things. I wanted you to have social position, but that failed, and I've learned now that I want you, our intimacies, pleasures, even if I can't have them alone. You'll never know what I've gone through to learn that I had to have you, George."

She was on her feet, her arms held out toward him. He didn't move. Eddie started for the door. George said, "Don't. Sarah, think this thing out, be sensible."

"I'm not going to think," she told him. "Damn being sensible. I want love too. You're my husband, this is our home, our room."

"*Your* room," he said as he went to the door awkwardly, getting in Eddie's way. "We'll talk again later. You've got to see it my way. What is over is done. Eddie, will you help me pack a trunk."

"No," she said, almost shouting. "Do you think I've come crawling to have you go noble on me? I don't care how many little bitches you've slept with! I don't care who you've whored around with! Your philandering means nothing to me! Damn your harlot!" She was on him, pulling him from the door, and Eddie tried to step in between. Rodman tried to tear himself away, but she was strong—her long arms holding him, her body against him, trying to smother him in an outburst of some kind.

Eddie said, "I ran down the stairs."

He came back to the bed and sat down carefully. He neatly mopped his face with a folded handkerchief and looked up at Abe with damp eyes. "They were up there an hour, Mr. Pedlock. He had a cut lip when he came down and he told me he'd pack later. It was my afternoon and night off. I came here to Ma. I was so sick that night Ma didn't sleep a wink. The first of the boils came. I never saw Mr. Rodman again. And now I'm no longer driving for Mrs. Rodman, of course, not since she's . . . she's on trial. I can't seem to get any strength into me. They were both wonderful to me. I'm all ground glass inside me stomach asking why and how did it all happen."

Abe held out a stogie to Eddie, who shook his head. "Eddie, off the record, do you think she and her brothers murdered Mr. Rodman and Mrs. Nash?"

Eddie nodded brightly, still in a trance of total recall. "Oh, yes. I've got no more proof than you have, of course. And if I did I wouldn't come forward with it or say in court I ever said any of this. But it has to figure that way. She's a very proud woman. And she begged him to come back to live with her. Have his girl, his bit of an outside fling if he wanted to, but she wanted to go on being Mrs. George Rodman. It isn't—wasn't—like her to knuckle under like that to the fact of his going off with this other woman, leaving her the laughingstock of the town people."

"Did Mikel Hawley ever threaten Mr. Rodman?"

"I never heard him. The two men, they got on very well. Of course, I don't know what happened after that afternoon. I never went back. I was having my boils."

"Eddie, it's important that Mrs. Rodman actually proposed

to Mr. Rodman that she permit him to have a girl on the side, if he continued to live with her as a husband. You know what I mean?"

"Going back to bed together—it was that plain, yes. I know you find that hard to believe. But I heard it, and it bowled me over, letting him have a woman up a back street. I never had anything to do with women, but I've studied them, watched them; there's a lot about them no man can really dig out. Mrs. Rodman, she had her odd side, if you want to call it that. And Mr. Rodman, he was the kind of man you couldn't help loving. He had something you can't explain, but I did understand, after I got over the shock of it, why she'd ask him back on any terms."

Doctor Wymer came into the room. "How about that drink and food now, Abe?"

Abe nodded. How much more could Eddie tell?

Andy Plates's neon-outlined bar and grill was having a busy night. Abe took one bite out of the corned-beef sandwich and sipped his beer at a corner table away from the juke box. He couldn't seem to get cool; even the treated air in the large modern bar didn't seem to make Abe comfortable. Abe looked up at Doctor Wymer on his second double Scotch.

"It's a hell of a mess, Sidney. This Eddie isn't a liar, is he?"

"No. He's a nice little guy. Complexes all over him like a lot of the Irish, and a bit inhibited. Oh, those goddamn Celtic mothers offering grown men the phantom tit. I'm not going to probe his libido for you, Abe, but I think he told you the truth. You're not going to put him and his boils on the stand?"

"It strengthens the motives for murder. I may use him near the end, before I put Maman Celie on the stand."

"I don't think Eddie will be impressive on the stand. He'll deny he told you anything. Sarah Rodman was another mother image to him. And Maman Celie may get loud laughs."

Abe took a big gulp of beer. "It's too bad, Sidney, that murderers don't have solid respectable citizens witnessing all their crimes, so the state can produce only certified, clean-cut witnesses, all of whom read the Bible, are good to their dogs, and walk old ladies across the street."

"Speaking of ladies, you call Fran again?"

"Yes, when you were at the bar. She's very angry at me. The kids waited up till nine to talk to me."

"Better go home, Abe. Get some sleep."

"I don't sleep. I toss and moan and try the case all night, and Judge Riggs bangs his gavel and Roger Tindell objects and is always sustained. Sidney, was George Rodman a good or a bad man?"

"Good is that which justifies the existence of the individual as well as his society. Did he harm that existence or seriously warp his society?"

"I don't think he did. He was outside its moral fence, but that's personal between a man and his emotional plumbing. There's no perfection in law. Hell, I know that. Even in art you get godalmighty awful messes most of the time. And in human relationships, when it comes to love it often drives out what ought to be, for something that must be done in passion without reason. Haven't you and me—I suppose—done something crazy along the same lines?"

Doctor Wymer laughed. "Stop playing the priest at confession. No comment. I see the human gut and nerve end blamed for lots of things. Integrated physical relationships should make of our lives a common happiness, Abe—not a hell—but most often our contradictory undisciplined actions lead to crimes people like you have to try in a court of law. This is no night for small beers. Barman, Scotch, and bring the bottle."

Abe said, "I'll have a bourbon. Ed Hightower, when he's lushed, gets mellow. Not cynical like you, Sidney. The chief says, 'Man, poor character, is inconsistent, distracted in his mind, and capable of great pain.' Think how George Rodman must have suffered. Maybe he welcomed that bullet, dying at the climax, like the last note of the love-death music of Wagner."

Sidney Wymer swallowed a large double Scotch. "Wagner was a lousy romantic; so was George Rodman, I bet. Reason isn't a dream, Abe. It's living honestly—in reality, among our sensations and impulses that count. Of course, people expect a minister to be all head and no genitalia. But take it from me, the life of just the imagination is not any good reason for existing. Harmony of all our parts and ideas must be carved out through conflicting desires and aspirations. To most men, my too sober friend, it's come down to this: How much will we sacrifice of our passions for harmony? The Reverend George Rodman found out he couldn't sacrifice everything. I mean, in mistaken kindness he didn't take his girl and run off soon enough. Barman, this is dreadful Scotch. Cognac; let's try that."

Abe said, "I'm finishing my bourbon and going home. I'm too tired to talk any more."

"Can diverse natures in us be made compatible? Can some peace be achieved within ourselves? I say yes to you, Abe Pedlock, if you bathe it in alcohol and Chanel Number Five. You know why women smell the way they do? That's to scare off the squares."

Abe was no longer listening. Somehow he had no clear image of George Rodman, and it was getting no clearer. The bar was emptying. He would drive Sidney Wymer to his house and take a cab home.

In the car Abe asked, "What did you think of George Rodman?"

"I was polite to him. When we met."

"Often?"

"No. Almost never."

Abe nodded. "I never really knew him. Only met him once, really. I mean, to talk to."

"What?"

"I said that—"

"Don't bother. I'm drunk, Abe."

"I can't drink. I mean, I can but I don't care to, much. George Rodman was in many ways like myself. Only from a different level. He too was an outsider but had the right godhead, genes, coloration, background, to be taken in without fear."

"Fear dresses me in the morning, blows out my candle at night." Sidney smiled and closed his eyes.

"He got in, I didn't. But he didn't really make it. You may

think I'm too sensitive about my position here. But look at George Rodman. He failed, and took up a love he felt was more real. Why didn't he make it? He had all the breaks, all the charm, grace, creed."

"Never heard of your George Rodman," said Sidney.

. . . I remember the last time I saw the two of them—George Rodman and Helen Nash. It was in April. There was a black rainstorm banging across the town, and I was standing under the leaking canvas awning of Jacob Yuron's Photo Gallery, water down my neck, streams of water falling. I was waiting for a bus. Fran had the car and had taken the kids for the afternoon to her sister's farm down Royal Road.

A large Buick came splashing up, and the door opened and a friendly voice said, "Heading up Ann Street?"

"Yes, but the bus must be waterlogged someplace."

"Hop in."

It seemed a shame to intrude my wet wool topcoat and soggy hat into the warm interior of the polished car. There was the Reverend George Rodman (not wearing his turned-backward collar), big, handsome, smoking a pipe, and between us in a transparent oiled-silk raincoat was Mrs. Nash, some songbooks on her lap, her delicate head on a fine, thin neck politely staring into the rain.

"I'm the Reverend Rodman. This is Mrs. Nash. We've been to hymn practice and I'm running her home."

"I'm Abe Pedlock, with the D.A.'s office."

"Of course. I know you. Met you at some charity affair my wife was giving." The rain ahead grew stronger. "Helen, I don't really like the new hymn we tried at all. Too Puritan. Listen to this, Mr. Pedlock.

"*Days and moments quickly flying*
Blend the living with the dead.
Soon will you and I be lying
Each within our narrow bed."

I said, "It's strong, but you must admit it can't be denied."

Mrs. Nash said, "It has a fine musical setting to it."

"Oh, music," said Rodman, smiling. "The words are the things I listen to."

The rain had increased in fury, and we sat in a kind of bubble of steel and glass, the interior womb-warm, and I felt the physical presence of us three. Helen Nash, young, rosy-cheeked, with a delicate face and very large eyes, her slim, rain-spotted legs ending in gray rubbers, and the interior of the car smelling of storm and healthy flesh and George Rodman's Dunhill "Royal Yacht" smoking tobacco.

George Rodman said, "Were you born here, Mr. Pedlock?"

"Yes. I haven't been away much. Didn't leave till I was seventeen—to go to college. Later I was in the Army—paper work, military courts in Washington. Then back here. It's a good place to be born."

"I was born in Ohio," said George Rodman, "and I can't get used to the Eastern Shore. The heat in summer, the storms in the bay." He smiled and turned to face me. "But I like it, in good weather."

Helen Nash shook her head. "I never liked it. You must be born here. If you don't like Robert E. Lee or never heard of the D.A.R., the women look on you as if you were a Negro or something."

I laughed. George Rodman smiled. "Helen, you must meet more people and find out they aren't very different from most of us. You hunt, Mr. Pedlock?"

"As a kid, rabbits, ducks."

"My father hunted a great deal."

Helen Nash said, "How could he do it?"

"It was rather dangerous then," said George Rodman. "Cape buffalo, lion. He was a famous hunter. Like my brother-in-law Mikel."

The rain had not let up, and I knew it wouldn't.

Helen Nash said, "I was thinking, wondering what this town was like before we came, when the Indians were here. Better off then, I would think, than they are now, clamming."

"As a Christian I can't accept that, Helen."

I sensed nothing between them or behind our banal conversation. It was either that I was dense or they hid carefully from the public the intensity that must have already begun between them. I felt George Rodman was not lying; he was a Christian not just because he was a preacher or said so. I sensed that he meant it. Yet I can't say why or see him too clearly. I just remember a man smoking good tobacco in a shiny car driving me to my door in a rainstorm, and then off they drove—the two of them—while I shook rain off my eyebrows and the wet elms flapped and beat around the house; and I never saw them again—not alive. . . .

CHAPTER X

AFTER MIDNIGHT

IT WAS MIDNIGHT before Abe was home, showered, wearing just shorts and a light cotton robe. He sat at the kitchen table forking strawberry shortcake. He had refused any other food. The cake was not one of Fran's successful ones. The strawberries were on the sour side; in the hot weather the cream had not whipped properly. Abe ate a section of the cake and looked across the table at Fran in her peach-colored dressing gown.

"It was good of you and the kids to save it for me. I had to get Sidney Wymer home."

"It's not one of my good cakes." Fran rumpled her short-cut taffy-colored hair and leaned across the small table. "You're very tired, Abe."

"I'm pooped. This day is never going to end."

"Don't talk. Let's just sit."

No jaded stability had yet set in with their marriage. There was a ripe kind of innocence about Fran that Abe cherished, a fine, dignified, symmetrical face, a particular dazzle that Fran had for him, something he couldn't explain to other men. They existed in a warm physical envelope. (Her luminous shiny eyes across the table show me I'm a very lucky man. The last few weeks have been hard on both of us. One has to walk carefully not to spill happiness. I should have come right home.) He ate and watched her as Fran sat looking at him in a kind of amused, persecuted silence that married men know so well.

(I wonder about Fran. Do I know her? Does she know how much I love her? She seems to live in an ivy thicket of personal reveries. That's how I first met her at that law school dance, in her formal white tulle. She was taller, larger, than most women, and very tanned, with her short hair almost pink-white. She gyrated rather than walked that night and had an amused yet plaintive look on her face. We sat on the steps outside the hall holding hands, sat on stones the violet color of dried lavender. Little secret pleasures are not really little. It took me a long time to know her. She was so real, but I was fooled and waited to discover what she was really like. In the end I knew au austere quietness was the real Fran. A healthy self-satisfaction. Her proud, clean look, a delicate equilibrium between an innocent maturity hard to believe and an animal curiosity about me, the male element missing from her life. Fran wasn't one to dawdle passion. One night we thought we were engaged; it was cocktail time in the suburban dusk and the Wurlitzer juke box down the road was playing banal Irving Berlin sweetness. A deep, inexplicable sympathy was between us. Later her sister was against her marrying a Jew. That dreadful year when it seemed it was all over. And I . . . I must rest or I'll collapse in court tomorrow.)

Fran was crying as Abe finished the last soggy bit of cake. "Oh, Abe, you don't know how I love you."

"Of course I know. My ego takes it for granted."

"You don't really know me. Sometimes I don't like myself. I bother you so in your work. I wonder when you'll find me out. Am I shallow and too selfish for you and the children?"

"You've had a hard day too."

"You need your sleep and we women are all crazy people."

"That's so they match the men they marry." Abe smiled, too weary to lean over to kiss her, too tired to follow deep-seated emotions. He was worn thinner than he would admit.

Fran put the cake plate and silverware in the sink. "The county chief of detectives called."

"What'd he say?" Abe stood up and stretched and frowned.

"Some information he had for you. Call him in the morning. It can keep."

Abe hid a frown. The heavy burden of duty fell over his head like an overlarge hat. "I'll just call back and go to bed. Go on up, Fran, and I'll look at Tom, too."

"He's a very sick cat. I should have listened to you."

Abe kissed his wife's warm cheek. She went upstairs.

Night-flying moths stumbled against the kitchen screen door. The wet, heated night air brought in the scent of freshly cut grass, the old-wood smell of a house that had baked in the sun all day. Abe put through a phone call for Chief Smith and waited; the only night sounds were the bumbling noise of a giant moth with very dusty wings against the back screen door and the train whistle of a freight someplace near Mills Spring blowing for the crossing.

"Hello, Chief Smith? This is Abe Pedlock. I'm returning your call."

"I've been digging in our cross-filing system for you."

"Come up with something?"

"You be the judge of that, Mr. Prosecutor. I had to backtrack more than five years."

"What turned up?"

"At a Fourth of July picnic eight years ago at Clam Beach, Thomas Nash was arrested for carrying a forty-five Colt pistol in his car and threatening to shoot someone."

"He was in Philadelphia at a meeting of toolmakers the night his wife was murdered. We even have the group photo of the event, and a hundred witnesses. Who'd he threaten to shoot? George Rodman?"

"No. Next day after the picnic a John Higgins swore that Thomas Nash had threatened him with the pistol; and he swore out a citizen's complaint against Thomas Nash to keep the peace."

"John Higgins?"

"Son of Big Ed Higgins. Yep."

Abe gripped the phone hard, feeling his damp fingers on its unpleasant, hard, shiny surface. "Big Ed's son? What was the thing all about?"

"The report, with old MacDonald's private notes on it when he was running this office, lists Thomas Nash as saying young Higgins was annoying his wife Helen."

"Annoying?"

"The note says Tom really caught his wife in a room at Moonbay Hotel on July the Fourth. The sheriff tells me young Higgins was quite a turf hunter. Always in trouble with girls. His old man, Big Ed, had to get him out of real trouble a dozen times. Stopped his son marrying that Mary Durant who works in your office, the sheriff said, by threatening to get her father kicked out as court clerk."

Abe was aware he was sweating profusely, the perspiration pouring down his armpits. "I never knew that about him and Helen Nash. Or Mary Durant being involved with him."

"John Higgins seems to have been in a lot of strange nests."

"Chief, I don't know where this can lead, if anyplace. Put a check on John Higgins, see if he still saw Mrs. Nash, where he was the night of the murders. It's crazy to think maybe he . . . maybe . . ."

Chief Smith's breathing was audible on the phone. "You never know about these shack jobs. Maybe they didn't break up —young Higgins and Mrs. Nash—after Tom Nash tried to pistol him. Maybe they carried on till Rodman took her away from him. Maybe young Higgins decided to get both of them that night, work them over, mutilate—" Chief Smith was really excited, Abe sensed. Chief Smith relished such details, away from open court testimony, when they confused him.

Abe became aware of the latent madness in the chief of detectives. "Go easy, Chief Smith. This could ruin my entire case against the people now being tried. You just check John Higgins' whereabouts, what he did that night, what he's been doing, how he's been behaving. And, Chief Smith, I don't have to tell you to keep your lip buttoned. Big Ed Higgins isn't likely to be amused if his son gets connected with the Rodman-Nash murders, even by just raking up an old gunning complaint. Don't let this one leak to the reporters."

"Me, Mr. Pedlock? I like this job. Don't worry. I know how to cover. I'll get a report on young Higgins to you soon as I have something."

"That's the stuff, Chief Smith."

Abe hung up the telephone. The earth had stopped breathing and rotating, he felt as he wiped his damp hands on his robe. (A hell of a note; it's too crazy to mean anything. Yet I have to follow it. It's puzzling; life should not be . . . so mean. It's my job to know. I can't go on trying the three defendants if there's a chance, a slim chance, somebody else was the murderer. Big Ed doesn't think his son killed anybody. Or does he? He just didn't want his name brought into the Rodman-Nash case. Suppose he did think so? Would he warn the D.A.'s office to lay off?)

The image of Mary Durant filled Abe's mind. Mary and John Higgins? She had been associated with Abe eleven years, ever since he was a young punk briefing cases for the not so successful law firm of Novak, Bixby and Silverman. That explained those events when . . . The censor that locked away things long ago refused to let Abe bring things back for inspection. Abe turned off the kitchen lights to avoid the moths, opened the screen door, and went out onto the kitchen porch. Tom the old cat lay on a tattered towel, his fur mussed, neck thin, the hairy stomach once so fat pinched now, the ribs showing. (I was searching land titles in those days—interpreting abstracts, representing small decadent estates in probate courts.)

"What's the matter, Tom—don't you like being a very old man?"

The cat did not move but only made a low, mewing sound. Abe

pushed a saucer of milk closer and saw it was curdled sour. He replaced it with a fresh dish of milk from the old refrigerator kept as an extra on the porch for the overflow of supplies. Tom made no effort to drink. Only the low, mewing sound and the slight rise and fall of the ribs showed the cat was still alive. Abe, full of Chief Smith's report, felt that only gravity held him on the porch floor.

(That bitch in my office, Mary Durant. She and John Higgins. It must have started right after high school. John Higgins. I remember him now. A fat-faced nun-and-priest-polished school-boy when I knew him. Had his own car at fourteen. Ran around with the rich Catholic crowd, played football for St. Mary's the year they beat Hawleytown High. His car killed that old lady on Royale Street after a drinking party at Zeller's. It cost Big Ed a lot to keep it from meaning prison. A farm for the old lady's husband, a reporter's son on the fire force, and the old D.A., Charlie Ford, got that judge's bench.)

Abe filled another saucer with water from the porch tap and put it down by Tom's side. Life was such a delicate thing.

CHAPTER XI

A MAN'S PAST

ABE DIDN'T GO up to bed. He thought. Tom, old, stiff, something inside out of order, yet the life force was there—did he have memory, regrets? (Mary Durant, voluptuous high-school flirt, and John Higgins, lecherous grandson of a famine-year mick, almost married.)

Abe latched the screen door and climbed slowly up to the heat-filled bedroom. Fran was asleep already. She had had a big day too—the house, the kids, worry over him and the cat. Abe ached with love of her in memory of other nights' sleep after satiety. He dropped his robe and got onto his side of the bed, glassy-eyed with fatigue.

(That year when Fran's sister was so strong against me and we broke up. That dreadful year when I went to Washington for the law firm, a new young attorney, not yet dry behind my briefs. And they sent Mary Durant with me to type the final papers, to settle the matter of the sale of the Lauder estate that owned the theater down there.) Bitterness swept Abe lying by the side of his sleeping wife. The old, unpleasant thoughts curly with self-contempt broke past the censor that had so long held it all walled up. Staring at the dark, warm night ceiling of the bedroom, Abe was back eleven years in time, in the parlor car of the Pennsylvania Railroad daily special, *The Senator,* going to Washington, D.C. . . .

"How's the show look to you?" Barney, the Washington theater manager, asked Abe after the dress rehearsal.

"I'm only here to arrange a sale of the theater for the estate," Abe answered.

"What do you really think of it?"

"Washington may like it."

Mary had been silent and sullen on the train journey and in Washington. She didn't want to go to the opening-night theater party.

Abe said, "The buyer of the theater will be there. We'll arrange the legal details."

Mary wanted to eat something before going to the party. Her color was high and her gestures were involved and desperate, as if expressing some problem with her hands and body. It was his first important assignment on his own. Fran would be proud of him—if she ever saw him again. The band was low and the food very good. He and Mary had one long, slow dance around the overwaxed floor. Then they sat down and ate a bit more.

Mary said, as the coffee appeared, "Ever have a dream when you must run and can't? I've had them."

"Everybody does. Let's get to that party."

"Don't rush me, Abe. I want to talk."

"You're keyed up about something, Mary."

"I've been holding something back—but I'll lick it. It's a man. Help me, Abe."

"Stop frowning." Abe took her hand in his. "Look, I was a pretty mixed-up person when I joined the law firm. Then you showed me the tricks."

"Oh, the hell with tricks. You don't need them any more." Mary swept a water glass off the table. It broke. Abe ordered two brandies.

Mary said, "Christ, is it worth it? The agony, the pretense to people, this love business?"

The waiter brought the brandy and silently picked up the bigger fragments of the broken glass. He went away.

Abe patted Mary's hand. "Look, I've been over the bumps myself."

"Oh, why do we get trapped? I want so to be happy and have people around me happy and like me. That's all. Ha—that's *all*."

"You were the dream girl of every high-school boy who knew anything about what it was all about."

"I feel ready to die tonight. Give me your handkerchief, Abe."

They sat, not dejected, just sad, and drank brandy, and both spoke rather poorly. Abe was already aware that love, accepted or rejected, in real life was limited by imagination and inhibition, and could reach no real pitch of perfect expression with words. That could be accomplished only by artists, writing later of what they had felt, in agony or ecstasy.

"Fran isn't going to marry me. Her sister is too powerful an influence on her."

"We'll be friends, Abe." Mary raised a hand like a small white flag. "Friends in misery."

"All right. I don't suppose we'll get to the theater party tonight if we keep drinking brandies."

"It's all on the expense account. I want to lie down."

"Yes, do that. You look very upset."

"You go to the party alone, Abe. We came here to do a legal job."

"I'll see. Come on, I'll take you back to the hotel."

"No, get me a cab. Any color except romantic pink."

He dropped Mary at the hotel and went on to the party, in an apartment on New Jersey Avenue—the dome of the Capitol gleaming through a bank of windows.

Abe didn't care much for the party. He had too many drinks, met the buyer of the theater, and had a few more drinks. He must have dozed off. He was not a drinking man. But he felt he could hold his liquor when he had to.

Abe came awake to find a colored singer named Mindee shaking him. It was very late. Most of the people had left the party. Mindee looked down at Abe. "Yo' sure sleep solid, Mistah Pedlock."

Abe struggled to a sitting position on the lumpy sofa smelling of cigar smoke, body powder and spilled drinks. He tried to focus his eyes, his mind refused to give any clear-cut orders.

"Party over?"

"Over for some. I'm still pitchin'. Phone call for yo'."

"What?"

"Just come in."

"Oh."

"It's a Miss Durant."

"Mary?"

"She says she hated to bust in on yo' kicks but it's very important. Sounds freakish to me. She on the tea?"

"My head is kinda . . . kinda . . ."

"Come on, the gal is waitin'. She sounds powerful troubled over somethin'."

Abe picked up the white gold-trimmed phone offered him.

"Hello. What's—what's the matter?"

"It's Mary."

"Hello, Mary. It's Abe."

Her voice rushed him. "Abe, I've tried to kill myself. Sleeping pills. In the hotel room. I can't keep awake. I don't want to call the cops or a strange doctor."

"Oh, hell."

"Please come over. Don't call anyone."

Abe said slowly into the phone, "Right away. Vomit, stick a finger down your throat. Walk. Walk your tail off. Be right over."

It was a strange cab ride through late Washington, images on Abe's mind, changing and shifting.

Mary met him at the door of the room wearing a nightgown. "I can't toss up much. I can't walk."

"I bought some milk. I'll boil it—got some mustard too."

"Abe, save me."

"I'll call the hotel doctor."

"No. No! It would ruin us both in Hawleytown."

"All right."

There was one small lamp burning by the bed. Mary in her yellow nightgown was making sobbing, sucking sounds now with her eyes closed. Her body shook and her naked heels drummed the rug.

Abe stepped on a small bottle and picked it up. Empty. He figured quickly. Too many—much too many to keep down. He carried Mary to the bathroom. His finger went down her throat in cruel, probing swiftness, as far as it could go. She gagged and went on gagging, and it was like the tops of the waves coming up. He kept shaking her with a violent persistency. He heated the milk by holding it under scalding bath water.

"Get this into you."

"Hold my head."

Abe let her keep it up a long time until she retched for nothing, and he saw the stuff hadn't been absorbed very much. To keep her awake he pinched her very hard on the naked arm, and then under her breasts, until she moaned in pain; and he stood her up and began to walk her around the room. Cruelly, with unflagging perseverance, he walked her.

She said, "It's all not worth it. Spoiling a hired bed. Eternal love, with time off for summer vacation and relatives for Christmas."

"Keep talking."

"Running away from hired afternoons in dirty rooms. Let me die, Abe."

"You don't really want to die, Mary."

Mary hung in a great lassitude over a chair. Abe didn't dare leave her and he didn't want to wake anyone in the hotel; every one was asleep. He just kept pinching her flesh, and when she showed by her moan she felt it, he walked her. Her arms turned blue from pinching. Mary keeled over. Abe took her back to the bathroom. There was nothing now in her stomach. It must have been four o'clock, and she was breaking into words that made no sense, struggling obstreperously. "The dirty dog . . . easy lay—goodbye, dear . . . call you sometime."

Abe stripped her, washed her, rubbed her down with heavy towels and bundled a flannel robe around her while she kept on saying, "It's too sad, so sad, sad . . . the important family . . . Big. Big shot . . . thrown over, kicked out . . . To save my old man."

Abe got some more warm milk. It was so hot it burned her lips. Abe had made it half brandy from a bottle in Mary's luggage. She shivered and gulped it, and after a while just leaned back and moaned. Abe had a big drink himself. He had never seen a woman built like Mary. Nude intimacies were not only limited and rare for him but in fact had been almost nonexistent.

Mary asked, "How am I doing?"

"You'll make it."

"Let's have another drink. Join me."

They had two stiff drinks each.

"Abe, you're a great guy."

"It was just you being low for a moment."

"You got the gate too. Was she fun in the hay?"

"I don't know. I'll never know now."

Abe went over and sat down on the bed and took Mary's hand. It was ice cold. Her eyelids, the brandy told him, were like smooth, multicolored glass, but the rest of her was pink and provoking. The pinched flesh was turning bluer where he had ruptured little blood vessels under the surface of the skin. Was it for real? Was he really with the high-school vamp, naked and warm in her open robe? She looked up, and Abe wiped her face. Her hair was wet, and Abe dried it. It smelled of some perfume.

Mary, spreadeagled on the bed, was looking at the ceiling. Her voice was husky and low. She seemed again in possession of her faculties. "They shouldn't leave that stuff around."

"You don't have to talk. Cover yourself."

Mary rolled out of the robe, arms out to him. She turned and kissed him. "Oh, Abe, all we have is each other. Nobody else cares."

He gripped her to him, aware of her skin, her body, his own driving urges.

> *Nay, but to live*
> *In the rank sweat of an enseamed bed,*
> *Stewed in corruption, honeying and making love*
> *. . . over the nasty sty—*

Abe came awake in the Washington morning to the smell of freshly brewed coffee and in a disordered bed. He didn't want to open his eyes, but when he did the white sunlight stabbed at his pain-soaked eyeballs and he was aware of the gong clanging inside his head, and the acid in him, of the dryness of the brandy working its way through his bloodstream and his kidneys.

He was in Mary's hotel room. Mary lay beside him on her back, arms behind her head, legs crossed, breasts high, her stomach rising and falling, the soft blond down on it highlighted in sunlight. Abe didn't look long at her; he was aware of the coffee smell. He looked at the portable electric plate and saw the small Pyrex bubble perking. He got out of bed and took the Pyrex pot off the glow. He found two plastic cups in Mary's baggage—she was a seasoned traveler—filled them and came back to the bed. Only when Mary opened one eye did he sense that they both were naked. He tried to laugh and set down the coffee on the night table. "Smells good."

Mary said, "I put on the coffee and fell asleep again. Pour me a black cup for the top of my head to float in. You can have the shower first. I've never been with a Jew before."

Abe smiled. "I'm too hung over to explain the nondifference."

After they had both showered, they sat together—she in a blue bathrobe and he in his shirt and pants, and they slowly sipped very hot black coffee. It did help.

Abe said, "How do you feel?"

Mary put her arms around him. "I feel, Abe, I made a jackass out of myself last night. Forget what I raved about. I don't usually lose control."

"All forgotten."

"Abe, you're a fine lover."

"I kind of took advantage of you."

"Don't be a dope. It was the right treatment and I wanted it."

"We've got to be at the local lawyers' at noon."

Mary looked at a small bedside clock set in a leather square. She stood up and tightened the belt of her robe. "Abe, I'm human, I like being liked. I don't say what happened here hasn't happened a few times before."

Abe put down his cup. "Mary, you get back into bed. I'll go alone to talk to the lawyers."

She held her head. "Maybe so. I'm spinning."

He got her into bed, pulled the sheet up over her, and leaned and kissed her lightly on the lips. "You're a fine, strong girl, and I'll put that in writing if you want it."

She put her arms around his neck. "Thank you, Abe."

Their affair had lasted two months and a few days. It was already over when Abe, walking past the public tennis courts on Greene Street, had run into Fran wearing shorts, a man's open-collared shirt, carrying a white sharkskin jacket, two rackets under a tanned arm. Like legerdemain they had come together without speaking and taken each other's hands with a fierce urgency. They leaped at love like acrobats over the heads of slower people and went together down to the river bank. He remembered he had whistled, like an inconsolable fool, *"Addio del passato,"* from *La Traviata*—not that he particularly cared for the opera.

It had been a rank and dismal two months and a few days with Mary Durant. She was, he knew, ashamed of him; he stood no higher in the social scale than her own father. A time of despair banged out in hired beds at out-of-the-way places. Of rutting and limply expiring under low pine ceilings of unseasoned lumber dripping resin, lying on musty sheets, smoking cigarettes in motel rooms where spiders printed etchings in dark corners. And Mary, with unsatisfied eyes, looked at him disdainfully before they again tried for satiety together, another frenzy of driving each other to endurances that meant nothing by the time they left, in separate cars, as the sun set low over the river. They never entered each other's private lives, never met new friends or shared anything but the almost daily animal battles of two hurt people who fought as silently as they could.

At the end Mary said she would be very busy for the next few weeks. Abe saw her that evening in the large yellow car of a city paving contractor, Matt Olsen, a big red-faced man with the jowls of a college athlete fifteen years after winning his letter in sports. The next morning Abe dictated a long legal brief to her with an expressionless ease and Mary took it all down skillfully.

When he again met Fran, Abe knew he had come through a futility as fruitless as his thoughts of Sarah Hawley. He and Fran were married a week later by the justice of the peace in Sand City, and Abe never again knew any other woman. . . .

(I must sleep. I must sleep now. This day must end. I must sleep. I must sleep and I must remember that I am trying Sarah for murder, and that what happened once long ago meant nothing . . . meant nothing. Mary was an accident, and she doesn't really remind me of Sarah; only in a certain little walk and the way she turns around, moving her entire body, not just her head. I love Fran, only Fran. The rest is youthful nonsense. The kind of crush a kid has for a movie star or a face seen once in the window of a passing train diner. I have come through to happiness with Fran—just the way it is in the corny TV shows, the movies, the placid, respectable, normal, accepted . . . way . . . the way . . . I must sleep . . . I must sleep now . . . I must sl . . .)

BOOK TWO

THURSDAY

CHAPTER XII

ANOTHER DAY

THE SLEEP WAS TROUBLED and fitful, the night room warm, and
on the damp bed Abe got little rest. He was aware of that phase
in his dreams when they became frightening as if seen in the
light of smoking red lanterns.

The hoot of the first factory whistle sounded, and Abe sat up
in bed to find the sun was already up. From downstairs he heard
the noise of the children at their food and the clatter of the
breakfast dishes. Abe was tired, worn from his fearful dreams,
and the memory of reliving Washington with Mary Durant. He
panted in the heat, went to the bathroom, shaved and showered
and came down to the kitchen.

Fran was wiping Davey's small fat chin free of oatmeal.

"Daddy," said Davey, "Johnny Winkle says you hang people on the courthouse lawn."

"No, Davey. Daddy doesn't hang people," said Fran, pushing a wedge of yellow melon in front of Abe. "He just sees they get justice."

Deedee, in stiff blue jeans and ballet slippers, looked up from the comic section in the newspaper. "We're going to do the trials of the witches in Salem in civics class at school—those that were burned. And because Daddy is in the District Attorney's office I'm going to play the judge. Hear ye, hear ye!"

Abe tasted the cold melon; his stomach refused to accept it, but he fought it down and followed it with a glass of ice-cold pineapple juice. He felt better as he looked at Deedee and patted her pale, neat hair. "They never burned witches at Salem, Deedee."

Fran said, "It's just a legend."

Abe swallowed his black coffee. "They actually crushed them to death between stones."

"Golly," said Deedee. "This will sure surprise Miss Wells. She said they burned the American witches."

"No. Records show otherwise."

"Oh, Abe, don't be legal," said Fran. "It's horrible enough either way."

Davey solemnly announced, "I'm going to vomit."

Fran shook her head firmly. "You do, Davey Pedlock, and no ball game in the park later. A child who tosses his breakfast isn't well enough to play ball."

Abe took two more scoops of melon and tried to swallow some toast. "You driving to the school today, Fran?"

"No. It's Mrs. Coleman's day for the car pool. I'll take you to the courthouse, dear."

Davey said, "Deedee, can I sit up front?"

A horn sounded from the curb, and the two children were gone after a sticky kissing of their parents' cheeks. Abe picked up the crumpled newspaper, avoided the front page, and settled back in the chair. "I'll go as soon as you can get ready, Fran. I want to get a county car at the courthouse and go see someone before court opens."

She put her arms around him from behind and kissed his ear. "Abe, you're going to break down. Just rest now, while I go see the cat; he's so weak. And then I'll drive you. It may rain today."

"Could be." He felt alone as she went to the back porch; the burden of the day was already pressing down on his head. He ached for long, cool, comforting sleep. To focus his mind Abe read slowly a column of print in the morning newspaper.

WIDOW'S WILL CARRIED OUT
PETS ALL KILLED

Mrs. Gladys Prockter, seventy-one, a childless widow, doted during her lifetime on her mansion full of pets, her fine big herd of black sheep, her cattle, pigs, ponies and barnyard fowl. So much, in fact, that the prospect of being separated from the animals by death preyed on her mind. So she fixed that up in her will—she ordered that her menagerie follow her to the grave.

Last Saturday she died while sitting in her favorite armchair, surrounded by her two spaniels, three cats and seven parakeets, in her thirty-room mansion.

Yesterday, while doctors inside the hoary mansion conducted a post-mortem on the widow to determine cause of death, a group of veterinary doctors, slaughter-men and officials of the SPCA gathered outside and carried out her last wish.

They rounded up 120 sheep, four ponies, two cows, two bullocks, three pigs, the two dogs and three cats and seven parakeets, and scores of fluffy chinchilla rabbits, pigeons, geese, ducks and guinea hens.

All day long the gunshots sounded across the quiet farm lands, and villagers down the road winced at each shot.

Then the widow's sister, Mrs. Christabel Taylor, followed the vets and officials around the yard piled high with corpses to make sure all the animals were dead. Mrs. Prockter's will stipulated that her sister must vouch that all the pets were killed humanely.

"It has been a most distressing day," Christabel said.

The Nash house of white clapboard and a stubby chimney stood near the edge of town in a meadow on which scratchy patches had been planted with flowers that grew rangy and wild, and sun-tormented vegetables were surrounded by wooden stakes connected by knotted cords. It was early in the day, and Thomas Nash was watering a row of hollyhocks behind the house. Abe came around to him through the gravel drive. Thomas Nash, the widower of Helen, was an elderly man who kept his back straight, his very white hair neatly combed. He was smoking a small, dark pipe. His voice was low and pleasant as he said, "Morning, Mr. Pedlock."

"Hello, Mr. Nash. I thought you might be up early before you went down to the shop."

"It's slack just now in the machine-tool business."

He put down the watering can and wiped his hands carefully on the back of his work pant. He led Abe to an unpainted bench under a grape arbor full of a purplish fruit.

"Mr. Nash, you didn't tell me everything," Abe said.

"Everything I knew." The old man reamed his pipe with a thick cleaner and blew through the stem.

Abe lighted a stogie, his second of the day already. "You didn't tell me about John Higgins."

The old man relighted the pipe slowly with a large kitchen match, the cords in his neck standing out as he puffed life into the pipe bowl. "I didn't think it had anything to do with the . . . the other matter. Let me tell you something. No matter what it looks like, Helen was a very fine woman and a good woman. She was eighteen when I married her, and me, I was fifty. A mistake. She was a romantic kid and wanted to get away from Spring Corner. I went out there to set up the machinery tools in the wood-veneering plant where her uncle was foreman. She was an orphan. To her I was a city man. I had a good car and I took her to roadhouses and she always drank one beer and listened to the juke boxes play. She was all legs and wore a small ribbon in her hair."

The old man looked off across the field where two boys were trying to raise a kite into the hot, windless sky. "I disappointed her in lots of ways. No, not just in lovemaking. I did in that too, of course. In other ways too. I'm a stupid man, learned my trade in the old Navy. I can follow plans in machine tools, but that's about all I can do. I didn't read books, and Helen read a lot. The house is still full of her book-club selections. Wasn't a book she didn't try. She liked to talk about people in novels as if they were real. Stuff I didn't follow very much. For me, a pipe, the sports page, a little digging in the garden, lots of sleep, and I was satisfied. I saw it coming—the first trouble. She couldn't hide anything that sounded dishonest. It wasn't in her. She grew into a fine woman in the ten years we were married."

The kite had crashed into some bushes, and the small boys were thrashing their way to it with the high cries of heated childish voices.

"I'd say John Higgins was the first. Know what I mean? She changed. It didn't calm her. It made her dreamy, careless around the house, redder nail polish, new hair-do. I was on a rush order to finish the special milling work on the dynamo that went out of order at Milltown. She went alone with some people we knew to a Fourth of July picnic at Clam Beach. I got back real early and drove down to Clam Beach to meet her. Some wise guy had tipped me off. I waited outside that hotel down there. That's what you came about this morning, Mr. Pedlock, wasn't it?"

"You had decided to kill John Higgins."

The old man—he seemed so free of trepidations and inadequacies this morning—knocked out the dottle of his pipe on his work-scarred palm. "I don't know. It was my grandfather's pistol. He had been a Federal marshal in some Western town. Got killed, I hear, in a card game. I always carried it in my car. I pointed it at John Higgins outside the hotel. I don't know if I would have shot him. He was scared, but he laughed and took it away from me. He swore out a disturbance-of-the-peace paper against me the next day. It was hushed up when his old man got wind of it. Everybody was very nice to me about it. I guess they all knew for some time about the two of them. Helen said she was never going back to him. I wanted very much to believe her."

"The affair didn't end there?"

"I never again tried to find out. Then Helen joined the church choir. They practiced three nights a week. Seemed a lot to me. But I no longer stuck my nose in. To be an old man alone in a house isn't something to look forward to, Mr. Pedlock. So much left-over life to get through."

Abe liked the old man—he had dignity, and no conceit

"When did she join the church choir?"

"Three years ago. Helen had a fine voice. Not much range, but a good quality. I can tell you when she and Mr. Rodman became serious about each other; I kind of skipped that the times we talked. I didn't spy. I heard nothing. But it was Helen tipped me off. She was like a delicate precision tool, true to form, but she had a way of reacting to certain conditions, pressures. She changed her way of doing her hair to a very neat, simple style. Dressed different, too. Didn't try to look like a girl any more. Subscribed to a longhair record club, held meetings in the house of women's clubs that helped children with bad eyes, rheumatic hearts. That was when I'd say it began with Mr. Rodman. I liked him, you know. He was a fine man. At first he came here when he drove Helen home, and we talked about heavy-duty engines. He had worked his way through college and the seminary driving a thrasher and binder on a wheat farm someplace out in the Dakotas. He knew a lot about heavy-duty machinery. Then after a while he didn't come to visit here any more. Sometimes late at night I'd hear his car stop way up the street under the big oak. There was a loose fanbelt hum he couldn't get out of it. Half an hour later Helen would let herself into the house. Go to her room. We'd had separate rooms for six, seven years. I thought that was it. It would go on like that. I'd live as long as I could and not be alone."

"How did John Higgins react to this new situation, Mr. Nash?"

The old man began to refill his pipe slowly from an old leather pouch. "About nine months ago Helen came in, around five o'clock, from shopping, carrying a net bag full of groceries, looking like she had been crying. She wouldn't talk; just banged into the kitchen and shut the door. I looked out our front window.

John Higgins was sitting in a sports car across the street. He was taking a long drink from a pint of whisky. He looked real angry. Then he threw the bottle across the street. It broke on our curb. I went out with a broom and a bit of tin and swept it all up. After that, you know the rest—what happened."

The old man put the unlighted pipe into his mouth, his hands at his side. Two small boys passed carrying a large torn kite. Abe heard the old man weeping. Abe got up and walked away, the stub of his stogie tasting dreadful. The meadow was full of bees, big rowdy fellows with fuzzy yellow pants. There was a ghost of wood smoke in the air, and below in the little fields a man was plowing, turning back the earth in dark furrows, turning back the pelt of the soil, preparing to fertilize it again. The white horse walked slowly, the plow moving in jerks, and the man behind making little *tisk tisk* sounds that came up to the garden. Abe looked at the old man.

> . . . in that drop of time,
> A life of pain, an age of crime.

Abe wondered where he remembered that from. The white horse had stopped to nibble at stubble. Overhead a hunting chicken hawk was marked against a sky the color of burnished silver plate. The town, a heated amber-colored mass, attracted him. He flew toward it. The white horse went on, chewing slowly. Abe found the county car hot to the touch, got in and drove off.

The few minutes alone with Fran that morning had again given focus to his purpose. (That's my big problem during this trial—keeping at least one toe dragging in reality. Mostly I just drift over the surface of the earth, and I feel it isn't real or happening to me. Then I think of the bad dreams, and in contrast the courtroom is there again and solid. The murders were real, the defendants are real. John Higgins is real. For all these, everything has shape, form, color. There are records, briefs, mountains of legal papers, courts, lawyers; fourteen—carrying two spares— real-live jury members. This heat is real and I am a human being whose sweat glands are active, whose tired mind is trying to think logically, and for just a moment, the one split second, when the *me,* the thing, the entity that is *I,* ticks, I know then I'm real my-self.)

Abe pulled up at the county building at twenty minutes to ten. He felt tired after his visit to Nash. The day promised to be as hot as yesterday. In the lobby Chief Smith appeared to be waiting for Abe, a long, thin bundle wrapped in brown paper under his arm.

"I called your home but you had already left, Mr. Pedlock."

"I went to talk to Thomas Nash. That affair with John Higgins went on a long time. He was bothering Mrs. Nash as late as eight months ago, if Thomas Nash isn't lying. What have you got there?"

"Let's go up to your office," said the big man, hitching the bundle tighter under his arm.

Mary Durant, in cool white silk, was sitting under a fan reading *The Hawleytown Home News.* Behind her the mottled calf binding of the volumes of *Corpus Juris*—lawyers' reports, an-notated—made a warm background. She looked up as the two men came in and said to Abe, "Mr. Hightower wants to see you before trial time."

Chief Smith said, "Maybe we better go see him with this right away." He patted the paper-wrapped object. "It's important."

Abe nodded at Mary. "Our witnesses been checked in for the morning?"

Mary nodded and folded the newspaper. "Tod is herding them into the bullpen. And I've inserted cards in the sections of Pepper and Lewis' *Digest of Laws* you want to cite."

Abe felt his scalp twitch and the skin on his neck grow flushed as he looked down at Mary and caught her scent. He remembered his total recall, last night in bed, of the dreadful Washington trip.

"Go ahead, Chief Smith," Abe said. "I'll be right in." Alone with Mary, Abe looked closer at her and said, "John Higgins' name has entered the case."

She looked up thin-lipped, showing her teeth in one corner of her mouth. "*That* bastard."

"Mary, it's going to be a hell of a hot day in court and the witnesses may throw me. So I'm not going to lead into this easy. When we two went down to Washington on that Lauder theater estate matter, you and John Higgins had just broken it up between you. That's why you tried the sleeping pills."

"You going to call me as a witness?"

Her overly sensual body almost made him gag.

"Now, look, Mary. Don't get huffy. You know damn well I'm not calling you. But I've got a problem. Did John Higgins ever impress you as the kind of lug who would kill a woman if she gave him the gate for somebody else?"

Mary's eyes had widened into a cat-canary expression. She seemed to struggle for breath and said as if enjoying the idea, "You think he never forgave George Rodman for cutting him out with the fair Helen?"

"I don't know. I have no prima-facie evidence. But it looks as if he was still trying to get her back. And Helen Nash wasn't having him." Abe leaned across the table. "Mary, we're friends. Real friends—no legal phraseology—you know that. Have you been seeing John Higgins again within the last year or so?"

Mary began to laugh—a little too high in key, too prolonged. "I see. I may not be all I ought to be. But I've got pride. When I've been kicked out on my pratt I don't go crawling back scratching at the door. And so you can nol-pros the idea."

The call box lisped on her desk. She pressed a lever, and Miss Munday's phone voice sounded. "Tell Mr. Pedlock Mr. Hightower is waiting for him."

Abe said into the intercom, "Coming, Munday." To Mary he added, "Maybe I've been trying the wrong case in court. Maybe I better go back to law school and get that job waiting on tables again."

Mary didn't anwer. She was staring at her pale nail polish.

Ed Hightower, in his office, was smoking the same corncob pipe, and Chief Smith was rolling a handmade cigarette with skill. On the roll-top desk the paper bundle had been opened; a rusting Winchester rifle lay there, its stock broken, the trigger guard crushed. Abe whistled. Chief Smith smiled. "Grappled it up near Barraclough Inlet."

Ed Hightower said, "It looks like the one you've been looking for."

"Find a shotgun too?"

"No shotgun. Just this. About six miles downstream from the duck blinds. Just luck."

Abe looked down at the rusting rifle barrel. "Can you get bore views and barrel photos to compare markings with those on the slugs we found at the scene of the crime?"

Chief Smith licked a cigarette paper with a thin edge of wet tongue and finished smoothing his handmade smoke into shape. It hung from his lower lip, the paper end twisted shut. "Already have made all comparison photos and tests for rifling scars on barrel and slugs." He lighted his cigarette slowly, savoring his moment, and looked up through the moving smoke. "First tests match. This rifle fired the murder slugs. On enlargements I'm getting made for rechecks, with larger prints, it will show up easy. You can show the jury real big charts."

"When can I have the big prints?"

"After the noon break today. Jacob Yuron's photo gallery is blowing them up real big."

Ed Hightower frowned. "We don't know who owns this Winchester, Abe. We haven't proved it belongs to Mikel Hawley. If it doesn't—*falsus in uno, falsus in omnibus.*"

Abe translated, "False in one, false in all. My case is wrecked."

Chief Smith said cheerfully, "I've been questioning Pete Maxon, Mikel Hawley's gunsmith. He hasn't recognized it yet. He will."

Abe said sternly, "You lay a finger in coercion on him, Chief Smith, and we're really in trouble."

"What makes you think I'd ever roust a respectable witness?"

Ed pointed with his pipe stem at the chief of detectives. "Don't quibble. We know your St. Louis record. Have you been through Maxon's files?"

"Yes. They mean nothing. The rifle's serial numbers, all identifying marks, have been filed off. I'm X-raying the filed sections.

Sometimes a shadow serial number remains in the steel from pressure of the dies. Mind if I get going on it? I'll have it in court this afternoon."

Ed Hightower shook his head, and the big man went off with the package under his arm. He looked down at the lawn, where the morning crew from the jail was watering the flower beds.

"Abe," he said, not turning around, "are good and bad more than mere subjective likes and dislikes? Are there objective ethical values? Reason, I've learned as D.A., will never conquer blind impulses. I gathered from Chief Smith you've dug up enough now to bring John Higgins' name into the case."

"At least we know why Big Ed wanted to have lunch with me. It wasn't the Hawleys' social position he was worried over. It was his son John, who was almost murdered once, or at least close to aggravated assault and battery."

"Don't jump at conclusions that easy, Abe. If that gun turns out to be owned by Mikel Hawley you've won your case. It's the *coup de grâce*."

"And suppose it belongs to John Higgins?"

Ed Hightower turned and stared down at his desk. "Justice Holmes said, 'Half of the law is always a lunatic, maybe the better half.' Where is John Higgins?"

"Chief Smith hasn't found him yet. We're not making the hunt official. I'm going ahead with the trial as I first planned it. And I intend to put Maman Celie on the stand tomorrow near the end of the state's case as my key witness. If only that damn jury were a little smarter."

"Abe, no stupid jury is as stupid as the lawyer who picked it."

"Chief, I deserved that answer. I have to get to court now. I'm going to read Mrs. Nash's love letters. What did George Rodman have to inspire that kind of writing?"

Ed pushed his hands into his pockets and sank his head down between his shoulders. "George Rodman. Have you noticed, Abe, what a nebulous figure he is? Everybody else is real and twice life size in the case. But Rodman has escaped us so far. He's an enigma. What motivated him beyond the old Adam—what was he really like, preaching God on Sunday and fornicating three times a week on damp ground after choir practice? Did he beg God for mercy on his miserable soul, did he pray to be made free from lust? Did he feel that human tragedy of temperament and desire leading the spirit by the nose? As I grow old, only motives interest me, not verdicts."

"I'll see you at the noon break, Chief."

"Make George Rodman real to that jury, Abe. If you don't, it isn't going to seem to them that you're talking of a real person. You ever meet him?"

Abe turned at the door. "Twice. Once at a charity affair. And once he gave me a lift in a rainstorm. Helen Nash was with him. I formed no impressions that I could build up in court as to the real man."

"George Rodman, I feel, may have been one of those people of sensitiveness and sensibility who, for survival, grew a super-ficially tough skin against the blows and the agonies of human life." Ed Hightower brought a fifth of bourbon out of his desk. "He had been taught that what he was engaged in was mortal sin and evil, but the scenes that tie us to reality are stronger than social morals. The burned child dreads the fire, the burned toast does not. Was George Rodman child or toast?"

Abe shook the doorknob. "I wish I had your time, Chief, to be-come a philosopher."

"You're not in gear for it; you're still too young, hopeful and free of the grape." The D.A. looked at the bottle and pulled the cork. " 'Ripeness is all.' That's a quote, son."

CHAPTER XIII

MR. TINDELL REGRETS

THE COURTHOUSE BELL began to ring the hour. Abe looked up at the back wall. The sign still read: THIS CLOCK OPERATES ON EASTERN DAYLIGHT SAVING TIME. It was ten-seven on the big court clock.

Judge Wilmont Riggs's right cheek was so swollen he looked like an angry squirrel. The cheek had a red tinge, and the judge sat sideways on the bench, head down. Abe turned and held up a bundle of letters Rod Miller had handed him. "I would like to enter these as an exhibit for the state and read them to the court."

"What are they?"

"They are the twenty-nine letters found scattered over the bodies and the scene of the crime. They have been identified as being in the handwriting of the murdered woman and are addressed to 'Dear George' and are signed 'Helen.' "

The judge said to the defense table, "Any objection to the letters being read?"

Roger Tindell rose, his hands grasping the lapels of his tobacco-brown jacket. "May it please Your Honor, we are aware of the contents of these letters. They are intimate love letters, and while I respect the legal skill of Mr. Pedlock, I doubt if he is actor enough—a good actor, that is—to read such personal emotional things properly, without the courtroom's bursting into ribald laughter."

Judge Riggs scowled and winced in pain. "One giggle and I'll clear the courtroom."

Abe said, "I'm willing to let any Theater Guild graduate at the defense table read these letters in my place." He saw Sarah

Rodman make her thin lips firmer and Mikel Hawley continue working a bit of paper he was folding in his big hands. Batty Billie seemed most at ease, resting, arms folded, a big breakfast inside, most likely, and feeling at one with his personal, simple version of the universe. His big, gray unblinking eyes stared, expressionless, at Abe.

Tindell waved off the offer Abe had made. "No, you read them, Counselor, in your melodious basso, if you insist on reading them."

"Four of these letters are directly involved with the evidence presented so far in this case, and—"

Devil Cavanagh rose in lazy slowness and said through his morning toothpick, "Not four. You read them *all*, Mister Pedlock. Your Honor, we object to hearing any material out of context. We want the entire group of letters read—in order of dating."

Judge Riggs, looking in pain, said to Abe, "You may proceed."

"I shall read the entire twenty-nine letters. Some are rather long."

"Go ahead, go ahead, get on with it," said Judge Riggs.

"There are no dates, no addresses. The order I read them in is my own, and the jury and defense may question my arranging of the letters. But there is no way of knowing their true order. However, I begin with a short note which seems to come early in the friendship of Helen Nash and George Rodman."

Tindell, fingering his Delta Sigma Rho key—from the renowned college debating fraternity—asked, "How do you know, Mr. Pedlock?"

"Elementary, Doctor Watson. It begins 'Dear Reverend Rodman.' All the other letters begin 'Dear George.'" Abe held up the letter to the light from the tall windows that made the pale brown ink on the tan-tinted paper stand out.

DEAR REVEREND RODMAN:

It was kind of you to bring me home all the way, and to lend me the volume of poems. I have never read Mr. John Donne, and I do not make much sense out of them.

*But I wonder that he being a minister should have writ-
ten about a flea on his girl and calling her his New-
foundland. Our talks are inspirational. I am no longer
desperate or feel I am the only sinner and beyond hope
of redeeming. You are like a breath of fresh air in my
life—which is, I know, isn't it, a commonplace way of
saying it? I must not take up your limited time so much
or so often. I am sleeping nights for the first time in
weeks. And I have written down the text from the
Bible: Thou shalt not follow a multitude to do evil. It
is a great comfort.*

Yours truly,
HELEN NASH

Abe without comment began the second letter.

DEAR GEORGE:

*No no no I cannot rest and cannot just exist without
writing you this hurried letter as to the way I feel. We
are at the fishing bay in a small, dirty cottage with two
other couples. Tom is fishing all the time, and everyone drinks too much. "I am two fooles, I know. For loving, and saying so." Oh, darling, how far this is from
everything we have said and have felt for each other.
Don't be angry that I write like this. I want to scream
out at Tom and beat together the heads of people fishing here, and kick out all the beer bottles. But I practice
control control control. I sit in the sand and read and
keep on my big sun hat because you said you like the
pale color of my skin and I feel like when you read the
Song of Songs that new way and everything seems perfectly clear as to what it is really about. Only honesty
between two people matters if, as you said, they don't
hurt anyone. And we're not hurting anyone, are we,
darling? No. No, of course not. I had a terrible afternoon this Monday with J. I didn't yell, but he came
into the house suddenly, slapped me and said dreadful
words, many of which I didn't understand. But I was*

firm—I only cried when he hurt me, and J. went away making remarks I'm not going to think of or repeat. You will be careful, my dear, if you run into him. He has a mean temper and when angry sometimes doesn't know what he's doing. I can't tell even you certain things between us, the crazy way he acted, the physical cruelty, but—I see Tom is coming up from the boat landing. Till we meet next time . . .

> *Love,*
> YOUR HELEN

Judge Riggs asked, "This person called 'J' in the letter. Have you identified him?"

"It's a problem, Your Honor." Abe didn't look at the defense table. (Have they found John Higgins out? Will they call him as a witness?)

Roger Tindell stood up. "Will the court tell Mr. Pedlock that the judge's question was not answered."

Abe smiled. "No identification to the satisfaction of my office has been made. May I go on reading?"

"Go on," said Judge Riggs, making a note on his pad.

The next six letters contained little but affection expressed almost breathlessly, and lists of books read, moods of unrest and of happiness. A letter written on yellow copy paper contained more:

DEAR GEORGE:

I am sure you didn't want to go to Boston and leave me, and that my letters help a little, but I keep thinking, He's in Boston, he's in his hotel room, he's making a speech at that stuffy dinner. I keep saying, My darling is walking across a street, he's not watching the traffic, and, oh, I feel if I try to keep in contact through our minds, through all the miles, all the cables between us, I will make you careful, and you will think of me, of us.

A woman fainted with a moan in the courtroom, and the bailiff and a clerk carried her out.

*It was wrong of you to talk to S. about me, even if you
didn't tell her who I was. Wrong to think that we can
ever be forgiven. Now when I stand and sing in the
choir and look into* her *pew I shall feel her eyes boring
at me, and I shall be sick to shaking because I feel that
she may guess it was me you were telling her about as
your true love. Women, dear George, know these things
—no, I didn't read it any place—because they are not as
honest and true as men when it comes to the emotions.
You're so right in saying the highest emotions come
from the lowest feelings sometimes. We women will
fight with anything at hand to keep what we have, and
maybe it's nature, maybe it's our greedy selves, but no
man understands what we can do and will do if we have
to. Sometimes I feel I'm offering my life to you in my
two cupped hands, and you can't pick it up.*

*Often I see no solution for us, not anything but to go
ahead as we have gone. Telling S. you were in love with
someone else, even if you didn't tell her who, may ruin
us somehow. I feel it. I don't care for myself alone.
There is only Tom, who needs my care and who is good
to me and I owe him some Christian duty. Beyond that,
I'm nobody, I'm nothing. You, you have position, you
have your fine work. I didn't believe in God till I met
you. I felt that anyone who permitted all those horrible
diseases, and the crippling of little children, dreadful
wars, the murder of millions and millions of people in
such horrible ways, that was no God I could believe in.
It was all—I once thought—an accident some place,
had no purpose and made no sense. And then you explained to me the meaning of faith, blind faith and the
goodness in the mercy of what you preached. Even for-
giveness and redemption. You made it real with all of
yourself when you made me real. Made me feel not
ashamed to live as myself, to enjoy, but also to sense
I am nothing and I am everything. I wish I could write
better, could say things with bigger words. There is*

dammed up in me such surging things I can't ever ex-
press, so much I can't say because the tools of saying
things are missing to make them mean things that can't
be expressed by me in ordinary ways. Oh, George, I
am rambling, thinking back, and you ask me to avoid
both. The weekend we spent in that cabin when I
went to see "my aunt," and we . . . .
. . . . *You see, darling,*
I am now able to write it all down and feel no shame.

Love,
HELEN

Abe had read the entire letter, including the last few frank
lines that made his face brick red.

Judge Riggs banged down his gavel once and asked Snooky
Durant, "Are there any minors in the courtroom, clerk?"

"No, Your Honor. Today—advised by Mr. Pedlock—we
screened out everybody under twenty-one."

Judge Riggs tenderly touched his jaw line. "I'll have no snick-
ering in this tribunal of law. Our English language is the result
of a lot of filling and backing, a great deal of trial and error.
Some of the words that have been read here today were once in
common usage and are part of our great literary heritage held
back for those times when the overused, overprinted language of
today fails to express fully what we want to say. So let no court
habitué think he is here for a thrill."

The judge rubbed his jaw, as if musing on his reading; then
came back to the case with a thump of his gavel head.

"It must be remembered that these private letters were between two people involved in an emotional complication and
not meant to be read like this in a court of law. Mr. Pedlock, I
must agree with Mr. Tindell that you are without romantic acting talent—this being in no way a criticism of your legal efforts.
You read them clearly, and that is all this court requires."

Abe smiled. "I am aware the stage suffered no loss in me. May
I go on?"

Judge Riggs nodded. Abe read letter after letter, short notes
and long. One he read more slowly than the rest.

DEAR GEORGE:

When I think we shall soon be gone away from this town, it's like fighting my way out of a dark, burning dream—you know, when you keep waking in another dream and that one also doesn't end in anything real in bed but another dream. Like those little Chinese boxes you bought me that fit inside each other and you wonder how can they go on. Sometimes I live a dozen dreams before I'm awake and hear the clock tick-tock on the night table, and in the next room Tom snoring, and then I get up and go downstairs and make coffee and write a short note to you. It's one of those times now. I want to say yes, we'll go away together—it's real. The first morning bus has just gone by. Soon, George, no one will know who we are and we'll be only the two alone—alone.

Love,
HELEN

Abe looked up. "I have one more and I am finished. Only four of these letters are vital to the state's case and show they were leaving and—"

Tindell's voice broke in. "Will the letter-reading continue, and will the reader not instruct the jury as to how to interpret the letters?"

"Mr. Pedlock, go on, finish reading, save your comments."

Abe lifted the last sheet to the light.

DARLING:

I have the feeling everything is wrong somehow, I feel haunted and spied on, and the weather even is against us. I have seen S. three times now this week. You tell me she is violent, shouting, threatening. You admit she is capable of violence, her brothers of bodily harm. It's dreadful, that last clawing talk you had with her. Wherever I turn I expect to see her watching me in that way, like a cold crystal dish. Perhaps I'm going crazy or maybe she is watching me because she knows

everything now and will still act. Oh, lover, come to me
tonight. Just for an hour at the old club off the road.
You know, where we first loved. Please . . .

HELEN

Abe handed the letters to Rod to have them entered as exhibits for the state and then turned slowly to the jury. He could
hardly speak. "I leave it to you to think over these letters. I am
very touched by them. It is a woman in agony. They show a fore-
boding of danger, an awareness of some coming disaster. I think,
whatever you may think of the moral issues, they speak for a
Mrs. Nash who was in many ways a sensitive woman, who was
able with her limited command of language to express a very
great and painful emotional experience. I do not say that sin
loses part of its evil by losing its grossness, but I do want you to
feel that the murder of these two was a cold-blooded plan, and
that four of the letters show that the defendants were involved
and aware of what was being planned by the two murdered people who never escaped in time."

Tindell was on his feet shouting, "Cheap soap-opera tactics!"

The next hour passed in admitting and denying, in rereading
and protesting. But when it was over and Judge Riggs had called
for lunch, Abe felt he had made it clear to the jury that Mrs.
Sarah Rodman had not been passive or merely hurt by the revealing of her husband's love affair. That she had reacted—and
violently. He was holding Eddie Desmond in reserve.

Rod Miller patted Abe's back. "Those letters did us a lot of
good."

Abe turned to Mary. "I want Eddie Desmond served with a
paper to appear as a witness. Maybe tomorrow. He witnessed one
of these violent scenes between Mr. and Mrs. Rodman."

Mary was fanning herself with a thin brief. Her blouse was
sticking to her damply. "I cried when you read those letters."

Rod said, "Some people, it really sets them rocking."

Abe turned away. The letters had touched him in a way that
his reading of them had not shown. (Damn this business of me
being so legal and hard. I tore Helen Nash apart and exposed her
body and parts like a butcher's sides of meat and skin and nerve

ends and organs. I took something beautiful, powerful and full of the highest agony of human love and I spread it thin—like butter—on the faces of everybody in the courtroom. She must have been a very wonderful woman.) Abe walked over to his office to change his shirt.

He called the county jail. Chief Smith said he had the witnesses ready. Abe stripped off his shirt and stood damply under the whirling fan. His neck rash was worse. Next year they must vote that bond issue for an air-conditioning system. He took three vitamin tablets and a drink of ice water. There was a tap on the frosted glass of his office door. Abe said, "Come in."

Roger Tindell walked in. "Smells like a bear cave in here, Abe."

Abe began to button his second shirt of the day. "How the hell do you manage to look so cool all the time, Roger?"

Tindell sat down, pulling up his trouser legs to show the white clocks on his thin blue silk socks. "Low blood pressure, I guess. Also I wasn't reading love letters in open court. Beautiful things, words. And to think she lived in this town and we didn't know her."

Abe began to smooth out the fresh shirt. "I can see her, clearly, even understand her. But George Rodman, he's still too damn fuzzy. Outside of court, he real to you?"

"I knew him very well, as a member of his church—but that isn't the man Helen Nash wrote to."

Tindell crossed his legs and took out an alligator cigarette case and then changed his mind. Abe pushed the shirttails into his pants. (Roger is bothered about something. For an Ivy League stuffed shirt he's not a bad guy. Tedium and melancholia are his buddies, I'd guess. And an austere pride in being a Tindell.)

"Abe, I'm here to kind of soften a blow. It could have come to you cold and official. But I told the board of directors at the country club I wanted to explain it to you. You're well liked. You're a white Jew and we know it."

Abe sat down and looked up, unaware his mouth was open. "I've been blackballed?" (Poor Fran, all those new tennis clothes and the cool evenings she planned on the club terrace, some little dinners in the trophy room and the big dance at Thanksgiving seated at Judge Riggs's table with the two other white Jews, Keith Rifkin (modern homes) and Monroe Greene (married a Delaware corporation). And New Year's Eve, all the best people blowing red horns under silly paper hats knowing there wasn't a better country club or better party in the country. All gone now. Oh, Fran, it will break your heart.)

Tindell leaned forward and took Abe's arm. "I'm damn sorry and that's why I'm here. I've always respected you, the way you stood up against the party machine on the crooked paving contract, and the way you kept town girls' names out of the news when the abortion ring scandal was broken up."

"I was only doing my duty, Roger."

"I want you to know I regret very much your not coming into the club."

"I suppose the quota is two white Jews to a club. I'm not a very good one. But you can't resign from a race like from a club. Let's forget it, Roger."

"It was something else. Not the racial bit at all. It wasn't. Don't think it was in this case. It's a feeling among the club members I know. You had a job to do and you're doing it. I said so to the board—that you're not going out of your way to smear the Hawleys. Or any of the old families of town. But you know some people's prejudices harden with their arteries."

"What's the sense in talking, Roger? I'm not joining the country club, and the worst of that for us isn't much. Just my wife will have to continue playing at the public courts and we'll entertain at the Walker House. You think there's a chance of a good fall thunderstorm?"

"Abe, once this trial is over I'll bring your name up again. Present you myself to the membership committee. The board may feel then—will feel, I'm sure—you showed taste and discretion in doing your job."

Abe looked at his watch. "We better grab a sandwich. Roger, thanks for telling me, yourself. I'm not going to put on an act that it didn't hurt. It does, like a kick in the groin. But it's worse for Fran. And we'll survive." (Sure we will. Only it isn't going to be easy to live at home till Fran's rage simmers down against the town and club. And I don't blame her for wanting the club. But society is based on a pecking order, and unless you're biting high on the perch you don't get anywhere. But I have a chance to be moved up to a high pecking perch. I can see what Roger is skillfully driving at in his best John O'Hara, Princeton-hero manner. I can almost see the sensory motor arcs in his brain spark when he says I'd be welcome up there where they worship the Golden Golf Club if I'd show taste and discretion. That just means *don't* put your eyewitness on the stand. Honor and integrity are just words; the most popular ideas are only fallacies unless lived out. I should be tempted, should struggle to resist, but somehow it's just my lousy duty the way I learned it, and that's all. A failing in me not to be praised as to how honest I am; it must show my lack of spirit in refusing a fine bribe. Well, no one any longer plucks out the eye that offends; we just wear a fashionable black patch for a while. Full integrity, I now see, is never a fully realized ideal; a battered conscience is the best I have.)

Abe put his jacket over his arm, already feeling his shirt begin to dampen on his back. "Buy you a lunch, Roger?"

"Be glad to accept, Counselor, only the reporters would make a fancy headline out of it. Let's make it a big dinner at Chichester House, wives and all, the day the verdict is in. Winner to pay, including a good vintage champagne."

Abe put his arm on Roger Tindell's shoulder. "Including a real fancy vintage champagne, whose ordering, however, I will leave to you."

Roger nodded, smiled, crinkling and closing his eyelids.

Judge Riggs looked in great pain in the afternoon. Mary Durant slipped up to Abe's side as the first witness was being sworn in. "Judge made an appointment for four o'clock with Doc Zimmerman to have a wisdom tooth extracted. If it's really impacted and if the surgery gets real bloody, he may be hospitalized tomorrow."

Abe nodded and walked toward the witness stand feeling warm

and tired. A tall, Teutonic-featured man with a wild blond mustache and close-cropped hair sat there with his arms folded like a military-school cadet. The thick lenses that covered his washed-out gray eyes blinked in the afternoon sun. The jury continued fanning itself.

CHAPTER XIV

THE DEFENSE OBJECTS

THIS CLOCK OPERATES ON EASTERN DAYLIGHT SAVING TIME, Abe read for the thousandth time and turned to face the witness.

"You do business in Hawleytown as the Maxon Gun Repair Service?"

"I do."

"How many gun-repair services are there in King County?"

"The plain fact is I am the only full-time factory-trained gun-repair man in the county. Some jewelers and a blacksmith at Connors Corner tinker around, try to repair guns and rifles, but I usually have to do their botched work over."

Rod Miller handed Abe the Winchester that had been grappled up from the river bottom. "I hand you a Winchester repeater rifle. Can you tell me anything about it?"

The witness took the rifle, turned it over and over, peered at its trigger and stock through his heavy lenses, fingering the bolt. "It's a sport model Winchester of their Series Four A, firing a thirty-two-caliber long cartridge. It's an automatic ejecting rifle with a screw sight and a curled walnut stock. Shoots up to three hundred yards accurately when in good working order. Somebody has smashed the bolt and firing action and the stock."

"So we are aware," said Abe. He looked at Tindell and Devil

Cavanagh. (I need their unwilling help in what I'm planning; so far they are sitting back in their chairs digesting their lunches, not interested in or objecting to my questions. Sarah Rodman is staring at the wall over the judge's head, a stare that she has changed little so far during the trial.) Mikel Hawley moved, as uncomfortable as usual at being indoors, in tight tailoring, a heat rash most likely between his heavy legs and most certainly on his large neck. Batty Billie played with a bit of glossy silver candy paper and seemed unaware of what was going on.

Abe turned back to the witness. "Could this gun, Mister Maxon, kill a human being if it were in firing condition?"

"If you aim at him and hit him. Or her."

"Objection, Your Honor," Tindell said. "We have no proof this rifle killed anyone, so the witness may be testifying as to what he doesn't know."

Judge Riggs said, "The witness will confine himself to being a gun witness. Strike the answer."

The witness said, "It's not a gun, Your Honor, it's a rifle."

Judge Riggs, dead-pan, said, "The court stands corrected."

Abe leaned toward the witness. "Mr. Maxon, how deadly is this type of rifle?"

"It can hit with a killing capacity anything, on a windless day, in good light, up to three hundred yards."

"And how close can you come to, let us say, living game?"

"Well, you can hold it against yourself and use it. There was the case of the banker at Turneyville who put the barrel in his mouth and with his big toe on the trigger, he blew off his—"

The judge was banging his handleless gavel. *Next* question, Mr. Pedlock. The witness will save his stories for his memoirs."

"Mr. Maxon, is this a common rifle? I mean, is it turned out in great numbers and can anyone buy it?"

"If they have the cash. It's a good rifle, easy to keep in order and, yes, I'd say fairly common. It's a standard model that doesn't change much from year to year."

"One rifle of this series is much like another, isn't it? Difficult to separate?"

The witness shook his head. "No, I wouldn't go that far. I

find every rifle has its own marks, scratches, sometimes even different screws and method of assembling. You know, those testing filings and adjustments made at the factory."

"No, I didn't know." Abe saw the defense sitting forward paying attention now. "Have you ever repaired this rifle?"

The witness kept turning the weapon in his hands and shook his head. "Serial numbers have been filed off. I couldn't swear I haven't handled it before. And of course I sell rifles. But I know I haven't repaired it. You see, I always scratch the letters P. M.—that's for me, Peter Maxon—on the trigger guard—here —very small when I repair a rifle."

Abe said very slowly, "You know who in King County own rifles of this model?"

That stirred the defense table; their chair joints creaked behind him. Abe waited for the witness to speak. "I handle, like I said, rifles of this model. But I wouldn't know if I sold this one to anybody in the county because of the serial numbers being gone."

"You have a record of rifles of this model you have sold, or repaired, for people living in King County?"

Devil Cavanagh was on his well-shod feet. Abe grew tense. (It's now they should put one foot in the trap. I want them to spring it on themselves.)

"Your Honor, we object to this line of questioning. Suddenly every man owning a rifle, and every woman too, of this make and model is now a suspect. And if he, or she, or it, or they should be in this court, and being tried on a mess of suggestion and innuendo, it still can't be made to appear as evidence."

Abe said, "It is a telling bit of evidence, I concur."

Judge Riggs said, "Mr. Cavanagh, you've made your speech. You want to object to the naming of the owners of a rifle of this model in this county?"

"Correct, Your Honor."

Judge Riggs turned to Abe. "Have you any reason to continue this line of questioning about an unidentified rifle that can have any bearing on the case being tried here?" (So the judge ha sprung the snare for me.)

Abe took the rifle, faced around toward the judge's stand. He felt like a ham actor padding a part. He could see Mary Durant at his table as she curled a corner of her mouth in wonder. "Your Honor, *this* is the murder weapon. And I enter it as an exhibit for the state."

The defense exploded. Objections flew. Several newspapermen went out to report to their wire services. Judge Riggs hammered on his desk. In the end, after the citing of many laws of evidence, he turned to Abe. "You have not presented any evidence that this is the murder weapon, Mr. Pedlock."

"I shall do so with my next witness, whom I will put on the stand if I can ask Mr. Maxon one more question."

"Only if it does not at this time relate to this being the murder weapon. And we will hold up accepting this as an exhibit for the state."

Abe turned back to his witness. "How many people can you name in King County who to your special knowledge owned, had, still own or have a rifle of this exact model of Winchester repeating rifle?"

The defense no longer was interested just in this part of the witness's testimony. Heads were together, discussing exactly what Abe's next witness might present.

Mr. Maxon took the rifle Abe handed back to him. "Well, I made a list this morning from my record books when I knew I was coming here to identify this type of model. The rifle came out in this redesigned model about eleven months ago." The witness took up a bit of blue paper stained with machine oil. "This model I've repaired, sold, or seen in the gun racks of these local sportsmen: let me see, yes, Doctor Wimber Brown, Mrs. Nellie Mae Boyd, Mr. Lawrence Lipton, Jimmie Welton has two of them—he takes deer parties out in season—Buddy Godoff, the Jilner brothers—all four have rifles of this model— Mr. Mikel Hawley, he bought one, Miss Murphy of Murphy Farms uses it on vixen that go after her chickens, Ken Tanney, Mr. Edward Higgins, Sutter Goodel, old Ram Potter, the game warden."

Abe turned briskly to the defense table. "Your witness."

Devil Cavanagh stood up and walked over to the witness and picked up the rifle from the witness's lap, hefted it, looked down the barrel, and made a comic Army drill gesture as he brought its stock to the floor.

Abe said, "We will let the defense borrow it after the trial for playing soldier."

"Mr. Maxon, your list makes no claim as to being complete as to all the people who own this model rifle in the county?"

"No, sir. Only those I know."

"There may be hundreds more of this model in the county?"

"Well, I wouldn't care to say how many more."

"You're an honest fellow and a skilled craftsman, Mr. Maxon. Tell me, is there any proof you know of that says this rifle was owned by anyone in King County?"

"I don't know of any proof."

"Are there any marks, or anything else, that identify it as being owned by any of the people you just named?"

"Objection," said Abe. "We haven't made such claims as yet."

Judge Riggs said, "Mr. Pedlock, you can't have your gun and fire it too. Answer Mr. Cavanagh's question, witness."

"No, sir. I can't identify this gun as belonging to anyone I named or know if it's owned by anyone in this county."

"You may stand down. Thank you."

Rod Miller called, "Miss Jane Keefe." A thin, large-boned girl in her late twenties took the stand. Suntan ran across a large Wellington nose. Her hair was crudely cut and badly combed, and her long fingers were stained with acids, nicotine, and ended in small square-cut fingernails.

"Miss Keefe, what are your duties with the county?" Abe asked her.

"I am in charge of the tests in the police laboratory and assist the medical examiner in his work."

"What schooling have you had?"

"I am a graduate of the University of California at Berkeley, where I majored in Criminal Medicine and Police Procedure."

Abe said, "The court is advised that such major courses are given there."

"I spent three years on the crime laboratory staff of the San Francisco Police. I did postgraduate work in medical evidence at Johns Hopkins. I was assistant to the city pathologist of New Orleans. I have been here in my present work two years."

"You have published some writing on scientific police work?"

"I have written sixteen articles on chemical and medical crime detection for the *National Police Monthly*. And a series of three on 'Microscopic Evidence in Criminal Procedure,' for the Protective League bulletins. I have had one book published, a year ago, *Unseen Witnesses,* a collection of case histories where laboratory processes solved the cases."

Devil Cavanagh drawled ironically, "Is the witness *also* a Phi Beta Kappa?"

Miss Keefe said without any change of expression on her face, "Yes, sir, I am."

Abe smiled and took some enlarged photographs from Mary Durant. "Will you identify these photographs, Miss Keefe, before we place them in evidence?"

"These two are cross-sections of the slugs that killed George Rodman and Helen Nash. Here are side views of the same slugs. All are greatly enlarged to show certain ridges and grooves, marked A, B, C, D, E, F, G, H. This is the true signature of the rifle barrel they were fired from. No other slugs fired from any other gun would have these groovings and markings."

"These photographs are unretouched?"

The witness frowned and plucked at loose skin on a yellow finger. "We never retouch a photograph without marking it as such. Now here are enlarged photographs taken with special lights of the test slugs we fired from the gun barrel. Here are again grooves marked A, B, C, D, E, F, G, H. They fit exactly grooves and marks lettered in the same manner in the slugs that were used in the two killings."

"Which proves, Miss Keefe?"

"Objection. This is mumbo-jumbo and—"

"Overruled."

"These, it proves, are the two slugs that killed George Rodman and Helen Nash, and they were fired with the rifle now in court."

Abe held the rifle shoulder-high with both hands. "This then must be the murder weapon?"

"Objection. There were also shotgun wounds that could have come from the fatal death weapon."

Abe said calmly, "Medical testimony has already been given that it is the medical examiner's expert findings that the rifle shots killed the deceased, and that the shotgun was fired later. However, I am willing to change my question. Miss Keefe, is this *one* of the murder weapons?"

"According to accurate, accepted, scientific police testing, it is."

Abe said, "I enter this rifle, the slugs and photographs as exhibits for the state."

"The clerk will accept them."

Abe nodded to the defense table. "Your witness."

Roger Tindell was whispering in Cavanagh's ear as if trying to restrain him from questioning the witness. Devil Cavanagh shook his head and stood up. "Miss Keefe, with all your very large education and training, have you found one shred of evidence that points to the actual owner of this rifle? Who is he? Can you tell us?

"We are trying through X rays to bring out the pressure ridges under the filed-off serial numbers. It may give us those numbers and could lead to an identification."

"Could, might, should, would—that isn't scientific talk. As of this moment there is no concrete evidence that identifies the owner of this rifle."

"Not yet, but—"

Judge Riggs banged. "Just say yes or no."

"No."

"Thank you, Miss Keefe. I meant no slander of the Phi Beta Kappa. That is all."

Abe wiped his face and neck and took the rifle. The heat was burning like acid in the late-afternoon dampness that made it the worst time of the day. He addressed the judge. "Your Honor, the state's next witness is not a friendly one. He is at present a citizen in residence at the county jail, no summer resort, on a game-law violation. I would like Your Honor to admonish the witness he *must* answer the questions put to him. And if he has any special knowledge not to withhold it."

The judge looked at the clock (half an hour till his dental appointment). "The witness will answer or be cited for contempt. And keep it short, Mr. Pedlock."

They had brought Vargis over from the jail and he now sat on the witness stand after taking the oath in a husky tobacco voice. His prison denims were washed and faded. His hair had been combed and he had shaved, pointing up the unhealthy skin of an outdoor man under lock and key.

"Mr. Vargis," began Abe, "I'm going to keep this short, as the judge asks, and to the point. You are caretaker of a cottage and private hunting acreage Mikel Hawley owns in the Inlet Marshes?"

"Yes."

"Speak up. You also take out hunting parties of Mr. Mikel Hawley's guests during the duck and deer season, take care of the food, camp gear and rifles and ammunition?"

"That's the job of a preserve caretaker and guide."

"You have handled, cleaned and put away the guns of Mikel Hawley at the preserve?"

"Some of them."

"Most of them?"

"Most of them."

"All of them?"

"Maybe."

Abe took up the damaged rifle. "Do you know this rifle? Take it, examine it. Good. You handle it like an expert, a man who loves guns."

The witness said, "Looks like any other Winchester thirty-two."

"This one ring any bell of memory; you recognize it?"

"They all—when standard models—look alike to me. Unless they have silver mountings or special sights, or letters cut and inlaid in the stock."

"Mr. Mikel Hawley's rifle have such extras?"

"Yes, they do."

"Mr. Vargis, I may be getting a little deaf. So speak very loudly. Do all Mr. Hawley's rifles have extra sights, silver mountings, letters cut into the stocks? Take your time answering. He must have a big collection, so think of *all* of them."

"Not all have the special fittings. Only the handmade special jobs."

Abe decided to ride with the witness on the next question. "You do not identify this rifle, then, as being from Mr. Mikel Hawley's collection?"

"No, I don't." The witness permitted himself a smile.

"But Mr. Mikel Hawley has a rifle of this make, this caliber, this model?"

The witness picked some lint off a pants leg and looked sourly around the courthouse focusing on no one. The armpits of his denim shirt began to stain with a darker blue. "Mr. Hawley had a Winchester of this model."

"*Had*—no longer has? Speak up. Tell us, has he or hasn't he?"

"Objection. The witness is being bullied."

The witness said, "He's not bullying me. I can take care of myself. There was such a model at the cottage."

"Where did you see it? What cottage?"

"In the game-preserve cottage."

"Your duties, you said, didn't you, included taking care of the rifles?"

"I didn't say; you said it. Yes, I oil and clean them. I don't do any repairs beyond putting a screw in tight."

Abe was pleased that the witness, in his cold rage, was answering properly.

"Two weeks after the murder of George Rodman and Helen Nash," Abe said, "Mikel Hawley gave a large party at the marsh cottage. There was a big crow shoot because the farmers' crops were being attacked by the birds."

"We do a lot of crow shooting. It's good gunning practice. I don't remember all the crow hunts."

"Let me refresh your memory. It was the day Mr. Mikel Hawley was awarded the silver cup by the Eastern Shore Game Preserve Society for getting a thousand marsh acres beyond Pierson Point made into a game-bird preserve. Remember that day now? You photographed very well with the party in the pages of *Town and Country* magazine."

"I remember it . . . now."

"What rifle was Mr. Mikel Hawley using that day?"

The witness grinned and answered quickly with relish. "He was using a Savage thirty-two and a Remington twenty-two. *Not* a Winchester at all."

"You're so eager as a good witness you've anticipated my next question, Mr. Vargis. He was *not* using a Winchester of this model I show you now. He owned such a gun, you said."

"Yes." The witness suddenly began to sweat in large drops. They ran down his face and dripped off the tip of his nose.

"Was the Winchester of this model that Mikel Hawley owned in one of his gun cases that day?"

The witness wiped his face with the back of both hands. He lowered his head. Abe turned to look at Mikel Hawley at the defense table. The big man seemed as chafed and bored as ever.

"Your Honor," said Abe, "will you instruct the witness he must answer, and answer faithful to his oath to tell the truth."

The witness lifted his head and bit off some words. "The Winchester was not in its case that day."

"Did you see it anyplace in the house?"

"No. I didn't see it no place."

Tindell rose, then shook his head and sat down.

Abe fired another question to the witness who sat facing him, contempt burning in him at what Abe had made him say. "Mr. Vargis, wasn't a silver-mounted shotgun also missing from its case and rack? And neither have been seen by you since in their usual place in the gun cases?"

"Yes."

Abe turned. "Thank you, Mr. Vargis. You've been a fine witness. I am finished with you."

Tindell rose and asked, "Mr. Vargis, continue to be a good

witness. Couldn't the rifle and the shotgun have been lent to someone? Borrowed, even stolen?"

"Mr. Hawley and me had the two sets of keys to the gun cases. He could have lent or given the guns away. As to robbery, we never saw any marks, and Mr. Hawley never reported anything stolen."

Tindell thanked the witness. Abe stepped forward. "Just a minute, Mr. Vargis. Did Mr. Hawley ever tell you the weapons were stolen or he had lent or given away either the missing Winchester or the missing silver-mounted shotgun?"

"No. He never mentioned either gun that day or since to me."

"You may stand down."

Judge Riggs wiped his face slowly and rose. "I have a medical appointment. The court will come together tomorrow at ten." The toothache raged red on the judge's cheek as he left the bench in a hurry.

Abe felt Rod's arm. "Not a bad day's work."

Rod Miller and Mary began to gather together the folders on the table. Abe sat panting and touching his heat rash.

"About time to call it a day. Rod, get that list of owners of this model rifle from Pete Maxon and check every one of them. Find out who no longer has their rifle, and if not where it went."

Rod nodded. "If they all have their rifles, it just makes it stronger that our exhibit is Mikel Hawley's rifle."

Mary Durant was at Abe's side, carrying several folders of material. "Going home early tonight?"

"I better. Fran may leave me if I don't."

"She's a good kid. Rotten about the country club."

"News travels fast during coffee breaks," said Abe, picking up his overstuffed briefcase.

The three of them walked back to the D.A.'s offices, refusing to talk to reporters who wanted more information on the rifle. Rod went off to get some papers. As Abe and Mary entered the hot offices, orchestrated by the flies buzzing in the heat of the window shades, Abe said to Mary, "What do you think of John Higgins and the case?"

Mary sat down, tired and crumpled, careless of how much leg

she exposed. Lighting a cigarette, she asked, "That why you had lunch yesterday with Big Ed?"

"He didn't say so, of course. See if the chief is in."

After working the intercom, Mary looked up. "Miss Munday says he left early. You going to put John Higgins on the stand?"

Abe ignored the question. "You ever go hunting with John?"

"No. We led, you might say, an indoor life. What if he or his father had a rifle like the one in court? Look, A.P., ever since that mad time in Washington, you and me, we've been pretty good friends. You've got a great case against the Hawleys. Stick to it. Don't take on the state political boss. John Higgins is a big, fancy-talking slob and skirt crazy, but he's too soft and spineless to kill any woman who gave him the brush."

"Would you have killed John if you had a chance, Mary, about the time you went off the deep end?"

"Sure. But I'm a mean bitch." She smiled, answered the ringing phone and looked up, poker-faced. "It's your wife. Wants to know if you're going home."

Fran sounded in a deep, spreading panic. "Oh, Abe, something has upset me so."

"Now don't give way to it. I'm going to be home by seven. I promise."

"Tom is dead. He's out on the porch all stiff and shaggy. He cried out just once, and then just sank down. It's dreadful. The children are crying."

"I'll have Miss Durant call the SPCA to have the cat picked up. Just put some newspaper over him till they get there. And don't let the kids touch him."

"I can't go near him. He was so unhappy these last few days. So lonely, so alone. No one at all cared for him. Poor little fellow."

Abe wiped his damp chin with the back of a hand and sighed. "I know, I know. I'm going to see Jacob Yuron, and be right home."

He hung up and said to Mary, "Call the SPCA. Our cat died. Have them pick it up right away in this weather. Fran is a little jumpy."

"Too bad. Were you fond of the cat?"

"No, that's the odd thing. None of us liked Tom. He was pretty snooty when we first got him. Cold and indifferent. When he got old and feeble he wanted us to comfort him, but it wasn't easy. Fran, I guess—well, she tried."

"Kids taking it hard?"

Abe decided to put his briefcase in the office safe. He left Mary calling the SPCA and went toward the office of Ed Hightower. Miss Munday nodded him in. Carl Vogelhofer, the other deputy district attorney, was asleep on the sofa, his mouth open, his shirt stained with sweat. The fan buzzing over his head seemed only to stir the warm air without changing it. Vogelhofer came awake as Abe walked in. Carl coughed himself upright and ran a gray handkerchief around his wet mouth. "Man, it's a killer. Papers say rain before morning. Ah, to love the earth and be wary of the earth."

"I don't think it will rain. No heat lightning. Where's the chief?"

"He phoned for you to wait for him. He sounded upset. How can he drink like a gentleman if you upset the applecarts?"

Abe sat down and let the fan breeze catch him in the back of the neck. "I refuse to ask what have I done now."

"Big Ed Higgins sent for the chief. You've been checking on all Winchester rifles in the county."

Abe looked up and grinned. The breeze felt good on his heat-rashed neck and his tired, warm blood felt full of soda-water bubbles. "Oh, so that's it. Well, all forces are calculable if we understand and don't fear them."

"What are you grinning about?"

Before Abe could frame an answer, Ed Hightower came in. His gray striped Palm Beach suit was crumpled. The yellowed straw hat on the back of his handsome head was about to slide off. He looked at Abe, grunted, went to his desk, got out the bottle of bourbon and poured himself three fingers into an old shot glass. He swallowed it quickly and recorked the bottle. "Too good for you younguns. Moonshine corn, and not a penny in tax paid. Well, Abe, your aggressive virility is certainly making my last days in office a busy time."

Abe leaned forward. "Chief, just tell me—Ed Higgins still have his Winchester rifle?"

"It was stolen out of his car at a hunt meeting in South Carolina. Canvas car top was cut, and rifles and cameras stolen."

"When?"

"About eighteen months ago."

"He show you the insurance report he filed on the theft?"

Ed Hightower sat down and put his feet on the desk. "Ed told me he didn't report it to the police or the insurance company. Said naturally he didn't want to embarrass his host, Senator Wendley, by suggesting the old family servants were thieves, if it was the servants."

Abe nodded. "No witnesses, of course? No reports anyplace?"

Ed picked up a corncob pipe, filled it and let Carl hold a match to it. When the pipe was smoking just right, he spit into the cuspidor and said in a tired old man's voice, "Abe, you've got to make up your mind. You accusing the Hawleys or John Higgins for these murders?"

Abe shrugged his shoulders. "I don't want to go into court tomorrow and ask for the death penalty for the three defendants unless I can eliminate John Higgins. And I must. I'm going to have Chief Smith bring him in for questioning."

Ed Hightower said, "Don't jump so fast."

Abe said softly, "I've got a hell of a problem of ethics, even forgetting the strictness of the law. I'm trying three people for murder, and I've got a lead that may point to another suspect altogether."

Ed said, "What do the law books say?"

"Do I stop the case? Ask for a mistrial? Or dismissal on lack of proper evidence?"

"It's your case, son."

"A hell of a lot of help you are. Carl?"

Carl rolled his eyes and pursed his lips. "Man, I'm just waiting to see how you get off this fly paper."

Abe scowled and rubbed his fist on his chin, enjoying the

rasping sound of his face stubble. In the heat his beard grew so fast he had to shave often twice a day. "*If* I ask for dismissal, I'll never be able to indict the Hawleys and Sarah again. If I ask for a recess, I have to give a good reason and Roger and Devil will smell something. I've got only one thing to do."

Ed nodded. "That's right."

"Walk the razor's edge, barefooted. Continue the trial and follow this lead on John Higgins. If it points to him, I'll ask Judge Riggs for a private hearing in his chambers and explain what's happened."

Carl said, "He'll eat your ass out for holding back that long."

Ed nodded. "And Roger and Devil will be in there, too, when you explain it."

Carl said, "It's smart to stop the trial now."

"I'm not smart," said Abe, head down looking at the soiled floor. "I'm just a work horse. I'm going to have John Higgins in for that questioning I talked about."

Carl looked at Ed Hightower as if they shared a small secret.

Ed sighed. "John Higgins left for Europe a week ago. Day before the trial opened. Big Ed told me this afternoon his boy is going to live in Rome; some Catholic business for the Knights of Columbus. Going to be gone a year or so. What are you going to do—extradite him? You know how the party depends on the Catholic big-city bosses and machines. And on the Irish-Italian national committee chairmen and big shots for support down here. We're in enough trouble in King County without dragging the Vatican into it."

Carl Vogelhofer reached for the bourbon bottle and poured two drinks into paper cups. He handed one to Abe. "Abe, you're most likely right the first time. Mrs. Rodman and her brothers committed the murders."

Ed smoked slowly and poured himself another glass of bourbon. "We haven't even proved that. Who's your first witness tomorrow, Abe?"

Carl looked over a sheet of reports. "We served Eddie Desmond this afternoon. He said he's going to deny anything Abe claims he told him last night. Said he was sick and had a shot in his buttocks from his doctor and his mind was wandering."

"He'll talk," Abe said. "His evidence will prove Sarah Rodman made one last effort to get George Rodman back, even permitting him to keep a mistress, and he turned her down cold. She threatened him. Then I'm putting Maman Celie on the stand as an eyewitness of the crime. And I'll get the crime lab to identify the serial numbers by X ray on the rifle and the state will rest its case." Abe stood up. "Any two out of three of my witnesses being effective is enough to get us a conviction."

Ed Hightower said, "The wisest man is he who devotes his life to one small subject—Indian arrowheads, butterflies or seducing servant girls."

CHAPTER XV

BEYOND A
REASONABLE DOUBT?

ABE CAME OUT OF THE COURTHOUSE. The bulky figure of the Reverend Winthrop Romar was coming toward him from the jail building. The man in shiny black waved to Abe; he was a man already aged and disintegrating.

"A very hot day, Mr. Pedlock." The voice was strained through some bronchial difficulty.

"Mrs. Rodman bearing up, I hope."

"Yes. She has her faith, and prayer. You, sir, don't believe in prayer, I suppose, like most of you modern people."

"Oh, no. I think it's a great help to lots of folks."

"But you see it, I'm led to believe, as symbols, objective correlations of promises no one can prove?"

Abe shook his head. "Don't pin me down, Reverend. I have no preconceived prejudices. Tell me, does Mrs. Rodman talk of the trial?"

"You shouldn't ask that. Not of me, sir."

"You're right, Reverend. I'm under a strain too. And I'm really pleased she gets comfort from her faith, and her prayers."

The old man's wide, wattled head nodded. "There is an inaudible invisible life all around us. Become aware of it."

"I agree with you, even if we don't perhaps mean the same thing. Good night, Reverend."

"Good evening, Mr. Pedlock."

The old man went away, walking slowly.

(I wonder, too, as he does, at the rich and silent qualities of the mystery of it all. But my mind doesn't run deeply that way. I better get on and get my visit over and go home to Fran. Fran prays sometimes, and the kids go to Sunday school and are taught, like that old man, to be kind and good. Yet the courts are always so damn busy with evil. The old man is a good old man, afflicted with a simple insight into everything but direct experience. And I better get a move on.)

Abe walked past the World War I memorial and as always thought of his father, who was only a brown fading snapshot of a scared boy in itchy khaki. Abe passed Mrs. Reid's genteel, neat rooming house. The jury were walking out to their dinner. Abe wondered if he had picked well and he wondered if these people were fitter than he was to arrive at a just and whole truth. He had not been impressed with the jury at first. When Judge Riggs had looked down at them, as their names were called, he had said, "Have any of you formed any impression or opinion as to the guilt or innocence of the accused? Answer simply yes or no, or raise your hands."

None had, and, raking the people from right to left with his eyes, the judge had gone on. "Now I ask if any of you know of any reason whatsoever why you could not enter upon trial of this case if you are chosen, with an open mind, bearing in mind that under the law the respondent is presumed to be innocent (Are

Sarah Rodman and her brothers innocent? Am I trying to forget John Higgins, the stolen rifle, the hiding out abroad under the strong protection of an alien church?) *until his or her guilt is established* (If only they find some serial numbers on that rifle with X rays) *beyond a reasonable doubt* (How can one ever be sure of any witness, any bit of evidence?). *And can each of you render a fair and impartial verdict* (Does the jury hate the rich or fawn on them? Do they dislike local society or envy it? Have they worked at the Hawley plants and been fired? Have they some-thing—a charity—to be grateful for, and so can repay some Hawley kindness with some help?) *based solely upon the law and the evidence given you here* (evidence of love letters, of gun experts, and of an old, old woman, half mad perhaps and crippled, who deals in magic) *in open court?"*

The double line of walking people passed Abe wtih nods and greetings, and one or two spoke some simple things about the weather. They went by on their way to the Walker House for thick, smoky pea soup, the county-paid-for steaks, the mugs of beer, the strong coffee and the apple pie.

A week and a few days ago they had been made jurors. Judge Riggs, his impacted wisdom tooth already aching, had said to Snooky Durant, "Swear in the jury." Snooky, always proud of his swearing, had cleared his throat and recited, "You do solemnly swear that you shall well and truly try and true deliver-ance make, between the people of this state and the prisoners at the bar (Sarah Rodman has been calm in the courtroom from the first. Mikel is always red of face and given to loud breathing, but he has calmed to an impassive mass of flesh and good tailoring. Batty Billie is just himself, a man who is not fully aware but doesn't mind being present) whom you shall have in charge, ac-cording to the evidence and the law of this state, so help you God."

"So help me God," the chorus had answered.

Judge Riggs had looked at Abe and then at the jury and said, "If any person, while you are out of this courtroom, attempts to talk to you, discuss this case with you, report it to me at once."

It had begun so well, Abe thought. He was so sure of his case, and now this damn John Higgins matter, and Eddie Desmond threatening to deny everything. How crisply, in legal jargon, Abe had handed up his first bit of evidence. "The People offer in evidence People's Exhibit One for identification as People's Exhibit One."

"It may be so received and marked," Judge Riggs had said, replying in style.

Abe stopped walking. What had been the state's Exhibit One? He had no idea. He could not think. Abe couldn't remember. The whole case had fled from him, and his mind was empty of it. Panic pushed against him and he looked around. He was standing in front of a vast pile of white brick, a building of fine colonial design. It was George Rodman's church. His name was no longer attached to the bronze marker reading, HAWLEYTOWN PROTESTANT EPISCOPAL CHURCH. As a boy Abe's entire high-school class had come here to the church to look at the famous hanging staircase and the sacred vessels presented to the church by Queen Anne before it had separated from the Mother Church of England. Mr. Booner had been the minister then, an old man with a red nose and very white hair, and he had said to the class through a small mouth, "Religion, children, is more than the history of church architecture."

Abe walked on, crossing curbs and moving along. Lee Street had once been the main street, but then Royale Street had been promoted by a real-estate group of Chichester Club members, and now most of the better shops and bigger stores were gone and only the flashier type of chain store and the usual long-established *Selling Out!* outfits were thick among the few die-hards who held out against a failing market on Lee Street. One was Jacob Yuron, who for fifty years had worked and lived in a small red brick building that carried a sheet-iron hanging sign in the shape of an old-fashioned box camera, on which were cut out the letters JACOB YURON'S PHOTO GALLERY.

Abe walked up to the simple low window of the shop and looked in at the usual parlor-sized photographic collection of football players in their high-school uniforms, fat, fertile Polish brides (aware as a queen bee of their reproductive value) and farm faces worn and tired, defenseless babies naked on a rug, serious and comic groups in reunion and at tables, visiting dignitaries opening a bridge or spading up a shovel of dirt, planting a splinter and stem of a tree. Time seemed airless and suspended, Abe decided, in these silver-nitrate images, as if something that should have passed quickly was stopped and could not start up again. An old-fashioned iron horse-weight held open the glass-paneled door to the shop. Abe walked into the smell of developing fluids, library paste, and the rattling old canvas wall pictures on which were painted castles and woods, landscapes and river scenes. They were no longer used much, but when Abe had been a boy he had enjoyed rolling them down and helping Jacob pose his customers stiffly in front of them.

"Hello. Who's there?" Jacob's voice, with its burry bite, came from the small yard behind the building. Abe walked out into the square of brown and orange earth. Jacob Yuron, old and rusty-looking, sat in a wire-repaired captain's chair salvaged from some bay barge, smoking a Dutch cigar. He was a huge man with big hands and large features rough cut as if unfinished. On the ground beside his chair stood a pitcher of wine and soda. Abe could hear the cracked ice moving in the pitcher.

From a ledge behind him the old man took down another big kitchen glass and poured Abe a drink of wine and soda. "Ah, you need this."

Abe sank down on a low bench and sipped the drink. It was tart and cold. "You always made good cool drinks, Jacob."

"You were a stinker as a boy. Always begging for ice or some hunting shoes that laced up the front or—remember?—a motor bike."

"Did I? Yes, I wanted a motor bike very much."

They sat in the warm twilight in the little square of unplanted earth fenced in by walls of raw weathered planks, the earth hammered hard except for where Jacob had a few rosebushes and two square feet of a heavy, old-fashioned lettuce that he liked to mix with vinegar, pepper and sliced cucumbers. Abe remembered the yard long ago, just as it was now. He an orphan, with poor relatives. A child born to a girl who claimed to be a soldier's widow but who had no wedding paper to prove it but did have poor relatives who worked the vegetable and seafood markets in the early-morning hours under gasoline flares. Abe had passed at last into the hands of the bachelor Jacob Yuron, who was not a relation, but who, over his gallery, had an extra room for a hungry and unwanted boy in shabby hand-me-down clothes. Jacob had dignified Abe's position by appointing him delivery boy, and later he had taught Abe to work the rack that dried the pinned-up negatives, and the polishing machine that put the high gloss on the prints made for *The Hawleytown Home News* society page.

The old man was a mystery to the town. His father, his grandfather, had run the Photo Gallery ever since the days of taking pictures on copper—with the daguerreotype process—the head of the sitter plastered white with flour and held in a rigid iron clamp. Jacob had gone off as a young man to Cuba, in the Spanish-American War, and there was gossip of a tragic love affair in New York City. On the death of his father Jacob had come back to Hawleytown and taken over the shop. A silent, solid man who kept no pets, lived alone over his shop, owned only two sets of books: Gibbon's *The Decline and Fall of the Roman Empire,* and Josephus' *Antiquities* and *Wars of the Jews.* He was a fine camp cook. Weekends Jacob fished in an old yawl he kept at Ike Barton's Wharf. He had, he claimed, no causes, no loves and no sadnesses.

Abe put down his glass on the packed ground. "Jacob, I've painted myself into a corner. Maybe I should have stayed with you and stuck to taking pictures of sassy wedding parties."

Jacob looked at his chemical-stained thumbs. "You're not trying this case scared, Abe—I can see that. The rest leave to the jury."

"I want more than that. And in trying for it I can do some people harm."

Jacob nodded and shook ash off his pale Deutsche Akademie cigar. "My grandfather, who started this business, tells a story of when he was riding in a coach to Washington from Baltimore, to take pictures of Lincoln's first State of the Union message. On a glass plate with the old box camera. It was raining and windy and they stopped at a crossroads to pick up some passengers who had to ride outside. My grandfather pitied them. Then, crossing Elhorn Creek, what happens? The coach turns over. My grandfather was a giant. You remember his picture that Matt Brady took? He came scrambling out of the mud and began to help rescue the outside passengers from the water. One little man he finds holding on to some reeds and he brings him ashore. To his horror my grandfather finds this man's head pushed down to one side, resting right on his shoulder. My grandfather—a powerful man—grabs the man's head in his two hands, hoping to pull it back to normal. He gives a yank. The man screams at him. 'Let me go! I was *born* this way!' "

Abe laughed and held out his glass, and Jacob poured him another wine and soda. The old man grinned. "Don't try to straighten justice's neck too much all at once. Just pull it out of the stream. That's enough, enough. How's Fran and the kids?"

"The heat isn't doing any of us much good."

"It's going to rain tomorrow. Cool off the town."

"What makes you so sure?"

"There used to be a play, on the Yiddish stage in New York, where the old *yenta,* the old hag, used to take her shoe off to let her toes feel for a storm. To tell it it isn't funny. I used to be a great theater-goer."

"What's happened to the Yiddish stage?"

"It's mostly all gone now, Abe. Second- and third-generation Jews can't speak or understand the *Mama Loschen,* the mother tongue, any more. But if you haven't seen Jacob Adler in *Der Yeshiva Bocher,* or the two wonderful Schildkrauts, father and son, in Schiller's *The Robbers,* you missed great theater. And clowns, how do they compare today to Mogilewsky as Kooneylemul; and women: Bertha Kalish or Mrs. K. Lipzin as beautiful immigrant girls. Anyway, I got bitten by the theater for a time. Now a little Gibbon is enough."

The yard was very still. The warm wind suddenly rattled a loose windowpane. Jacob Yuron took a sip of wine and soda.

"Abe, lots of things drive people crazy, or near it. I guess we'd be the same kind of folk even if we were selling dill pickles from a pushcart on Division Street."

"I intend to go ahead with this trial as I began it. You were in Cuba with old Hawley, took pictures at the hunting cottage for years."

The old man held up his hand, palm up. "I think I felt a rain-drop."

Abe shook his head, stared at the heated sky. "No, you imagined it."

"You want to ask me, Abe, could the Hawley boys really murder someone?"

"I was sure until the last two days. There is a slim chance, a very slim chance, there may be another suspect. Not connected with the Hawleys at all."

"To you, hunting is killing, the murder of little animals and big ones, too. But to the gentry, and I went out with them a lot at one time, for deer and mallard and teal, and the great Canadian goose, it's part of their education. I was the official photographer for them. Mostly they were satisfied to kill this small game. How many carry it over to their private lives? Well, you hear of accidents cleaning guns, or someone who didn't know it was loaded. We're all animals, Abe. We need outlets against the pressures on all sides. Some take it in women, some in drink, like our friends Doc Wymer or Ed Hightower. Some in power, like Big Ed Higgins. You take it out in an idea you're keeping the law. Other people write books, sail ships, hate their neighbors, give little kiddies candies in parks. I'm not sure I'm beyond the patness of conventional morality or orthodox religion. But man will never be domesticated, Abe. A fair brain case, a thinking, laughing and weeping creature. I try to avoid him as much as I can after business hours. He's dangerous. Any of us, all of us, are capable of murder. Any of us. Give us the right reflex to trigger some emotional charge of developing fluid in our glands and it's done. A mess on a floor—a body to hide."

"No, I can't believe it's that simple."

The old man looked again at his stained hands. "In Cuba I

killed several men. One with these bare hands. Ever hear a neck crack? For that I was decorated, twice. Then I killed a young woman—never mind the details—running a car off a bridge. I meant to die with her. That was my young romantic period." The large onyx-textured eyes of the old man looked directly at Abe. "So you *see?*"

The old man divided the rest of the pitcher between them.

"Mikel Hawley is like his father, and I knew them both well— photographed all their game heads, developed their hunting camp pictures. They never learned how to focus properly. Mikel, the heavy elder brother, always back from murdering lions and elephants and zebras in Africa. Mikel, tanned, prematurely gray, humorless. And those big blue veins—like a road map—in his nose. Bragging of hairy chest, brute force, male manners. We suspected there was something wrong in him—something he hid behind the false hairy gestures.

"Sidney Wymer thinks Mikel's a throwback to the fur thieves, slave-ship brokers, those that banged heads, cocked a snout at the watch, and fopped with the best in the old City of London. But in this modern world where there is no musketry—no king to brawl for—he has become a hunter. Mikel, as his hunting films show, has blown thousands of little birds apart, murdered hundreds of deer, hartebeests, elks, moose, springbok and big brown bears. He has massacred thousands of baldpate, gadwall, blue-winged teal, merganser and canvas-back duck. Sidney says he's killed baboons, cynocephalus, brighter than Mikel."

Abe nodded. "But that's only sport—not murder by our law."

"I know. I shoot game birds myself."

"Not as a life's work, Jacob."

"No, I like duck meat, a good section of venison. But Mikel, he kills not to eat, not for hunger—just to blast and tear, to shatter bone, to stand warm and dry in rubber and wool when a shoveler duck comes spinning down under his shotgun, broken and torn—and then to hold the still warm cadaver in his hands and feel the flesh die against his palm."

"Jacob, you're not addressing a jury."

"Mikel Hawley's purpose in life is to kill expensively from

Lake Tanganyika to Greenland. To thrill. Such a man should have gloried in the late war, but he spent a calm two years of inherited privileges with other rich men's sons in the Naval Patrol in Phelem Bay."

"It's not legal evidence he is a man killer."

"To kill at Ugyr with the three-thousand-gauge Smith Express, with the black beaters, think of the pleasure he got in the shattering damage of huge slugs, tearing backbones and kidneys apart in the primeval forests, salt licks, waterholes. He also enjoyed bullfights—if the tauromachia was good and deadly; he of course understood the need of the lousy moment of truth. Abe, don't brood if you have legal evidence that points at Mikel. You've at least got there a man who *could* murder and enjoy it. Shall I make some more wine and soda?"

"No. Fran is holding dinner."

Walking away from Jacob Yuron's shop, Abe wondered what Ed Hightower really felt about the trial. (I always had such a dislike of alcoholics before I got to know the chief well. Was my father a drunkard? There's no way of ever knowing now, I suppose. It depresses me to see good men drink too much and it makes such a bad mess of a human being. That first time Ed Hightower called me to his office. He had been drinking and the bottle of bourbon and some glasses were on his desk. Miss Munday was in the outer office playing the typewriter in ragtime, like a musical instrument. I didn't like this very handsome old man. I could believe he had been the most attractive-looking man ever to stand for the bar in the state. I think I showed my distate for him then, and the bottle of cheap corn whisky.)

Abe remembered in detail that first meeting with Ed Hightower, the first of many.

"You're the new deputy district attorney, Abe Pedlock? Well, I hope you work out. The party thinks you're all right."

"I've been in practice and I'm fairly well known."

Ed Hightower closed the bottle with a slap of the cork by the palm of his hand. "Drink the local bootleg product. For a lawyer it's the best. Doesn't give him expensive tastes."

"Yes, sir."

"Cheap tobacco, laughing, vulgar women, poor-boy pleasures like fishing, looking at a landscape. Inness, the master of the Hudson River school, painted some down here. Didn't know that, I bet. And do you think your job is romantic?"

"No. I come from the other side of the tracks."

"Lawyers from this side get phony too. Anybody can be a Hemingway hero. Unflinching stupidity, claret-colored blood, high-school French and smoking guts. Fancy-named liquor, involved and tricky sexual encounters in sleeping bags sold by Abercrombie and Fitch. It's all a fake. Any steer in a stockyard can die game. And make a dead-pan face at the world as they cut its throat. It's harder to live, harder to think, harder never to pose as a brave man. Welcome on board, A. Lincoln Pedlock. I'm drunk but can walk."

(I hated the chief that night. That ironic old bastard with his fine face and fine education gone to seed in a small job. But I was wrong. The chief is an honest man, completely indifferent.)

CHAPTER XVI

THE CAT WAS OLD

ABE WALKED on up Royale Street past the corner soda fountain smelling of cold marble, vanilla and hot-house grapes in sawdust, to the shoeshine booth where one of Maman Celie's grandsons was just finishing polishing a wide black-and-white shoe on the thick leg of Snooky Durant, the court clerk. Abe looked at his watch and got up on the other chair beside the clerk. The sky was crackling to a faint blue glow on the horizon.

"Storm before morning, Mr. Pedlock."

Abe shook his head and touched his wet, tender throat. "It can crackle like this for three, four days before it storms." He touched again, softly, his heat-rashed neck. A small portable radio sang as the coffee-colored boy began to slap shoe polish on Abe's dusty shoes.

> *Woke up this mornin' feelin' bad*
> *Thinkin' about times I've had.*
> *Yo' went out and stayed all night—*
> *Do yo' think that's treatin' me right?*
>
> *Oh, yo' shouldn't do it at all*
> *Shouldn't do it at all . . .*

Snooky grunted his way off the chair, extracted two shiny dimes, and dropped them into the pink palm of the boy. Snooky said to Abe, "Judge Riggs mighty sick man tonight."

"His tooth?"

"Yep. Close to an hour chopping out that wisdom tooth at Doc Zimmerman's. Had to cut through solid jawbone, I hear."

> *I'm tellin' yo', lover*
> *How do yo' strut that thing*
> *Night and day . . .*

"Think there'll be court tomorrow?"

"Well, Mr. Pedlock—" Snooky adjusted his wide belt over a melon stomach, pulled at his tight pants crotch for comfort, and scratched himself under the armpit of his tobacco-brown linen suit—"if it were anybody else but ol' Riggs I'd say no. But if Judge Riggs can crawl, he'll be in court. But don't rile him up. He'd just as soon cite you for contempt as larceny when he's mean. Of course, he most likely will be swollen up like a poisoned pup. If so you'll have a day off, Mr. Pedlock." (Snooky remembers me and his daughter Mary. Look at him leer at me.)

Gettin' sick and tired of th' way yo' do
God, Mama, gonna pizon yo'!
Sprinkle goofer dust on yo' bed—
Wake up some mornin'
Find yo' self dead. . . .

"See you, Mr. Pedlock. Yes, sir, see you."

The boy began to slap his shaggy rubbing cloth across Abe's shoe tops, waggling his hard, small buttocks and rolling his kinky poll. (Maybe I'll sleep all day tomorrow if there's no court. I'll call Mary first thing in the morning to check and after the kids get to school I'll get back in bed and relax, relax . . . No, there's so much to do. I want to . . .)

"You goin' to the World Series up in New Yo'k, Mr. Petlock?" the boy asked, spitting on the cloth for a water shine.

"Can't get away."

"Man, they sho' been hittin'."

(When the trial is over I'll take the kids and Fran and we'll go out to her sister's farm and swim in the stream and fish in the river and mostly just loaf and rest and eat too much and in the morning wake up with Fran in the big four-poster and the sharp, sweet smell of sunny country.)

"Yo' done."

"Take out the price of a paper."

Abe handed over some small silver coins warm to the touch. He felt foul and dirty in his sweated clothes, his neck hurt and itched, burned like a singed finger. Every part of him was slack and wobbly with fatigue. The radio had a new tune.

Oh, I love to hear my baby
Call my name.
She can call it so easy
And so doggone plain.

He picked up a copy of the evening paper without looking at its front page and walked slowly up Royale back to Lee Street. Then to Ann Street, which seemed hotter than the rest of the town. There was a warm wind stirring, driving bits of dry, dusty paper and street mess ahead of it. The heat lightning overhead was blinking like bloodshot eyelids in the hot sky. The house looked good when he came up to it. Abe went in past the gate, up the red brick walk, past the lawn on which a whirling sprinkler still turned. He turned it off at the old brass outlet faucet—getting one trouser leg slightly damp. He went in through the back porch and into the kitchen and past the arch to the dining room. Fran sat at the table with Davey and Deedee, who were holding her close; all three were weeping. Tear-stained faces turned to stare at him.

He had closed the door carefully behind him. "You all been chopping onions?"

Deedee ran toward him and buried her blond head against his body, and he patted the thin, tanned neck. She whispered, "Oh, Daddy! Tom, he died, and the man with the little truck came for him."

"Yes, dear. He grew old and died."

Fran looked up. "It was dreadful. The man from the SPCA came an hour ago and just picked Tom up by his tail and carried him out dangling like that to the street without covering him, and tossed him into the back of the truck like just nothing at all."

Abe, arm around Deedee, came to the table. "Tom didn't feel anything. He was gone."

Davey wept openmouthed, wide-eyed, not from loss, Abe suspected, but as an actor, as part of the scene, as an active member in a family drama. "My cat has gone."

"Now, listen, all you characters," Abe said firmly. "It wasn't very nice the way the man took Tom away. But he couldn't hurt him any more. Remember that. It's something we had and kept and it wore out and you hate to see it thrown around."

Deedee smiled and wiped her face with the back of her hands. "Like my Japanese doll when Davey pushed in the top of her head."

Fran stood up. "You look worn out, Abe. Why don't you soak in a tub of cold water and come down to dinner in your robe."

"A bedtime party!" shouted Davey, attaching himself to Abe's leg by four limbs and grinning up at his father, showing the spaces where two baby teeth had been.

"No, Davey. Maybe this weekend we'll get into robes and have an old-fashioned bedtime party."

Davey released the leg. "I'm hungry."

Deedee took the newspaper from under her father's arm. "Your picture in tonight, Daddo?"

"I didn't look," Abe said, starting toward the bathroom.

"The funnies, the funnies!" yelled Davey.

In the hall Abe looked at the phone pad and asked over his shoulder, "Anybody call me, Fran?"

"Just some reporters. Nobody from the office. Abe, maybe you better lie down for half an hour. Your face is so white."

"No, I'm all right." A volley of thunder shook the house overhead like heavy stones rolled over a wooden floor. "Maybe it will rain and break this heat. It's the weather, not the trial, that's getting me down. Well, maybe it's both—wearing me ragged."

He could hardly get up the stairs; his shoes seemed enormous and made of lead. There was a pain riding across his chest and he held on to the doorknob before he opened the bathroom door. He half filled the tub. It was better in the cool water, lying naked in a tub which was just too short for his long, hard body. Abe uncoiled slowly, and all the secret corners of his body gathered in a relaxing coolness. He smiled at pleasant images coming to him as he soaked, personal, private things and only half formed as he absorbed the coolness.

The bathroom door opened and Fran came in with a glass tray on which were two large martinis. "The kids are reading the funnies. I thought you'd like a quick one. I went easy on the vermouth."

"I hope the Bar Association doesn't hear of this. Naked bathroom orgies, wild drinking of exotic mixtures." He reached up his head for her kiss and tasted the martini. "Umm, just right."

"It's the twist of lemon peel and *very* dry. Oh, Abe, I was shocked over Tom. It . . . it seemed such a disrespect for life and death."

He lifted Fran's chin as she bent down to examine his heat rash. "It's been hard for you. I know."

"I'll survive. Rub a little of Davey's zinc ointment on your neck. I heard about the country club turn-down this afternoon."

"Oh, damn." Abe gulped a swig of martini. "Some blabber-mouth at the PTA?"

"No, I went in for a bottle of vermouth for tonight, at Ringel's. Mrs. Tindell was there. She said she was very angry at the club's membership committee; she was too effusive in her regrets."

"I've already had the sorry-old-chap slap-on-the-back from her husband. The hell with them. The hell with all of them."

"She invited us to a garden musical at their house next week."

"The hell with that too." The bath was spoiled. The drink needed icing. The load was back on the top of his head. Fran rubbed his wet neck; it hurt but he didn't move.

"Abe, you enjoyed their musical last year. What did they play?"

"Some longhair corn." (It was chamber music—a trio—by Ravel, but I'm not going to admit I liked it. The water is getting warm. The drink is too strong, and Fran feels angry, hurt, re-jected by her society.)

"We're not much of a social success, are we?" Fran said as she stood up, her wonderful, slim, naked legs within his reach. But he did not touch them. "Abe, you had a fight with Ed Higgins, too, the 'Town Talk' column in the morning paper hinted."

"Hand me a towel. The hell with Ed Higgins too, the whole party and political machine. I want out; Lord, how I want out. Out and peace, just you and—"

Deedee's voice came from below. "Something's steaming on the stove, Mommo."

Fran ran off, and Abe got out of the tub and dried himself, rubbed some white salve on his neck, and got into his pale-yellow sleeping pants of the thinnest silk. Over this he put his lightest dressing robe and went downstairs, his feet swollen and too tight in the old red slippers. Already he felt warm and sticky, worse than when he had stepped into the tub.

The table in the dining room overlooked the garden, a garden slightly neglected yet usually pleasant. But tonight the warm wind was brittle and unpleasant, and the sky continued to crackle like breaking pottery, but no rain fell. Davey choked on the cold lamb roast and had to be slapped on the back. Deedee wouldn't eat the iced jellied soup. Fran had a burn on her arm from the stove that somehow had not acted properly while the artichokes were being boiled. The dinner frittered away, and they moved into the living room.

The TV set's glass front was soiled with fingermarks, and Davey added a few more as they watched an inane comedy of bickering and banal situations. Then Davey kissed his parents good night and Deedee went into the small back room called The Den (after she announced she was going to write an essay entitled "The Old Pine Tree at Ormsbee Farm" as part of her homework).

Abe and Fran sat in the living room drinking iced coffee, and every time rolling thunder clattered overhead Abe looked out past the screens to see if it was raining. It wasn't.

Fran tenderly rubbed a finger over the burned area on her arm. "It hasn't been a good time for us, has it?"

"For us personally it's been all right, Fran."

"Oh, Abe, I'm not complaining. It's just it's all so unfair. You getting stuck with this daffy trial that can ruin you, and Ed Higgins against you, and other things."

"The country club?"

"All right, the country club. It's small of me and shows I'm a snob and have no character to want to be where I'm not wanted. But, I looked forward to it so much." Fran began to weep. "God knows, Abe, I don't want a Cadillac or gowns from *Vogue,* but I did want to play tennis at the club and have the pool for the kids, and the fun of meeting our friends in decent surroundings, not that dreadful blue-plate dining room at the Walker House. Being able to repay dinners by giving a party for six or eight at the club isn't too much to ask, is it?" She fell against Abe and put her arms around him, and he felt the emotions shaking her. "Oh, Abe, I'm ashamed of how I feel about it. But I can't help it. I've always been your honest girl. I'm ordinary. I want success for you, and what success brings. I want a better, newer house and good schools later on for the kids. And a polished kind of pride. Now you know what you married. Just a stupid farm girl who wants what isn't coming to her and things that to other people maybe aren't worth having."

Abe pulled up Fran's head and kissed her cheek. She came over on his lap. When she wept and was emotionally excited there was a wild sensual disorder about her that made her mellow and very desirable. And even in his weariness and his numbness she was the only woman for him. "Now, Fran, it's not stupid and those things are worth having. They're the material rewards we work for. So they aren't the greatest things in the world. Maybe there is philosophy and literature and all kinds of arts and causes that are more important. But for us the things we want have values. They mean we belong, we fit in. I understand. I know just how you feel. I know what we've lost. I truly do, darling."

"Abe, that doesn't make it any more acceptable. I'm a no-good bitch to torture you like this. What's the matter with me?"

"Don't talk about it any more."

She sat on his lap and sobbed, and he held her in his arms. (We're miserable, both of us. And we've hurt each other. It's all as wearing on her as on me. If she hadn't married me, she'd be the wife now of a Buick dealer, or a professor of soil chemistry at the college, and she'd have no social problems, or two half-breed children, or a husband who isn't a fashionable *goy*.)

Later she looked up and smiled and wiped her eyes with her fingers. "I better close some of the windows in case it rains." (Davey wiped his tears away sometimes with the same gesture.)

"I don't think it will rain. Just end-of-summer heat lightning."

"It spoiled the upper-hall wallpaper last time."

"I'll close the hall windows when I come up to bed."

"Don't sit up too late, Abe. I've never seen you look so worn down."

"All right. I'll just go over some notes I want to make for examining the witnesses. It's too hot for me to sleep anyway."

"But you must sleep, dear. Try."

"I'll try."

"Abe, all those stories about Sarah Rodman as a girl—are they true?"

"Not admissible as evidence. You know that."

Fran was facing him, looking a him directly with what he called her "country girl" stare. "The stories about what a fast kid she was. And the boys running after her."

"She was a Hawley and we peasants below the castle walls always gossiped about the quality."

"She screwed everybody, didn't she?"

Abe shook his head. "I don't like the use of that word—not by you anyway. Besides, *everybody* meant a hell of a lot of males. Must be fifteen thousand hereabouts able to perform the act. No, don't listen to gossip. Sarah was a wild, rich kid, and spoiled, but she had a certain grace, a kind of way of walking and talking that couldn't really be vulgar."

"You ever sleep with her, Abe?"

(What the hell is going on here? What's gotten into Fran? But it's nothing; she's just a woman and asking questions, and that one hit home without Fran's knowing it. Well, let's see how good an actor I am.)

"Several hundred times. Maybe thousands. I had a large Italian racing car in those days, and we'd run down to the Florida coast and live it up in a suite, with a built-in jazz band and free champagne in every room. We were favorites with the international set. I'm surprised you never heard about it."

Fran wrinkled her nose and laughed. "You ought to be writing Hollywood movies." She kissed his cheek and said, "Get some sleep." She went upstairs slowly.

Abe sat down at the dining-room table, laid out his notebooks, took some documents from his briefcase and began to make notes on a ruled yellow legal pad. He worked, as usual, with great concentration. He turned on the news broadcast and then sat damply unhappy in the flickering lightning listening to the far-off roll of thunder. He heard someone lightly banging the brass front-door knocker. To keep Fran from being awakened, he went quickly to the front door and opened it. Against the dark street background Jake Barton stood out, big and uncomfortable in a jacket and straw hat, a long shape under one arm.

"Hello, Abe. I'm late, I know."

"Come in."

He led Jake Barton into the dining room, pushing the papers aside and wedging the most important ones out of sight under the briefcase.

"You peddling brooms this late at night?"

"Something better."

"How about a cold beer?"

"All right." The fat man sighed and looked over the room. "I like these old houses. High ceilings and solid woodwork."

"My wife's house," said Abe as he went into the kitchen to get the beer and two glasses. He felt he should be wary of Jake Barton's late visit, but his protective nerve ends that worked like an emotional and physical thermostat were tired and could not now let him become involved in worries or fears.

He came back into the dining room carrying the opened beer bottles, their green-brown surfaces sweating coldly on a tray, with the two best glasses. He poured and they sat facing each other across the genuine 1842 Shaker table Great-Grandfather Ormsbee had made. Sipping a malty coldness, the men relaxed. Jake Barton put down his glass and placed a large hand by the side of his hat resting on the table.

"Abe, I guess you know Ed Higgins has been pretty riled at you."

"I know. And I don't want him to get fiesty at me, but I couldn't go out of my way to do something that I couldn't let myself do. That sounds naïve. It doesn't sound right to a political boss, I'm sure. But I don't give a damn any more."

"You're low, Abe," said Jake Barton, taking up the long package and beginning to unwrap it slowly, like a careful man, unknitting the heavy hairy twine that held it together. He rolled up the twine with a saving gesture and opened the green wrapping paper. A shiny rifle appeared in his hand and he handed it to an openmouthed Abe. "Take it. Flew it up from Richmond, where it was found this afternoon in a pawnshop. Some thief pawned it four days before the murders."

"It's the Higgins Winchester?"

Jake Barton nodded and took some papers from his pocket and pushed them across to Abe. "Here is the original bill of sale. Here is the pawnshop record. Here is the factory order number and Ed's filled-in form registering the serial number. Also an inventory sheet of the rifle and serial number made two years ago for the insurance company, even if it was never reported stolen."

Abe looked up, blinking, and wiped his damp face with the flat of one hand.

"Mr. Higgins was sure worried, wasn't he?"

"Well, Big Ed is no fool. He wanted to be sure, but like you and me he didn't really think Johnny was capable of murder—this kind most of all."

"He sweated over it, though, Jake." Abe permitted himself the "Jake."

"Yes, Abe, he did. If you've read the Russian novelists—I've been wading through a few—you realize the human mind hasn't been probed very deeply as to what it can do or think of."

"John Higgins could have killed George Rodman and Helen Nash, but now it doesn't look so."

"Now we know."

"Mr. Higgins wanted me to have the proof? And tonight?"

"You never have had any solid evidence Johnny didn't do it. This is it."

Abe took a deep suck of beer. "I'm not going any deeper into it."

"Smart boy. Abe, if Johnny did do it, I wouldn't be here; as for Big Ed, I think he'd face it, not hide it."

"I hated the idea of bringing the state's case to a conclusion with this hanging over me."

"You're a stubborn man. But don't take in too much ground."

Abe stared at Jake Barton, eying him over the rim of his beer glass. "I have only the defendants on trial."

"How does it look?" Jake Barton was standing up stroking his hat. "You going to use your eyewitness?"

"It looks good. Yes. And tell Mr. Higgins he owes me nothing and I owe him nothing. I know I'm on his shathouse list now."

Jake Barton was expressionless as he held a hand toward Abe. "Not if you win this case. Big Ed wants winners in politics, not friends. Let's get together sometime, Abe."

"Sure, Jake."

Abe saw his guest to the front door; he was too fatigued for anger or for involved thought. He locked up the rifle and the papers and, forgetting about the windows, went upstairs to bed. As he undressed he wondered if the cat was put out, then remembered the creature was no more, incinerated by now, as if it had never existed. He felt great mortal fear.

In bed he closed his eyes and told himself he must sleep. (I must sleep. I must rest. I am in great trouble tomorrow. I am going to bring on an eyewitness who has no social standing, no acceptance in this town. It will be easy to destroy her. But she will not be destroyed. I will win this case, convict for murder, and I shall be destroyed with the convicted. This town will not accept a man who convicts Hawleys. They may even have to change the name of the town. But I cannot help it. If I had a father, a name I was sure of . . . Was my mother ever married? What do I want to be but what I am, a very ordinary man who knows law and knows he is honest, plodding, and has a wonderful wife and children, the kind of pleasures the intellectuals laugh at? But I want—I've been dozing—let me think of something else. Ed Hightower—I know how I was when I met him and we talked. Was he already my father image?)

BOOK THREE

FRIDAY

CHAPTER XVII

RECALL AND
DEPARTURE

THE WARM, DRY WIND was a little wilder near dawn, when Abe at last fell asleep. He no longer welcomed sleep even if he needed it. The dreams that came to inhabit it left him weaker than when he went to bed, and he would come awake and feel the *thump thump* of his heart pounding and the hot blood pushing through his protesting veins. But now he slept deeply, and when the dreams began to appear they seemed harmless, even pleasant. He was suddenly very young and callow again, and going to the state university, a shabby young man always in need of a haircut, and his long arms sticking out of the too short sleeves of his jacket. It was a bone-white winter day. There had been a sudden and rare snow and a brisk frost.

On the cliff the white stone and rough brick buildings of the state university were chill and lovely in the snowy landscape. The wind made a great copper clangor. Hidden were the badly chosen Latin mottoes, the vulgar memorial gates, the sacred, holy colonial barns, the square, paper-box-design gym, the bad bronze statues of chin-whiskered old frumps, founders and pirates who had disgorged before they died. All were now only little snowy pinnacles along the many short, precipitous ravines that led to the highest tower. Youth slept, dreamed of Greek sophists, football, ankles, the future. Only Abe was walking without an overcoat, not mindful of the weather. He was going to his grubby little room now to study.

On the steep street leading to the Science Hall stood the run-down white Regency house of Mrs. Fluter. Professor Fluter had been bitten by a fly years before in far-off Afghanistan while hunting the remains of Bahram Gur's palace. He killed the fly instinctively. A week later the fly killed him. Mrs. Fluter, after desolate tears, put out a sign for boarders. Widows learn to face incontestable truths, and cheap rooms for poor students could but didn't show a profit.

The dream almost faded as he opened a book, *The State and the Church,* by Monsignor John Ryan, and a voice like Big Ed Higgins' began to read the marked text.

> *Catholic Principles of Politics* . . . But Constitutions can be changed, and non-Catholic sects may decline to such a point that the political prescription of them may become feasible and expedient. A Catholic state could logically tolerate only such religious activities as were confined to the members of the dissenting group. It could not permit them to carry on general propaganda nor accord their organization certain privileges that had formerly been extended to all religious corporations. . . .

Big Ed's voice faded. The weather became pleasant. There was music that suggested fugitive miscellaneous pleasures as the dream shifted facets.

Abe was kissing Fran in the Tindell rose garden, which became a deep forest among china-blue hydrangeas, and the fountains played and seemed sheeted metal, wet and slick, and spun rainbows in the sun. Pelléas took Mélisande in his arms, and the landscape was one with the lovers. The shaggy barked trees, the spinning waters of the fountain, the serried tides of a dimpling sea. The voices of the leaves, the smell of mignonette.

And he loved her and held her close—and he kissed her. The wind was so like the sound of cellos. The splash of the fountain was so like the chords of horns and harps.

Abe looked down on the face of the woman in his arms and, leaning way over, he kissed her again with tremendous enthusiasm. The music welled up and entered his body, and he stood in a forest among the waters of a silvered suspended fountain.

A tamer forest—a glass-enclosed forest of *Philadelphus coronarius,* of California poppies and many roses—white Killarney tea roses, sweet of scent. The Tindells were famous for their love of planting. Chinese Blairii, soft-odored, filling the nostrils, fogging the senses. What was he doing here even in this dream? Pastoral artifice or real? Cockeyed somewhere, pleasant too. Not to think, just glide with the sleep. It had happened fast, would it pass quicker?"

Half rueful, he let the woman go, and Fran looked up at him quizzically. "You are very sweet, my love." Or so it sounded.

"Fran, darling," and it seemed so little, so silly to say, yet how was he to show the tumultuous ache that beat within him?

He took her close again, and his arms were tight around her. Sweet passion—of man and woman close together. He kissed her again, and she postured closer to him in solemn, triumphant gratitude. The white, sunny odor of her was half of this moment, half of this music that seemed to be coming from his own fingertips, from his own bones and tissues and flesh and blood.

Fran leaned back against the mock-orange plants and patted her hair into place. And not looking at Abe, she said softly, calmly now, and with the perfect control of women in that natural plausive way they recover so soon (women are full of so many inestimable qualities), "I think we'd better go back before they miss us."

"If you say so."

Inside, the applause was very loud. "Superbly done" was whispered through respiratory gurgles. Someone touched Abe, and he turned around. Judge Riggs, all his teeth pulled, took Abe's arm.

"Well done. The best-prepared murder case in years. You deserved the verdict." Devil Cavanagh's voice shouted, "Begorra and me boyo, sure now me knobby lad it's a poor mouth I make not to tell ya ya clobbered us from Killarney to Dublin, oh the Pedlock himself, and they cheered when ya rose so modestly now to answer that the Supreme Court bench was too much an honor, much too much too much much . . ."

Abe came awake to hear the night rain lisping on the slates of the roof just over the dark bedroom ceiling. It was cool and comfortable, and a fragment of dream made clear one must conceive truth and eternity and participate in them. Fran slept, facing Abe on her side, and he covered her with the sheet. The sound of the rain increased, racing in the gutters; the beat of it on the roof, the cool sense of it there, and strong, rested him as nothing had for several days. The good taste of the dream was still with him, and he flexed his toes and savored some satisfying bits of it that he remembered; but most of it had been torn apart as if by the rain and wind and was gone.

Abe got up and in his bare feet went to the big double windows facing the street. Spray cool and refreshing came through the screens, but he didn't mind. He inhaled deeply the damp air and felt clean and scrubbed. The street below was slick and black, the gutters flowing thick brown under the reflecting light from the corner. The flogged leaves on the lawn trees lay flat and droopy, taking the beating of the rain without protest and in silent leisure. Even the death of the cat when it intruded on Abe was an event on another planet.

Abe toured the house, closing the windows in the dining room, making sure the fairly new kitchen door didn't leak in rain at the bottom. The whole house was cooler, and as he moved slowly in physical contentment on his bare feet, he felt revitalized. Deedee was sleeping proudly on her back, her mouth slightly open and her small, delicate hands (ink-stained) folded on her little chest. Davey had a wet mouth, and a damp thumb was stuck into one cheek. He was scowling in some dreamed competitive game, deeply asleep. Abe came back to the bedroom and listened —as if to a fine watch—to Fran breathe. He hoped their relationship would return to what it had been, that the harm done by the trial and their defeat in the town's social wars could still be mended. Abe had a tremor of terror as he got back into the bed by his wife's side, a shiver of apprehension that he had lost her. So brooding, yet now cool and comfortable, he fell asleep and awoke only when the pale-green light of morning came through on his eyelids. The rain had stopped, but the day was pleasant, sunless as yet, and the smell of wet leaves filled the house.

There was the dark curtain of new rain clouds in the morning sky. But the day itself was smooth and the heat was only a memory. The courtroom would again be comfortable. The air would taste washed clean and the light that came in through the long open windows should carry the quality of green restfulness. There was a suggestion of thin lime-colored sun, but it no longer had the power to burn.

Abe had come finally awake with the phone ringing in the hall downstairs and Fran's voice answering and calling him. He had come down aware of the freshness of the rebirth of his energies. Mary Durant's brisk voice connected with his ear as he held the phone to his head.

"Judge Riggs's wife has called. He's continuing the trial today as usual."

"Is he well enough?"

"He thinks so. It was, I heard, a brutal operation he had."

"Not so good for us, Mary, if he's in pain and hating all the world."

"He says court at ten A.M."

"All right. Have Rod check in the witnesses. Any word from Miss Keefe in the police lab?"

"Yes. All negative. They can't get any serial number on that

busted Winchester, even by deep X ray. All they can prove
is that it was one of the murder weapons."

"That's enough," said Abe, invigorated to a cheerful acceptance. He hung up and went in to breakfast. With Fran and the
kids, he sat eating a stack of wheatcakes with farm honey from
the Ormsbee family bees while the two children bickered and
appealed to him for trivial decisions.

Dressed and eager, Abe walked slowly to the courthouse block
in a freshly pressed suit, smoking his first sweet-tasting stogie of
the day. In his office Mary informed him Rod had the witnesses
in court. Abe went in to Ed Hightower's office and told him
about Jake Barton and the recovered Higgins rifle.

"Of course we'll check, Chief. But I'm pretty sure it's the
Higgins rifle. I'll go along with the local opinion that John
Higgins isn't the murdering type."

"If you accept, I accept. You think Sarah Rodman and the
Hawley boys are the homicidal kind."

"I do. Under their emotional triggering."

"One must never talk too rationally about human behavior
or its fantastically irrational qualities, Abe. Its perpetual unrea-
son remains baffling, even if some would say all generalizations
are glib. Still, I think you're right about the Hawleys."

"Jake Barton said the same thing you did. Anyway, Ed Higgins
is off my back. Even if he'll never forgive me for digging this up
in the first place."

Ed Hightower's still handsome face, topped by the beautiful
gray hair, moved up into the full light of a window. "Abe, right
now you can still wind up the case with what you've presented
so far: circumstantial evidence. And the judge may declare it a
no trial or the jury may bring in a not-guilty verdict. A mistrial
at the most. And you'd still be pretty much a young man who did
his best. You presented cause for murder, evidence of other
shooting sprees, et cetera."

"*But*, Chief . . ."

"But, if you present direct evidence of the crime, put that eyewitness on the stand, she may fail you. Or be dreadfully dis-
credited. And if you do get a guilty verdict on that testimony,

it may not stand up on appeal. And if the defendants need something new for an appeal, who knows what they'll find? They could dig and find out about John Higgins. Could claim he had *another* rifle, even a stolen one, and for a great climax in court, even say he walked off with Mikel Hawley's rifle. Was John Higgins ever at one of the hunting parties with the Hawleys and —Well, you know how I'm building a whole new case, theirs, on one cobweb. Any lawyer can."

"What are you trying to say, Chief?"

"I'm not trying, I'm saying it. Don't put Maman Celie on the stand if the jury will not accept her. Now don't think I've sold out to the Hawleys, or to town prejudices, or am resting in somebody's pocket. I'm thinking of you, Abe. It's better for a man when you're a young punk to take one step back than two steps over the edge of a cliff. Let the jury decide on the evidence so far. Call this a hunch of mine, fidelity to the inspiration of reason, but I have a feeling your eyewitness means big trouble. She's too too bizarre, that old bag."

Abe smiled and patted the lean back of the district attorney. "It's not an order, is it?"

"No, Abe, it isn't."

"Come down to court and watch the evidence. I may bring the state's case to an end today."

"Have the world by the short hair, eh? The two-finger grip?"

Ed watched the younger man leave his office and went to his desk. He got out his bottle and sat slowly sipping a drink while the courthouse bell began to ring the warning quarter to the hour. Below, many people tried to move toward the courtroom. Cameramen and TV mobile units were active in what the old man thought of as their mean business, ugly business. Ed Hightower began to recall the names of several men who could be lured into Abe's job of defending the public weal when Abe was gone. None seemed to satisfy him and he had another drink, sipping it more slowly, enjoying it. All the other bright young men were ambushing success like Indian raiders; mostly they were conformists in tight little foreign cars and caps, victims of the urban syndrome: worship of the bitch goddess success; and slightly schizoid. Men like Abe, solid, honest, ordinary, were rare. And going to be rarer. Odd that ordinary men with codes of honor should be so rare. The new-brewed whisky was stronger than he had thought. No one took time to age anything properly any more. He corked the bottle, put it away and, getting his old Panama off a chair, put it on at a rakish angle and went out past Miss Munday. "I'll be in court, Miss Munday."

"The attorney for the flour-mill case is coming in this morning with his depositions."

"Cover for me, Munday. Cover."

Ed Hightower went down the public stairs, able now to endure his share of the morning's uncertainty of reality. He belched corn alcohol and said out loud to no one, "If one has a lawyer for a friend, one doesn't need enemies."

Judge Wilmont Riggs sat in chambers (one fairly well-dusted room, with a small toilet off it), an ice bag held to his crimson, swollen cheek, a flick of dried blood on one corner of his mouth. Snooky Durant, as court clerk and dresser, was busy at the old fumed-oak wardrobe brushing down the judge's black robe. Facing the judge, seated on old comfortable chairs, were Abe Pedlock and Roger Tindell. The table clock read four minutes to ten as an electric impulse stirred one hand.

Judge Riggs shifted the ice bag higher and said in a thick voice that seemed obscured by a thick tongue, "I suggest, gentlemen, we give this case to the jury end of this week. In fact, let's make that a strong order. Is there any reason either of you think it can't be done?"

Roger Tindell, wearing a well-brushed blue suit and a soft Ivy League collar with short wings, a rich blue-purple knitted tie, shook his head. "I have no idea, Judge Riggs, as we don't know how much longer the state will continue its rather hazy methods. I am formally asking, Your Honor, that you dismiss the jury and declare the state's case not valid and unproven when court opens."

The judge flipped a thick report on the table. "Yes, yes, I read your request, Tindell. It's in order and too long. But I intend to let this go to the jury. All papers a judge has to read are too long. Write a brief as if you're sending ten-word telegrams and make judges happy."

Roger Tindell slightly turtled his head, as if conceding that this rejection were some small, eccentric gesture on the judge's part. "I shall again make the request to *nol-pol* the trial in open court. For the record, Your Honor."

"Request away. It goes to the jury. Mr. Pedlock, have you many more witnesses?"

Abe smiled. "I was taught, Your Honor—by a man who taught us both—not to give away my procedure in judge's chambers before the opposing counsel. But this time I don't mind saying the state will most likely present only two more witnesses to prove its case."

"Good," said Tindell. "I mean to there being only two more witnesses."

"Unless, of course," Abe added, "we should have supplementary evidence come to our attention. Judge Riggs, the state would not object to postponing today's court or shortening the session if you should feel your tooth bothering you."

Judge Riggs tossed the ice bag to Snooky Durant and accepted a freshly filled one. "Tooth is *not* bothering the court. It isn't there any more. It's where it *was* that is knocking my damn head off."

Tindell made a slight sound of sympathy. "The defense joins Mr. Pedlock in agreeing with the bench to any desire it has to carry over to tomorrow or shorten the session today."

Judge Riggs changed hands holding the ice bag. "Snooky, my robe. At least this weather is bearable." The judge—so small and worn—stood up while the clerk helped him into the robe. "I must warn both of you I am in no mood for melodrama and grandstanding." He looked at the small clock. "Court in one minute."

Roger Tindell touched Abe's sleeve as they walked out into the hall and crossed it to the courtroom. "You golf much, Abe?"

"I'm not bad. I used to caddy as a kid on the old Colonial links."

"How about a game Saturday afternoon at the country club?"

Abe stopped and pivoted on his heel to face Tindell. "Thanks, Roger, no."

"Think it over. Your wife can join us and Mrs. Tindell for dinner. There's a good roast beef Saturday night, and a dance."

Abe shook his head. "I don't like my meat seasoned with wormwood." Abe regretted the words at once. He put his hand on Tindell's shoulder. "I'm sorry I said that. Let's go beat each other's ears off this morning. Maybe in a couple of weeks we'll try golf."

They crossed to the door of the courtroom, held open by a bailiff, and moved into the loud excitement of the refreshed trial room.

CHAPTER XVIII

ON THE STAND

THE COURTROOM WAS COOLER than it had been in weeks. Someone had propped open the windows, and a cool breeze came softly from the lawns where the jail crews were cutting the grass. Judge Riggs sat up too sternly in his chair. It was noticeable to the courtroom that he had a swollen cheek and that he patted it from time to time with a large handkerchief wrapped around something that was most likely a small ice bag. He had crisply ordered the defense to stop presenting briefs for *non-poling* the trial and had chewed out the deputy district attorney, A. Lincoln Pedlock, for referring to something the judge had already stricken from the records two days before.

Ed Hightower, sitting at the state's table, smiled and whispered to Rod Miller and Mary Durant, "Old Riggs has his dander up.

He could throw out a few contempts of court if his pain gets any worse."

Mary Durant balanced Abe's notebooks in a neat pile in front of her. "Just what is dander, and how does it go up?"

Abe, standing facing the bench, said briskly, "The state calls as its witness Edward Desmond."

Rod Miller looked around to watch the small, slow figure of Eddie Desmond cross to the stand and take the oath. A prowl car had stood by since dawn at the house of Desmond's mother— just in case. Even now the bailiffs had been tipped off to see Eddie Desmond didn't slip out of the courtroom.

Eddie was neatly dressed in a tan starched shirt and a worn brown suit that was freshly pressed; his short hair was damp with water, a lock loose over the wide white brow. He took the oath, gave his name in a low but clear voice and, when Abe faced him, showed no hostility, and no interest either.

"You are employed by Mrs. Sarah Rodman as chauffeur, Mr. Desmond?"

"No, I am not."

Devil Cavanagh, looking as if he had a hard night behind him, was sitting well forward, legs apart, in his chair at the defense table. His bloodshot eyes were half closed, his hands clasped together in front of him. He looked ill.

"You were once employed by Mrs. Rodman as a chauffeur?"

"Yes."

Devil Cavanagh leaned toward Sarah Rodman, seated near him, and whispered to her. She said something back, hardly moving her lips or turning her neck. Abe noticed the Reverend Romar in the back of the courtroom, the old man's white hair the color of aged ivory. (So she has her spiritual defense present too?)

"When did your employment terminate?" Abe asked.

"July twelfth. I got sick. Never went back."

"How long were you employed by the Rodmans? Dr. and Mrs. Rodman, that is, as joint employers."

"Two years and ten months."

Abe nodded and pretended the delicacy of the situation

needed discreet weighing of questions and short pauses to think. This was a very hostile witness. Eddie must be led in at a tangent to testify properly. "You were, I believe, a very handy man to have around. You helped fit drapes at the Rodmans', arranged for plantings."

Devil Cavanagh mocked Abe's voice. "He was a handy man. Your Honor, we don't object to it; we shall not challenge the witness on what he did for his pay. This matter is all trivial."

"Get on with it, Mr. Pedlock," said Judge Riggs. "What do you want to ask this witness?"

Devil Cavanagh moaned as if his head hurt very badly. "We doubt that he has anything vital to the case to ask."

Abe said, smiling at the jury, "Who's delaying the questioning of the witness now?"

The judge rapped loudly on the bench. Abe turned and shot words at Eddie Desmond. "Is it not a fact that Mr. and Mrs. Rodman wanted to send you to college, educate you at their expense?"

The witness answered expressionlessly. "I have no such recollection."

"Did you live at the Rodmans' during your period of employment there?"

"I did."

"Over the garage in what is called the chauffeur's room?"

"No."

"The guest bedroom on the same floor as Mr. and Mrs. Rodman's rooms?"

Devil Cavanagh was on his feet. "I object to any personal details relating to the relationship of the witness to the dead man and his wife as being outside the proper material questioning of this witness."

The judge scowled. "Mr. Pedlock, I don't like this line of questioning. I too want to know what its purpose is."

Abe turned innocently, watching the witness out of the corner of his eye. "Not for any exotic vice out of Roman history, as the hot Mr. Cavanagh would suggest, to confuse the court. I want the witness to tell the court of his life with two people who were very respectfully fond of him. Two childless people who treated him not as a servant but as a son."

The objection rose loud and in a roar. Abe banged on the witness rail. Cavanagh rolled his eyes in a saintly unnatural agony; Tindell began to wave his notes. Judge Riggs at last hammered silence into the court. "The witness will answer any questions pertaining to his relationship and life in the Rodman house bearing on the case, after the court takes fifteen minutes."

He rose and went out quickly to his chamber to suck crushed ice.

Ed Hightower turned to Abe as the deputy district attorney came to the state's table. "Why the uproar?"

Abe sat down and touched a stogie in his pocket and wondered whether he should go out for a short smoke. "I want to frighten the witness into a rage and soften him up so he'll answer what I want to ask him—answer properly without thinking it out."

Ed Hightower asked, "You think he will?"

"No idea."

Mary Durant said, "The Desmonds are all high-gummed Irish."

Carl Vogelhofer came up to the table. "Abe, I have your prize package in the bailiff's room. In a strong wheelchair and her son standing by. She's ripping today."

"Maman Celie been drinking?" Abe asked.

"No. I just brought her one gin. To 'oil de throat,' as she says."

"Good enough. When she's called, just wheel her in. Slowly. And don't touch her. Let Jim Caesar lift her up into the witness chair." Abe turned to Rod. "Have you the marked medical report from Sidney Wymer as an exhibit?"

"Yes."

"He promised to be here himself to testify, if we need him."

Mary Durant shook her head. "Not today." She made a gesture of drinking from a glass.

"Damn," Abe said as Ed smiled and patted his back.

When Judge Riggs came back and reopened court, Abe rose and went slowly up to the witness. "Mr. Desmond, the Rodmans were very good to you." Abe looked over at Devil Cavanagh, mouth open already. "As people to work for."

"I liked working for them."

"You were often present when Mr. and Mrs. Rodman discussed personal affairs?"

"I don't recollect any such times," Eddie said indifferently.

"Shall we pinpoint it, together? For instance, the day you helped hang the drapes in Mrs. Rodman's room. Remember that day?"

"Yes."

"Mr. Rodman came in and in front of you said to Mrs. Rodman that—"

Devil Cavanagh was on his feet pumping his arms up and down. "Is the witness on the stand or is the brilliant wonder boy of the D.A.'s office? Is this a trial at court or a rehearsal for a lousy B movie? I object to telling the witness what he is supposed to have seen."

Abe turned slowly to the bench. "I ask the court to warn the ornament of the Northern bar, the expensive import from New York City, that his language is an insult to this court and the office of District Attorney Edward Hightower. If he is trying to insult *me* personally, I don't fight duels."

"Trying? I said this, Your Honor, to—"

Judge Riggs was banging his handleless gavel down hard. His swollen cheek was a Chinese red. "I will hold both attorneys for contempt if this kind of exchange continues."

Roger Tindell was trying to hold Devil Cavanagh back as he shouted, "I suggest Mr. A. Lincoln Pedlock go back to law school and learn how to examine a witness."

"If the court will recess for five minutes, Your Honor, I will punch a head."

Abe moved quickly to the defense table and reached over for Cavanagh's coat collar. He was aware that all this was no sudden outburst of irrepressible rage on the part of the defense lawyer; it had some plan and purpose, and Abe suspected it was to show the witness he could defy the examination; that he was being questioned in the wrong manner. Under the fire and smoke of

Devil Cavanagh's bombast, Abe knew, was a thought-out trickery to cloud over whatever Eddie Desmond would testify to. Few judges had ever kept Devil Cavanagh under wraps.

Abe swung his fist at empty air, acting too now, and Rod and a bailiff pulled him off Devil Cavanagh. Tindell and Snooky Durant held the defense lawyer against the table, straightening his jacket collar. Sarah Rodman and her two brothers showed their first amusement during the trial.

Judge Riggs spoke in a harsh, dead-level voice. "The court will take fifteen minutes. I will see both the state and defense counsels involved in my chambers, and perhaps they can tell me why they both should not be held in contempt of this court."

There was a thin line of smile, objective reached, on Devil Cavanagh's face. Abe looked over at the witness. Eddie Desmond had gotten the message if the wide, wise look on his face was correct. Abe bowed to Cavanagh and said, "You first."

Devil Cavanagh laughed. "Sure, why not."

Judge Riggs had already gone into his chambers. Cavanagh and Abe followed him in. There was a buzzing excitement in the courtroom. Batty Billie sneezed and Sarah Rodman handed him his handkerchief, taking it from his jacket pocket. Ed Hightower, seated at the state's table, watched her closely, wondering how she could remain so cool, so controlled—but for the small smile. He must talk to the Reverend Romar about her. Romar's mind wandered a bit, but he was a good sort. They had been at Yale together. Mikel Hawley still was restless; the slight tic under his right eye had become a grimace, and now Ed Hightower noticed he rotated his left foot continually when he put one leg over the other and sat back. Or he did until Sarah leaned toward him and nudged him with her shoulder, after which he would stop rotating his foot for a few minutes.

Ed Hightower turned to Carl Vogelhofer and Rod Miller at the table. "If there is a contempt ruling against Abe, I want you, Carl, to take over the questioning of the witness."

"How do I proceed, Chief? Hard or soft?"

"Abe wants to bring out that Eddie Desmond heard George Rodman tell his wife he was leaving her and going away with

Helen Nash. And Sarah Rodman said he could have his girl, keep her, but he would also have to remain her husband, share her bed. George Rodman turned her down in disgust. It's a very vital point to prove such a situation existed in the Rodman household. It's the perfect motive for murder. And most likely triggered the killing. For Sarah there was no solution. Proves the old saying: Life is not a problem to be solved but a reality to be experienced."

Mary Durant had been talking to her father, the court clerk. She came back to the table with her loping, sensual walk and sat down in a flurry of her wide skirt. "Pappy says the judge is in no mood for lawyers hamming it up. He's going to get real tough."

Ed Hightower nodded. "Cavanagh played it as he saw it. He had to stop Abe softening up the witness enough to really talk."

Rod looked at the court clock and began to rearrange the table papers. "He's really chewing them out. They can't enter in the records for appeal that the judge had a tooth pulled."

Ed Hightower was staring at Sarah Rodman. The rather wild girl had become this cold, icy woman in court. It often happened that way. People change under crisis. Good education. He wondered whether she had ever read the old lines on adultery among the gods and how it was punished then. How did it go? As he stared at the woman, the lines began to flow back into his memory.

> Even the Sun, who with his central light guides all the stars, has felt the power of love. This god was first, 'tis said, to see the shame of Mars and Venus; this god sees all things first. Shocked at the sight, he revealed her sin to the goddess' husband, Vulcan, Juno's son, and where it was committed. Then Vulcan's mind reeled and the work upon which he was engaged fell from his hands. Straightway he fashioned a net of fine links of bronze, so thin that they would escape detection of the eye. . . . Now when the goddess and her paramour had come thither, by the husband's net and by the net so cunningly prepared, they were both caught and held fast in each other's arms. Straightway Vulcan, the Lemnian, opened wide the ivory doors and invited in the

other gods. There lay the two in chains, disgracefully, and some one of the merry gods prayed that he might be so disgraced. The gods laughed, and for a long time this story was the talk of heaven.

Groups had formed in the courtroom. Some people drifted out for a smoke. A juror was slyly removing a bit of breakfast from between his teeth. The reporters went out for a stretch in the hall. Someone chased out a small dog. A bailiff opened more windows. The clock hands moved very slowly. The witness studied his fingernails.

Abe came out of the judge's chamber wiping his face. Devil Cavanagh followed, walking, Ed Hightower thought, like a bulldog that had been kicked hard in the rear but wasn't admitting it. In court Judge Riggs tried to assist in keeping the dignity of the attorneys at a proper level, but it was known that he was a hide-ripper in his chambers.

The judge came in, red-faced, smiling a little grimly, forgetting the pain in his jaw. Snooky Durant handed him the ice bag wrapped in the large handkerchief and announced that the court had reconvened.

Abe came over to the state's table to pick up his notes. He smiled tightly at Ed Hightower as if he had been looking too long into a bright light. "I wouldn't like any more of those."

"Contempt?"

"Suspended till after the trial, and our conduct till then will have a bearing on his final decision."

Judge Riggs called out crisply, "Will the counsel for the state continue with his witness?"

"In a moment, Your Honor."

Ed Hightower said low, "Want Carl here to take over for a spell?"

"I was thinking of that. And taking the witness stand myself, swearing the oath and telling what was told me by Eddie. But that would only start a new hassle. No, I'll go on."

Abe walked over to Eddie Desmond, who now sat with his arms resting on the chair, his fingers meeting. "Mr. Desmond, what was your illness, the one that caused you to leave your employment with the Rodmans?"

"Boils."

"They still continue to bother you?" Abe leaned close, as if feeling sorry.

"They do."

"Who is treating you for them? Can I get you a rubber cushion?"

"No. Doctor Wymer." Eddie unconsciously shifted his weight in the witness chair.

"Doctor Wymer! Why, he's a well-known and skillful surgeon. He must know you pretty well to treat you for such a minor thing as boils?"

The witness shouted, "If you had 'em, you wouldn't think they were so minor!"

Abe joined in the laughter. Even the judge smiled.

"I beg your pardon, Mr. Desmond. I am sure they are a major source of discomfort to you."

"I once drove for Doctor Wymer. And he was the only doctor I knew. He liked my mother, used to come and talk to her."

"When did Doctor Wymer last treat your affliction?"

"Monday night."

"Your mother's birthday, wasn't it?" Abe was being very friendly.

"Yes."

"Did Doctor Wymer come alone?"

The witness said softly, aware where this was going, "No. You were with him, Mr. Pedlock."

"It was a fine birthday party, and I enjoyed it. Where did Doctor Wymer treat you?"

"On my rear end!"

There was laughter.

"No, no. Where did he examine you?"

"In my room."

Abe looked at the defense table. Heads were close together there. Abe turned cheerfully and asked, "That the upstairs room where you and I talked that night?"

The witness nodded. Abe said, "The room we talked in? Don't nod. Yes or no?"

"Yes, my room."

"Did we talk about Mr. and Mrs. Rodman?"

Roger Tindell rose. "We object, Your Honor . . . that . . ."

Judge Riggs waved his arm. "Sit down. This questioning is in order. He was asked *did we,* not *we did.*"

"We talked," said Eddie Desmond grimly. "I told you just what I told you when you took a statement before the trial. Nothing else."

"Yes, we have your statement. In our talk did you expand it a bit? Did you mention the plant-watering, the curtain-hanging in our talk in your room?"

"It didn't seem important to include it in my first statement."

"Oh, yes it is. Tell the court, did Mr. and Mrs. Rodman discuss something the day you were hanging the drapes?"

"Nothing important. Just ordinary things."

Devil Cavanagh relaxed. Abe frowned, walked over to the jury, then walked to the bench. Stall, he said to himself. Don't give the witness the idea you'll finish with him soon. "Your Honor, may I indulge the patience of the court by taking my time? This witness is a key witness. I must get him to recollect what he told me Monday night."

Judge Riggs said, "I can't try your case for you."

Tindell stood up. "There is no corroborating witness that this witness told Mr. Pedlock anything beyond what he first told in his statement. Will he continue the usual questioning?"

"Yes. Mr. Pedlock, continue with your witness. If you can't handle him, you have two men at your table who can try."

Abe walked back to Eddie Desmond. He sucked in air and stepped back quickly, his cheeks flushed from the judge's talk. "Mr. Desmond, I give you a hypothetical situation, which means a kind of imaginary situation that doesn't have to relate to you or anyone else. An assistant district attorney—doesn't have to be me—is told by a witness—now, remember, this is just an imaginary case." Abe glanced at the judge. Would he permit this line of questioning? Judge Riggs was rubbing his cheek with his hand-kerchief-covered ice bag.

Cavanagh growled, "Perhaps we should hold this hearing in a hypothetical court on Cloud Nine?" He made no further protest.

Abe went on. "As I say, Eddie (no use being formal now; *Eddie* is good enough), imagine a talk between these two people in which the witness tells the lawyer from the D.A.'s office he heard a husband—any husband—tell his wife he was going away for good with the woman he loves, and the wife tells him she doesn't care if he keeps a girl but he still has to stay and be a real husband to her. This situation could lead to murder and—"

Roger Tindell was raging mad on his feet. For the first time during the trial he was beyond control. "This whole line of questioning, Your Honor, is an outrage! It not only brings before this court imaginary situations, for which there's no shred of evidence, but plants an impression of events which the defense cannot permit to be offered even in this form in any court of law!"

Judge Riggs nodded. "Mr. Pedlock, this matter as you present it may be proper, but I can't let it continue much longer. Even if you continue to say it's hypothetical." Judge Riggs tried to hide a smile. Abe suspected the judge enjoyed the situation used against Devil Cavanagh.

"I will just ask the witness about one more hypothetical incident and not continue any longer, if it does not help his slipping memory."

Judge Riggs waved Tindell down. Abe faced Eddie Desmond. "And imagine this imaginary husband saying to his wife no, he would no longer be a husband to the wife—that he was leaving town with his girl in a day or so. Now, Eddie, would you think such evidence, if it existed, could lead to the fact that, with other proof, the wife in her rage would plan to harm bodily, even murder, her husband and his mistress?"

Tindell was up again. "I move that the entire so-called hypothetical questioning be stricken from the record and that the jury be instructed to disregard it as having no bearing on this case now being tried in any way whatsoever."

"Objection sustained. The clerk will strike the entire set of hypothetical questions from the record, and the jury will disregard them and draw no inference that any such scene ever took place."

Abe said, "For the record, Your Honor, I protest that this sort of question is permissible and has been used and accepted in court."

"You may protest, but the question is *not* permitted by *this* court."

Abe turned to his witness. "Eddie, did you witness such a scene as I have just described?"

Judge Riggs banged his gavel. "Mr. Pedlock will not continue this line of questioning, or I will remove him from the case."

Abe looked at his witness. He had done as well as he could. No matter that it was struck from the records, or they were told to disregard it, the jury now had something to mull over. Human nature couldn't be walled off by a judge's ruling. He glanced at Ed Hightower, one corner of whose mouth was curled up in an ironic expression. Abe said, "Your Honor, I was carried away. I apologize to the bench for my zeal. I am unsatisfied but finished with this witness."

"Your witness," said Judge Riggs to the defense table. The courtroom buzzed, also unsatisfied with the witness. Abe panted from his efforts.

Tindell stood up and said, "No questions."

Court Clerk Snooky Durant announced, "The witness may stand down."

Abe walked slowly back to his table, staring directly at Sarah Rodman. She gave him back the look, and Abe had a memory of the beautiful, dark, cruel eyes of a hawk that he had once found storm-battered one morning in the yard of Jacob Yuron when he lived with Jacob as a boy. Worn, tired, the hawk's eyes still held the shiny defiance that begged for no mercy. And showed no quarter in its fight with the nature of things as it bit Abe to the bone on one finger.

Judge Riggs looked up. "It's ten to twelve. Court will break now and come together at two."

Abe sat down with a spine-shaking thump, and Carl Vogel-hofer patted his shoulder. "You got more out of him than we expected."

Abe shook his head. "Stubborn little bastard."

"Loyal, Abe," said Ed Hightower. "Where did you learn that hypothetical-question trick?"

"There's a legend Abe Lincoln once pulled it in a railroad damage case for a widow who lost a leg in an accident."

"How did it turn out?"

Abe said, "In legends the hero always wins."

Ed Hightower stood up and bowed to the Reverend Romar. "I have to go to City Hall."

A man in janitor's overalls came in and placed a ladder under the courtroom clock.

CHAPTER XIX

NO GIN FOR THE
WITNESS

ABE, BEFORE LUNCH, first went visiting Maman Celie in the bailiff's room. She was in blue and yellow, cheerful in her wheel-chair, smiling and rolling her head and heavy silver earrings as Abe took her hand. "Oh, is many people here today who will hear the truth, Mr. Pedlock."

"We certainly hope so, Maman Celie."

"I run a *Houmfort,* a temple for the God Legba and the goddess Yida. Is more than the cutting of the throat of a chicken for sacrifice and the selling of ouanga charms and bags."

"How much more?"

"I am the spirit of Legba. I know. *Tout trois ont le pouvoir de vous*. That's Port-au-Prince French."

"Just tell it as it happened."

Maman Celie said, "I do, if the Lord of Gouede Oussou is willing. I sure could use a spot. Sure could."

"No."

Jim Caesar, smoking a poor gift cigar, puffed out a cloud of smoke. "She sure seems worth more than ten dollahs a day as a witness."

"Never mind that. I'm putting her on the stand as soon as court convenes. You order anything you two want for lunch by phone from the Walker House."

Jim Caesar folded the ten-dollar bill Abe handed him. "We might be able to put away a bit of food, eh, Mama?"

"And a big gin," said the large old woman.

"No gin," said Abe. "And only one beer. We must be bright and alert this afternoon. Jim, remember. No gin, or I'll put you away on the county work gang."

Back in his office Abe lay down on the worn couch and closed his eyes and kept them closed until Mary Durant brought in the lunch tray.

"Come on, A. P.," said Mary. "Bright-eyed and bush-tailed—this is no time for catnaps."

Abe groaned and sat up. "That little bastard Eddie Desmond."

"Imagine Sarah Rodman humbling herself to accept a husband with a girl."

"I thought women understood women."

Mary unfolded a napkin. "Clap yourself around this Boston clam chowder, breaded veal cutlet, apple pie and real black coffee. I bet this is the first real meal you've eaten since the trial began."

"If I eat this, go see Maman Celie doesn't get any gin."

"Promise you'll finish everything."

The chowder went down well. But Abe gave up on the cutlet and just forked the pie. He was swallowing the coffee, black and without sugar, when Ed Hightower came in and sat down facing him.

"I said, Abe, I wasn't going to interfere. But I can't let you go entirely naked into the arena."

"It was a shabby morning, Chief, and I know it."

"That kind of witness—one like Eddie Desmond—you can't help. And you got the gist of what he could have testified to the jury. But about this Maman Celie, I'm giving you advice. Get her on right after lunch, and go directly to the point. And fast. Don't shilly-shally. Ask whether she was there and what she saw. Who were they? Don't build it up or drag it out. Then turn her right over to the defense for cross-examination. If she holds up long enough and doesn't go voodoo, you've got a good chance of a conviction."

Abe pushed the pie plate away. "That's all there is to it?"

"Cut and dried, like Indian deer meat, Abe. You've come along fine so far. Don't get fancy now. Your witness can't stand much handling, so quickly does it." Ed Hightower stood up and slapped Abe on the back. "At a certain point a trial is on its own. Nobody can control it. Just keep your head and remember other stale but true mottoes."

"I'll remember."

The old man went briskly out of Abe's office, heading for his own and, Abe knew, a swig of the office bottle. Abe got up and again felt a tight band close across his chest as footsteps sounded. Rod Miller was back, and Mary Durant. Rod said, "Judge Riggs is in great pain. But sent out word he's going on with the afternoon session."

Abe scowled. "The judge take any drugs? I don't want a dreamy judge floating on the bench."

"Just a drugstore painkiller," said Mary. "Why don't you suggest we postpone court till tomorrow?"

"I can't, damn it. I can't. Maman Celie is just right now. Prime. I don't know how she'll be tomorrow. Rereading Doctor Wymer's report on her, I get scared. Is the doctor in court?"

Mary shook her head. "Not yet. I'll check again with his office."

"Yes. I may want to put him on right after Maman Celie if I have to."

The coffee tasted bitter and acid in his stomach.

Judge Riggs brushed away any suggestion of postponing any court sitting. "Get on with it, gentlemen. And stop trying to hold hands with the bench."

Abe had a larger burning sensation in his stomach and a feeling that his fingers were unsure of their touch or unable to pick up objects. He called Maman Celie as a witness. It was a grand entrance. Her son wheeled her in, and the old lady looked around with big, shiny eyes, very serious and happy. Cameras had been forbidden in the courtroom, but Rod Miller had managed to get a few into the bailiff's room just before she was called, and Maman Celie had enjoyed posing, with gestures.

The defense table stared blandly at the witness about whom there had been so much rumor. Abe looked over at Sarah Rodman. She had her usual pallor; there was no expression worth reading on her face. Abe thought he detected a throbbing of some vein in her temple, but it may have been a trick of lighting and the way her hair fell. Sarah's lips were dry, and for the first time since the trial began there was no trace of her pale red-blue lipstick on them.

Mikel and Batty Billie Hawley had settled down in their bored indifference to enjoy their large lunches; reports were they ate well. Only Devil Cavanagh seemed galvanized into a wild-eyed restless activity. The time was coming for him to perform, and Abe, as he walked to the witness, had a cold, involuntary shiver up his back as he wondered how the imported trial lawyer was going to act. He was never an easy man to work against if the newspaper reporters didn't overdo it. His reputation of courtrooms wrecked was notorious. But Judge Riggs was a stern man.

Maman Celie had stated her name and taken the oath seated in her wheelchair. Abe nodded to Jim Caesar. "Will the witness take the stand. Help your mother, Jim."

The large black man and a hefty bailiff strained to lift the big woman from the chair; slowly they got her bulk seated as a witness.

Roger Tindell wanted to say something to the court, but Devil Cavanagh, with a brutal gesture, shut him up. Abe was fully aware now that Devil Cavanagh was moving in on the defense and had taken over as he always did when the chances were desperate and other lawyers refused to take them.

The voodoo queen sat with regal bearing in the witness chair, arms folded across her massive breasts, a shape square and solid, like native carvings.

"Maman Celie, you know Sarah Rodman?"

"I does."

"Where and when did you meet her?"

"At my house in Dark Town. She come several times to visit me to get from me the charm to bring the love of the husband who had gone to another bed."

Judge Riggs said, "The witness will just answer directly the question asked by Mr. Pedlock."

Abe turned to the judge. "She was answering my question, Your Honor, as to time and place."

"Don't instruct the bench, Mr. Pedlock. Go on with your questions."

Abe turned back to Maman Celie. "Did you know any other members of her family?"

"The brothers. Mikel Hawley, he always with her when she come, very scared, to my house. The one touched with the black wing of the crow, he come once too."

"What do you mean by the black wing of the crow, Maman Celie?"

The old woman grinned and tapped her head three times.

Devil Cavanagh said, "Let it be recorded, Your Honor, that the witness questioned, by gesture, the sanity of one of the defendants."

Abe asked Maman Celie, "You mean what by that gesture?"

"He is one only the gods understand."

Judge Riggs rapped on the bench. "Mr. Pedlock, we will strike all references to William Hawley's mental state expressed by your witness. She is not, I believe, a medical authority."

"Only to her own cult."

"Get on with it."

"When did she come to you? Give us dates if you can."

"When the moon was low in March—and twice in June—at the high and low of the horned moon."

"On the night of July eighteenth, what were you doing?"

"I was out with my daughter-in-law Goldskin, on Leap Road."

"How do you date this trip to Leap Road?"

"It was the full yellah moon, first night. When the blood-weed and the manfork yarb root is right for tearin' up. I have marked it for the best picking night."

"How did you get to Leap Road?"

"Goldskin, lazy girl, she push me slow in my chair up Leap Road. I am old and I tire in the leg for long walking so I am always pushed to the road. But the sacred plants I hunt alone—I send Goldskin away—for it is the true way that the special thing is collected alone by a goddess of the—"

Abe glanced at Ed Hightower, frowning, and said quickly, "Maman Celie, your position among your own people is already well known, I'm sure, to the court and the jury."

Devil Cavanagh said, "The defense does not object to a lecture on voodoo, black magic and other mysterious rites and rituals that the state's witness is entertaining us with. How much would she charge to remove a ghost?"

The judge banged his gavel.

Abe said crisply, "Maman Celie, what happened after you got out of your wheelchair that night and sent Goldskin away?"

"I walk down toward the old boat club. There is a water spring there where the blood-weed grow thick. Then I hear voices come up from under the big tree. I start to go away for I do not want to meet nobody. There is a blast of a shotgun, and—"

Abe held up his hand. "How do you know it was a shotgun?"

"When I am girl in Haiti I go hunt after green parrots for a pepper stew with my pappy, Hugo Dumas. I know what shotgun sound like."

"Go on."

"Then quick-like *bang bang*, two shots. Not shotgun. Close together." Abe did not interrupt. The old woman, aware she held the courtroom with her story, nodded. "Close together like clap hands."

Judge Riggs had stopped rubbing his cheek with the ice bag.

"I turn around. I make up mind to go away quick. I lose path to road and then I see under the big tree in moonlight what I see."

"Take your time. Describe it all."

"I see standing up Sarah Rodman holding shotgun. And Mikel Hawley holding rifle. And laying on blanket on ground under tree are one man, one woman. Man is moving some, arms, legs, hurt like hellfire; then he too is still. Woman she drop shotgun and cover eyes with hands. I make up mind this no place for old nigger lady when white folk angry enough to shoot each other cold dog dead. They shoot me maybe if I make a sound. So I go back to road and to wheelchair. I call Goldskin, but she not around. I make up mind. I scared; I wait. Ten, fifteen minutes. Then big car pass me and in it Sarah Rodman and Batty Billie in back seat and Mikel Hawley driving like devil on tail, laughing. And I feel the red blood pouring, pouring, and I have a sense I see fresh dead on ground under tree with moon captured by branches."

Abe interrupted quickly. "Did you see either of the two guns in the car that passed you?"

"Yes. I see the guns sticking up alongside of driver Mikel Hawley on seat of car."

"Which way was the car heading?"

"Into town. Then Goldskin find me and I sass her out and say take me home, there is blood on the moon and it is no good night for hunting the sacred yarbs. I make up mind I tell her nothing. Goldskin stupid girl with flapping mouth, and Jim Caesar my son fool to marry anyone so young. But man must have woman, and he no listen."

Abe looked at Devil Cavanagh, who stared back at him with a smile on his lips bracketed into contemptuous corners. Abe stepped aside. "Maman Celie, can you point out and identify here in court anyone you saw that night at the old boat club?"

Devil Cavanagh made no move to object.

The old woman nodded at Abe and pointed a heavy hand ending in surprisingly small fingers with long nails. Her bracelets and the strings of coral-red beads around the wrist rattled. "I see at that table over there Sarah Rodman, and next to her Mikel Hawley, and next Batty Billie Hawley."

Abe said, "His proper legal name is William Hawley."

"Whatever the name. These three I saw standing over the dead bodies."

"Positive in your identification, Maman Celie? You are under oath."

"As sure as the blood-weed grows they were there with guns, and Maman Celie see it."

The court was quiet; the room seemed to inhale and exhale in time. The jury was leaning well forward.

Abe turned to look at Ed Hightower. He wanted to go on. Ask more details of the witness. But Ed gave him a slow shake of the head. He had made his points. He had his eyewitness testimony on record. Don't push his luck. He could always re-examine if he had to. Maman Celie had testified well. It was the time for a gesture and to get Maman Celie off the stand.

"Your Honor, the state has made its case, produced its eyewitness to the crimes, identified the people who murdered George Rodman and Helen Nash." Abe half turned to the defense table. Sarah Rodman had her mouth open slightly, and Mikel Hawley was rubbing his mustache as if it itched. Batty Billie appeared unmoved. "Your witness," Abe said quietly.

Devil Cavanagh leaped to his feet and went quickly up to the witness, moving on a trot. This was the real man, the skilled courtroom actor, the dangerous, slum-bred shyster who never failed to exploit some tricky detail for the good of the defense, and who had a sense of the dramatic that impressed jurors, if not judges.

"Now, Maman Celie—" his voice was loud but kind—"the defense is not going to question anything you said here today because it can all be proved or disproved by you by just one simple thing. If what I am about to ask you is so, then you saw something at that club. But if what I am about to ask is not true, then everything you have said is a lie, a big lie, a dangerous lie, and the whole case against my clients is worthless, foul, and a falsehood, and an insult to the intelligence of this court."

Abe turned around. "Mr. Cavanagh, you're here to ask questions, not dictate bad detective novels."

"Sit down, Mr. Pedlock. This is my court *now,* and my witness." Devil Cavanagh shouted, "*Maman Celie, stand up.* Maman Celie, you walk toward me. You prove to this court you can walk, prove to this court you did walk that night, walked when alone in that wheelchair on Leap Road! Come on, walk or be proved a perjuring crazy voodoo liar. A liar!" Cavanagh was screaming. He took several steps backward and waited. The courtroom was in a polar silence but for the tick of the wall clock as an electric impulse moved one hand forward slightly into time.

Maman Celie rolled her head as if it hung by a thin thread and gripped the arms of the witness chair. Her eyes opened very wide. Foam appeared in one corner of her mouth. The judge held tight the handleless gavel in his hand, raised it over the bench but did not knock. Abe had frozen in position near the state's table, and the band across his chest was so tight that he was aware he was struggling to breathe. (It's clear now that Devil Cavanagh, always the gambler, is betting everything on one fast toss. One big toss of the dice. If he knows as much as Doctor Wymer in his report, he knows a lot.)

"Come on, Maman Celie!" Devil Cavanagh took two more steps backward. He was now ten feet from the witness stand, and the old woman hadn't moved. "Walk just these few steps!"

Maman Celie fought air into her lungs and shrilled, "I will it. I will it. I do anything I will. I am the Maman Celie, the one who can and will. I walk!"

"Then stand, witch or woman; get up, stand! Walk!"

Abe wanted to protest and began silently to phrase some objection. But Ed Hightower was at his side and a lean hand gripped Abe's elbow. "Stay out of this. It's his act now."

Maman Celie strained. Maman Celie rolled her head again, looked down at her big, black, shaking son, up at the judge, and then with a last lost effort she fell back in the chair without being able to move her feet.

Devil Cavanagh was addressing the bench. "Your Honor, the defense demands that this court trial be terminated, stopped now, the jury dismissed and a direct verdict of insufficient evidence be handed down from the bench and the defendants released as free citizens."

Judge Riggs hammered his gavel hard over the rising noise of the court. "This court is still in session and I demand silence and orderly conduct. Bailiff, quiet them down or clear the courtroom." Judge Riggs looked down at Devil Cavanagh. "As I stated before, this trial will go to the jury." The judge turned to Abe. "You have concluded the case for the state, I believe?"

Abe looked around the court for Doctor Wymer. He felt Ed's grip pressing his arm hard. "The state may have medical rebuttal later."

Devil Cavanagh didn't wait for Abe to say anything more. He modified his voice to a rasping, direct crow of victory. "Your Honor, the defense was prepared to bring in many respectable witnesses to show that none of the accused could have or would have committed such a crime. That their interests and backgrounds and character were such that the very idea is ridiculous, and also to produce evidence that the state had no case at all. However, with this last so-called witness it should be clear just how lacking in any real evidence the state's case is. So the defense moves that the case go directly to the jury without calling any witnesses or presenting its now not needed evidence."

Roger Tindell was struggling to his feet to protest Devil Cavanagh's sudden move. Sarah Rodman with a powerful yank pulled him back into his chair. Devil Cavanagh was addressing the jury. "We rest the defense's case because of what you have just seen— or not seen—in this courtroom."

There was a great, growing uproar in the courtroom. Reporters were leaving on the run to file copy. The bailiffs were pushing at people, and the jury had become animated and was involved in head-nodding opinions. Judge Riggs banged for order. Maman Celie was being lifted down by her son and a bailiff, down into her wheelchair. Her eyes were closed and she was muttering something that was not clear or understandable. "*Le bon temps —temps—viendra, viendra.*"

Jim Caesar wheeled his mother toward the bailiff's room. Abe, leaning back against the table, watched her chair go out through the double doors. He sat down with a thump. Rod Miller and Ed Hightower and Mary Durant all talked to him, but Abe never remembered a word of what they said. He turned and looked at the court wall clock.

"I was never any good at waiting out a verdict." Abe scowled at the ceiling and ground his back deeper into the office sofa.

Mary looked down at him and handed him a glass cloudy with frost. He took a deep drink, tasting lemon and powdered sugar. "Thanks."

Mary looked at her wristwatch. "They've been out eight hours. Going to be locked up for the night."

"That's bad. Somebody there is throwing a stiff resistance to popular answers."

"For or against us?"

"Any gossip? Anything at all?"

"Nothing. One of the lady jury members thinks she's pregnant. But she doesn't blame anyone on the jury."

Abe grinned and handed Mary the empty glass. "Some New York reporter invented *that*."

"The reporters want to see you."

"Keep them away. I gave them a statement. The state rests and accepts what the jury brings in. Justice will be done."

"You worded it better than that."

There was the sound of running feet and the bang of a door. Abe looked at Mary, who had picked up the phone. He waited, taut—goddamn it, as jumpy as a newly made lawyer with his first auto-fender case. Mary hung up the phone. "Chief Smith's boys just arrested a pickpocket who was working the crowd. Nothing from the jury tonight."

"Turn out the light. I'll just nap here."

In the bright white sunlight the courthouse grounds printed themselves on Abe's eyeballs. He needed a shave. Two days now since he had thought of how he looked. He shaved slowly in his office; the feel of the razor blade was good on his skin. What the hell was the matter with the jury? Couldn't they make up their minds to a simple yes or no? It was no picnic being on a jury in this weather. You'd think they'd want to go home and take their shoes off.

Ed Hightower came in and said, "No, no verdict yet."

Abe powdered his jowls and sat down. "I woke up with the shakes last night. Teeth knocking together. Had it bad."

"They have to come in sometime."

"The reporters seem to think we should keep it alive with fancy statements."

Mary was suddenly at their elbows. "Jury coming in. Judge Riggs calling court for the verdict."

Abe felt the shaking start in his ribs as he got up quickly.

There was an undersea buzzing in the courtroom. And even with the strong sun, someone had turned on the overhead lights.

Judge Riggs looked pale and laundered as he turned to the jury, and his voice had a rasp to it. "You have reached a verdict?"

Ed Hightower whispered to Abe, "Judge smells something. He's angry at the jury."

The foreman, who had the pert thin mouth of a churchgoing man with a temper, said, "Well, Your Honor, we've been talking and counting and—"

"Have you reached a verdict?"

"We have not. We can't. We seem to—"

Judge Riggs banged on his desk top. "Do I understand that this jury has been unable after all this time to reach a verdict?"

Abe looked over at Sarah. She had folded her arms and was staring directly ahead of her, but her eyes were not in focus. Abe tried to think of what images, thoughts, emotions, ran through her body, through her head. And he failed.

"This jury, Your Honor, is locked tight, so there isn't any chance of any verdict. One way or the other."

Devil was turning an expressionless face—only the curl of the mouth seemed pleased—to the bench. "It would appear, Your Honor, that—"

"*This* is the bench's business," said the judge. He looked sadly over the heads of the reporters, who were animated and ready, and he sucked the space where the offending tooth had been. Casual and tired, but with dignity, he spoke in a voice that carried only past the first row. "The clerk will record that the jury having after a long period of time been unable to arrive at a verdict, the court has decided this a mistrial. Stop those people running from the courtroom!"

(Why doesn't it hurt or mean anything yet? Will the pain be very great when it comes? So Roger wants to shake hands.)

"Abe, there's a corny old saying."

"You can't win them all."

(There goes Sarah, eyes right in front, not a change in the color of her skin, not a shake; just all inside, hidden away, if there is something to hide now. Walking, on those long, wonderful legs, between her lawyers and the two cops who are pushing back the reporters.)

"Mrs. Rodman, just a short statement."

"What do you plan to do now?"

"What will you do until the new trial starts?"

(The double doors flapping, smell of dust and dry heat and the grass outside. Sarah Rodman is gone, her two brothers gone, her lawyers—Roger neat in victory, Devil happy as a mick at a fancy wake. And all the little clerks and free-loaders. Mary is crying. I didn't expect that.)

"Come on, Mary. Get the papers back in the office."

"You have to hand it to her the way she took it."

"That's class." (Was my tone mocking enough?) Ed Hightower came back from talking to Judge Riggs, who had popped out of sight with a swish of black robe. "He'll hear pleas for a new trial tomorrow morning. I want to talk to you about that, Abe."

(Why is Ed giving me that Ivy League look suddenly? He's even fully sober. *The Hawleytown Home News* must have had three editions ready. The newsboys are already yelling, "Hawley murder case ends in mistrial.")

Ed's back moved quickly away in space and through the double doors.

BOOK FOUR

DAYS OF
THE WEEK

CHAPTER XX

AMONG THE RUINS

FOR THREE DAYS there had been rains driving in from Hatteras, great sheets of green water falling into the summer-dried town and the surrounding Eastern Shore. Gullies had run red with eroded clay, and the back roads of crushed oyster shells were still unpassable. But it was cool again as the fields drained and the sun was out like a shout. Every object had a washed-out faded-denim look, even the clouds in the tightly stretched blue sky. Abe had driven into Hawleytown from the farm, Fran's sister's place, Ormsbee Farm, where they were staying for a few days after the trial. It was, Abe suspected, a foolish errand that had brought him back to town. But the compulsion had come and he had given way to it. Abe had slept sixteen hours their first night at Ormsbee Farm, and ten hours the next night in the old, soft mahogany four-poster. The poison of fatigue and frustration was gone from Abe. Only a kind of indifferent numbness remained, and he could not shake it loose; it could no more be fought than one fought cigar smoke. He turned the muddy car onto a street of well-taken-care-of trees and sparsely set, wide, solid houses of the more expensive era of several generations ago. (I delivered papers here when I was twelve, dropping with a toss of a wrist *The Hawleytown Home News* on bluegrass lawns that still had iron deer and often a garden with a shrill peacock in it. I helped Jacob Yuron set up his old old-fashioned box camera at society weddings in lots of these houses and held the flash powder gadget and later plugged in floodlights. It's all now further away in time to me than Roman history.)

Standish Avenue was wide and smoothly paved with imported red Belgian blocks. Huge elm and maple and oak trees were making amphitheatral glens on street corners. The lawns were closely clipped.

Not all of Standish Avenue was considered exclusive. It ended at the town limits in fields of truck gardens, a place of bean poles and tomato plants and the grubby little shacks of the vegetable gardeners. There were many outcroppings of reddish schistose rock. It was in this section of Standish Avenue that Doctor Sidney Wymer lived his life, with his personal devils, behind slatted shutters.

Abe's car ran off the smooth Standish Avenue paving and went by a red clay road to the brow of the gully-cut hill. A house stood there, a huge, fretwood-trimmed, turreted, towered house of the General Grant period. Melancholy with ivy, but proud. It was of brownstone, with bays, set in a huge neglected garden where old-fashioned flowers grew wild and bluebottle flies zoomed. There were nux vomica in tubs, and goldenrod. There was even a small faded darky (rusting badly) holding out a hitching ring and standing on a stone base labeled, in a rolling script, *Wymer*.

Abe went up the brownstone steps and pulled the brass bell handle. The shades were all down, and unkempt pots of flowers stood on the window sills, scattering petals down on old weather-washed bricks.

The door opened, and a Negro he didn't know stood there blinking at the sunlight, smelling of formaldehyde and soap. Abe followed the Negro down a hall and into a mid-Victorian living room. It was a shock to Abe to see a room like this in the town: wax candles in ormolu candelabra, rosewood buhl; high-backed black-walnut sofas; gilt and old-rose wallpaper and, in heavy frames, the departed Wymers. They were men with long chins, and many had that wild stare that the heir of all this also had about him. And some seemed dull and fat from existences that had grown rhythmical and serene. A family, Abe felt, was fine to have—in any condition.

The Negro motioned Abe to the stairs covered with green carpeting. Upstairs there were rubber plants in brass pots and more pictures, mostly landscapes. There were books, old tomes in shattered calf, with fine bindings, sets and sets, and odd volumes in strange tongues about queer subjects. The roof leaked, as some streaked and soggy books showed. Caffieri moldings hung loose from the walls.

In the huge front bedroom there was a big bed with rams' heads carved on the posts. Doctor Sidney Wymer lay in the middle of this bed watching a few stray sun rays creep around the heavy black blinds that were all pulled way down. Cushny's *Pharmacology* lay open on the night table.

Abe entered, and Sidney turned his head. It was a head more fleshless than ever; the skin was badly cured into a dirty-white leather and stretched over the skull by an unskilled taxidermist of little birds and squirrels. There seemed to be no body at all under the sheets.

The large eyes watched Abe, and the slack mouth opened slightly from between a little smile.

"I haven't been well. Haven't been seeing people. But you phoned during one of my more lucid periods."

"Been working too hard, Sidney?"

"No. Drinking too hard. Care for a drink of whisky? Poussin —two brandies."

The Negro called Poussin shrugged his shoulders and poured small glasses of pale amber liquor.

"Staying for a while, Abe?"

"No. We're at the farm for a few days."

Poussin went out. Abe sat back in an old-fashioned rocker, and Wymer finished his drink and looked at the strontium-yellow ceiling. Outside, far off, there was the *hock hock* of a hoe hitting the earth in some garden patch, and the buzz of insects in the unkept flower beds in front of the house.

Wymer, breathing loudly, made a painful mouth and licked his lips. "What do you plan to do now, Abe?"

The runners on the rocker creaked as Abe leaned forward toward the bed.

"Are you going in for mind-reading on the side?"

"I never tell my methods. That is one of the reasons for my success in *homo stultus*. When you entered that door, I knew at once you had kicked over the traces and were here in humiliation and anger. The tilt of your jaw, the slope of your shoulders, the way—oh, hell, fill my glass. What are you planning to do?"

"No plans," said Abe. "No plans at all."

"Well, you got a mistrial. That's better than a not-guilty verdict on your record."

"I felt, after the jury was out nine hours, it would be not guilty."

"Abe, are they going to be tried again? A new trial?"

"That's up to Ed Hightower. They've been freed on bail and are all home now, with the blinds drawn."

The man on the bed stared at Abe. "Forget it. And if there is another trial, take my advice. Let Hightower, that raunchy old owl, do his own dirty work. Don't you take it on."

"I doubt that I'd get it anyway, Sidney. I came here to ask you about something else besides your health."

"Sure. If it's money, maybe I can help. Or a letter of introduction to somebody in Washington? New York?"

"No, Sidney. Why didn't she walk?"

"Oh, Maman Celie?" He said it slowly, frowning.

"Yes. Why didn't she walk when Devil Cavanagh asked her

to in court? Even a few steps. If she had just gotten up. Why didn't she?"

"Abe, she couldn't."

"But she walked in *her* place. We saw her."

The man on the bed nodded. "Sure she did then. But by the time you put her on the stand she couldn't any more."

"Why not? Why didn't you tell me she couldn't?"

"I didn't examine her the day of the trial. I was—well, here, sobering up, more or less. I let you down, Abe. I confess it. But my friends must get used to that. I should have examined her and warned you."

"What happened to her?"

"A series of small strokes. Most likely in her sleep. She wasn't aware of them, probably. But it's small strokes that often add up. A little blood vessel in the brain ruptures, the patient wakes up feeling hazy, has difficulty moving his fingers, his hand, his leg. But he goes on living as if nothing has happened. It can take days or even years sometimes before it turns critical. That's what happened to Maman Celie. She had a series of strokes, I'm sure, the night before the trial."

"Would the jury have believed her if she'd walked?"

"That we'll never know, Abe. Don't let the office use her as a witness if there is another trial."

"Bad as that, Sidney?"

"I examined her yesterday. Left side and arm completely paralyzed; can't lift her arm. The mouth is dropped down lopsided. And what I saw when I looked into her eyes I didn't like. Speech is thick; isn't going to last much longer. Maybe the mind will soon black out. I hope so, before there's a big stroke that will leave her just a dumb bundle of vegetable unconsciousness. I see I depress you, Abe. Let's have another drink."

"Don't you have to be at the hospital?"

"I've a bright young assistant now who does all the dirty work. I save myself for the seventh inning, the operation. Don't look so horrified, Abe. I'm the only surgeon within twenty miles who knows there has been any medical progress made since Lister. Pig gelders is what most of the local Hawleytown talent is.

It's a fine town, isn't it, Abe, and we love it. That's why we have
to go on getting out of bed in the morning, the few of us who have
anything on the ball. You're the only lawyer in town who can't be
bought and who can do more than get a real-estate lease drawn
or defend a chicken thief. I don't mean the others are all crooked,
but they can be bought by social position, women, drink, political office. But not you—or am I wrong? That's why you have to
feel you didn't do so badly. If you pull tracks out of here now,
who is going to defend the law? Young bucks who are brown-nos-
ing for big corporations or sharp boys like Carl who are cynical
and keep their eye on the pot? Or handsome old men like Ed
Hightower or ugly ones like Judge Riggs who haven't the jism
any more to take it day after day?"

"Can I do anything for you, Sidney?"

"Don't want to talk about it? All right. How's Fran?"

"Not too happy, I suspect. It's been a real setback for her. The
Ormsbees were always stiff-necked, and they didn't care for me
in the family. Fran's unhappy. Don't think it's just because we
got blackballed for the country club. Fran isn't petty when you
understand her. You have to see it from her viewpoint."

"You don't mean it can wreck your marriage?"

Abe hunted for a stogie and found he didn't have any. "I
didn't say that. No, I guess. Hell, I don't know. Women aren't
fancy, noble creatures the way they are in novels. They're human, angry, aware of how hard it is to make a place, a living
after a wrong start. And her sister isn't making it too easy for
Fran to see me at my best."

"Pull up the shades. I feel garrulous."

Abe pulled up the shades. Sunlight came walloping in, showing new details of the room. Books, bottles, clothes and string-
tied piles of magazines filled the corners. Dust, in dignified
lethargy, was everywhere.

Doctor Sidney shifted himself to a new position. "Maybe
you're right, Abe. Get away from here. I have an uncle in Los
Angeles who controls some big firm, popular trash for the half-
wits that live in the sun out there. Lots of legal jabberwocky out

there for a lawyer. Oil, lumber, fish, movies, TV. I'll talk to him about you on the phone tonight."

"No. Not California. No seasons there, and no grace or style. Just that big dumb ocean. And from what I've seen of the natives when they come east, they're all like that big prize fruit you see at fairs—huge, pretty *and* tasteless and without flavor, as if forced to grow regardless of their own wishes. Hawleytown is my home. Maybe I'll get some setup in Baltimore and go in every day on the ferry."

Sidney Wymer looked around. "Do you see my socks any-place?"

Abe took the socks from the floor and handed them to him. "Could Maman Celie have walked the night she says she saw the murderers standing over the bodies of George Rodman and Helen Nash?"

"Yes. The old girl was strong and has amazing will power."

"And *if* she walked, she saw it. She wasn't affected? I mean, her mind? Nothing like visions or drug dreams?"

"No, Abe. She either saw it or she was lying. She wasn't soft in the head in any way to have hallucinations. And forget the case. Every hero soon becomes a bore. Hand me my pants."

Abe did, and left.

Abe started back to the farm by the river road, but instead of driving south to the old Brook bridge, he drove across the Chichester River by the town bridge that led to Barraclough Manor. He didn't know why he wanted to drive past the old Hawley place, but something inside him brought him there. He was aware of the fundamental misleading of himself when he avoided the results of his own actions. Sarah Rodman and her brothers Mikel and Batty Billie had been released on bail. Eli Chaucer, the old family lawyer, had found a judge to sign the writ of release, and a bonding company from Baltimore had arranged everything quickly.

Abe, blinking in the freshly washed day, looked up at the bulk of the Hawley house set in its emerald gardens and terraces over the river. (They're home now, and I wonder what they're doing? Did I come past the house hoping to see Sarah Rodman walking in one of the gardens? No, she'd be inside, dressed in a patterned, colorful dress, I suppose, after all the days in plain dark clothes in the courtroom. She's smoking too many cigarettes, staring out of the tall French windows of some upper room. Staring at what? I don't know, and I don't know what her retained memories, full of implications, can be. She's changed a lot, and yet, underneath, has she changed at all from the dignity and despair of the young girl I touched for moments? And how do I feel, who tried to convict her of murder? The heart has a secret memory—corny as it sounds—and I was, when very young, in love with her.)

Abe's car passed the main house, and the gates—locked—and the road led back closer to the river. The big red brick shapes of the old Hawley carriage house—now a garage—and the wooden dog runs came into view. Abe slowed for the steep climb down and the sharp curve in the road. (I'll never understand Sarah Hawley. I guess she found money and social position a short reprieve from reality and then a horror—and the hopes of her marriage a kind of slow torture that ended with two dead people under a tree. If she did murder, or aided in it, should she be punished any more? "There is a fundamental duplicity about the law of any peaceful society," Ed Hightower used to say. Yet to try the Hawleys again in a court of law for murder is something the town must do or the whole system could become vulnerable to dissonances and disorders. However, that's not my problem any more. I'm out of it. Some other young deputy D.A., full of prunes and principles, will indict Sarah Rodman and her brothers for a new trial. I'll be across the bay looking for a job, or opening a crummy law office in East Baltimore, among the stockyard workers and the clam dredgers.)

Abe stepped savagely on the gas pedal as the car reached the bottom of the drop, and the road ahead went on straight and level between the river elms on one side and the berry patches and sumac leaves turning red in spots on the other. (Mikel Hawley, chin up, freshly shaved, is drinking the family Scotch or bourbon, just a little too much of it. And if there are glass cases of hunting rifles up there, he isn't opening them. A drink in his big fist, an H. Upmann cigar, long as they come, in his hard-muscled mouth, not talking much, aware, like most hunters, I suppose, that luck is the one reasonable divinity one can believe in; *if* Maman Celie had taken just a few steps his sporting stalk with the law might see Mikel now in a stinking jail cell under sentence of death. And I would have beaten the Hawleys, the best people in town—me, an outsider, who doesn't really belong. But the outsider never wins. My kids will be insiders, and *their* kids. But let them stay free of the Hawleys.)

Abe frowned; he wanted to get back to the farm as quickly as he could. Brooding like this didn't help much, and his child-hood memory of the sacred books insisted that one must forgive (but that was not to forget). And his own personal life needed attention. (What was Batty Billie doing back there in the big house already a monument out of another era? If they've let him, he's out in the gardens most likely with a slingshot, trying for the sparrows, a blank façade with empty baby-blue eyes. One of the few people I know who is not a hypocrite in his pleasures.)

There was a cool wind, and the river road of crushed oyster shells over the sharp smell of tar was smooth. As Abe looked past the abstract patterns of the windshield's shine, the enigma of Sarah Rodman rode with him.

CHAPTER XXI

THE SILVER MORNING

FRAN AND HER SISTER had been making apple butter, and now hundreds of glass jars stood on their heads on the back steps cooling, and in the morning they would tighten them and store them in the vast earth cellar with its rough rock walls under the house. Deedee and Davey ate their supper, sleepy and swollen with weariness from playing all day on the farm. Fran's sister drove away in her old car to attend a cattle auction for the next two days. The hired man in the bunkhouse under the big elm would be gone the next morning for his day in town. The sun set slowly; the twilight came with a flutter of moths. Abe and Fran sat smoking on the screened porch, silently watching the fireflies signal each other in the small old-fashioned garden and along damp earth walks. Later the crickets and tree frogs took over. Tossing away stubs of tobacco, Abe and Fran went up to bed drugged by the mood of the night and the unreality of the time they had been through during the trial. Neither had spoken much of what was inside them, and it seemed no time now, here on the old farm, to express resentments, angers and disappointments. They slept in the front upstairs room papered in little Victorian flowers, and the four-poster with its cord springs and heavy mattress was restful. They fell asleep at once.

Abe had grown used to the seasons changing at the farm. Another one was spinning into place. It was one of those silver mornings when he got up, as the sun came up without effort and shone brightly without much force. The mad little red squirrel had climbed up the boll of the big elm tree overhanging the farm and complained of his wife to the big sleeping chimney. Later a toad had come out of the vegetable patch, his warted skin wet with beads of dew, gorged with insects and grubs. Like a wet handful of mud, he had deliberately plopped himself across the terrace and disappeared into the tall ferns where Fran's sister was trying to raise some Frau Karl Druschi roses. The diaphanous fronds tickled the toad's belly.

The big bees were already out, buzzing around the cornflowers and Sweet Williams, and somewhere men were burning brush, and a blue haze came up across the lake bringing that smell of wood ash and washed air that lifts one's nose to the hills.

The toad went on his way, plopping himself along the garden path, past the tubs of poinsettia plants, picking up a dividend in the way of a gnat as he went.

Abe could hear Deedee and Davey in the hayfield on the next farm, where there were spotted puppies to play with. The children appeared only at meals. Tanned, soiled and happy, they swallowed food and rushed off again to be with the farm children and do whatever children do on a farm. Abe wondered what they actually did; he had never spent time in the country as a child.

Fran was in the barn seeing the hired hand milking the herd before he left for the day. When Abe came back from his early-morning dip in the stream, he almost stepped on the toad, but neither molested the other, and each went on his way. Both thought it a fine day, although the toad, Abe suspected, was not conscious of his thought processes. Smiling benignly, the toad speared a bluebottle fly.

Abe pulled his terry-cloth robe tight around himself and reached for his first stogie. He set fire to the rough end and sat down on the porch chair deliberately to think.

Behind that door, in a bed that still carried the impression of his own body, had slept the only woman who mattered to him. Fran. Generous impulses throbbed in him when he thought of her. Abe puffed at his stogie and watched an ant climb over his big toe. He was a small, shiny black ant and he was rolling home a stolen insect egg twice his size. (The nerve of these mites; no sense of the inevitable.) Overhead, the angry red squirrel still chattered away on his limb, frisking out his plumed tail in jerks of temper.

What did he and Fran want? He wanted Fran; for always now, all the time, forever, with no fluctuations of the emotions. And what else? The kids, of course—and something to do with his life. What was that poem he used to read to Fran?

> Lying awake between the strokes of night
> I saw my love lean over my sad bed
> Pale as the duskiest lily's leaf or head
> Smooth-skinned and dark
> With bared throat made to bite. . . .

(Swinburne never had kids, you can bet on that. No doubt about it, I am a child-lover, a baby-pincher, a goo-gooer, a lifter of milk-colored babies, a gurgler to sour-smelling, toothless infants. They should have more children. Sons, daughters were something to have in this world of shifting values, of confused, discordant ideas, to pamper, spoil, educate and bring into adulthood, to annoy in old age, to leave behind one.)

Abe stood up and tied the bathrobe belt tight around himself. He saw what he would have to do. There was a painful ache in his jaw as he gritted his teeth together. His smoldering exasperation against himself grew. He would go down to Baltimore tomorrow and see what was available there for a lawyer. He gritted his teeth again.

"Well! You swallow a frog this morning?"

He turned at the sound of the voice and saw Fran in the doorway. She had returned from the barn and was now pulling a white rubber cap over her taffy-colored hair. Her simple flared blue robe was open, revealing her slim, tanned legs, hard and shapely, ending in firm, square-nailed little toes gripping a pair of red wooden clogs. Her solid breasts were flexed high as she snapped the chin band of the bathing cap closed under one pink ear. There was a bright efficiency, an awareness of life, about her.

"You look, Abe, as if you were ready to murder someone and just waiting for an excuse to plunge the dagger in."

He tried to smile, but he shivered. The sub-something, Wymer called it, with his Freudian nonsense. Was there an infinitesimally small idea in him of how much he feared losing Fran? She showed him the pink tip of her tongue. Grabbing a towel, she kissed him quickly, firmly, warmly, and went running down toward the stream. He watched the girl run. She was built to have children. The wide, beautiful, full flare of her hips, the slender torso.

Now to cook breakfast since they were alone. He was proud of his cooking; loved it with an old maid's fussiness, cherished the idea that he had the genius of a great chef in him. But all Fran would ever let him cook was breakfast. Slim chance to show his talent with food at that, but he would do his best. (Women have a natural perversity about men cooks.) Griddle cakes, pork sausages and coffee what is coffee.

He turned and waved. Far out, Fran was swimming with powerful strokes, cutting the deep indigo blue of the pool the dammed-up stream made under the willows, swimming with strong, regular, expert sweeps. She turned over on her back and floated, her limbs stirring slowly, just keeping herself afloat among some lily pads. He thought of his college course in English Lit., of Ophelia dead in the water for love of Hamlet.

> Too much of water hast thou, poor Ophelia,
> And therefore I forbid my tears; but yet
> It is our trick: nature her custom holds,
> Let shame say what it will; when these are gone
> The woman will be out . . .

Abe scowled. This was no time for the gloomy verse. It was time for breakfast. Sad poems lead to physical and emotional indigestion. And that woman was Fran, not poor Ophelia. The breeze had changed and blew from the cut fields. The farm crops had been cut—the late timothy, the rye and the heavy-headed red wheat stacked to dry in the sun. He could smell the sun-sweet odor of the curing forage. Far out, Fran still floated, her white rubber cap like another lily.

He would try a fondue. Fran had liked that mess of cheese, eggs and butter when they had been camping on their honeymoon, really together for the first time. He could cook as good a fondue as the best of them.

Fran looked across the breakfast table set on the terrace. She had very bravely eaten most of the fondue and was now finishing her second cup of coffee.

"Want to talk, Abe?"

"I think we better. We've been avoiding it."

"What are you afraid of?"

He refilled his own coffee cup, his face was expressionless, as if he were preparing in court to question a doubtful witness. "Of only one thing. Are you going to leave me, Fran? Losing you is what I'm afraid of. I don't mean just you taking the kids and going. Of losing you even while we're together. Tell me, Fran, how is it between us?"

She frowned. "I'm a determined girl. I don't give up easy. I didn't marry you because you'd be district attorney or a member of the country club. Or get me a big house in Barraclough Manor."

"That's good, because right now we haven't got any of those."

"You've lost faith in yourself since the trial, Abe, and you were so sure of yourself all during the hell of the trial. You've let yourself down."

"I'm scared of what it's done to us."

"It's not your fault. I showed you how much a place in the social scene meant to me, how much I wanted that goddamn country club full of high-nosed snobs. And now, Abe darling, you've begun to doubt me."

"I never said that—just that way."

"You don't like my sister and she doesn't like you. You know what she said last night before she left?"

"I can guess."

" 'Fran,' she said to me, 'you be good to Abe. He needs you now, and that's what a wife is for—marriage is for. He's been through a dreadful time and he's getting sentimental about himself. All hard men do. I know because before William died I could always tell what was the matter with him by the way he got sentimental over himself. Abe's a very good man; don't let him destroy himself with bad sentiment.' That's what she told me, Abe."

Abe looked at Fran and said nothing. She held up her cup. "Do you have half a cup more?"

He poured with a steady grip on the old Dutch coffeepot.

"She's a tough biddy, your sister."

"That's better."

"And she's so right. I'm carrying my personal portable wailing wall."

"Very good coffee," Fran said with solemnity.

Abe sank back in the chair and looked at the sky. Little cumulus clouds dotted the pink sky, moved in the direction of huge white nimbus masses shaped, it seemed to him, like little clowns.

"It's a good day for fishing."

Fran came around the table and sank down onto his lap. She rubbed her face against his cheek.

"Fran." He looked at her. He felt something he couldn't put into words; there was no eloquence at such a time in him. He knew because he had tried. Time and again. He knew he was— out of court—one of those silent men who stumble over their tongues when they try to express certain emotions. "Fran, we're not leaving the town. I'm going over to Baltimore tomorrow to see some people who talked very big about wanting somebody in the firm like me, when I couldn't take a job. We'll see now."

The hay cutter on the next farm began to click and rattle.

CHAPTER XXII

THE DUTY TO DOUBT

LATE IN THE AFTERNOON of the next day a small and battered car came past the fieldstone posts of Ormsbee Farm.

Ed Hightower, in sport shirt and hunting jacket, got out. "I don't live far from here. Just eighteen miles down the road. Nice farm, Abe."

"My sister-in-law runs it. Her husband died ten years ago. Of course, it doesn't really pay its way."

"No farm does, unless you run it like a factory and don't try to love it or live on it. Abe, I came over because you worry me."

They walked down toward the stream.

"You mean, will I want to be prosecutor when the Hawleys go on trial again?"

Ed rubbed his chin, as if to test how long his white bristles were. "No. It's been decided there isn't much sense in another trial. We haven't any new evidence, and Maman Celie's condition is so bad now she'll never be accepted in court. Maybe she shouldn't have been the first time."

They sat down on an old log bench. Abe shrugged his shoulders. "You're still the D.A., Chief."

"Now, Abe, don't get bitter. Our job is to see justice in process, even if most people think the D.A. wants only convictions. This time the Hawleys had the benefit of our court's ideas of what is evidence; next time it will—or should—work as well for somebody who hasn't their power and money. Don't you see, Abe, they were entitled to that doubt. It was your duty, of course, to apply the law and the duty of the defense to fight you, and for the judge and jury to work it out their way. You'll find out yourself more of what it is like when you're the District Attorney."

Abe shook his head. "Not a chance now. And anyway—"

Ed Hightower broke off a section of mint leaf growing at his feet and chewed a bit of it thoughtfully. "Both Jake Barton and Ed Higgins spoke to me about you for the job. They want you to run, and that means being elected, with the party behind you."

"Why this sudden change of mind about me?"

"A smart political machine wants the best young man. It isn't as if you can order by the dozen bright, honest young men who know the facts of life. You can't order them from a catalogue."

"Give me one good reason why I should take the job now. Besides the facts I need the money and that the prestige is important. I put all that aside when I thought it over."

Ed Hightower chewed slowly and spit at a passing hen. "It's bigger than you know, and older—this matter of dishing out law. Wait till you're as gray as I am and discover that your limits of effort are set by time. Stingy time, too. Then there is another limit, a limit set by man's mind. Between these limits we run, flogged by passion and reason. Those of us who know this and yet can still bear the responsibility of our actions, we're marked men. You're marked that way, Abe."

"Is that enough? To know one is marked?"

"It's all the angle of vision, Abe. To you I'm a poor excuse for a D.A. But I've kept the office fairly honest, and the law gets work done here with less injustice than in most places. I'm old now and I'm mellow with drink and all I want is to last a few more years on a judge's bench, brooding a bit on the meaning that lies in the simultaneous occurrences of ordinary and special things. Take the Rodman-Nash-Hawley case. Even there no action took place in isolation. Look how it dragged in the town, and the social pattern and the political parties, religion and even the taboos and the fetishes called the color line and the country club. Yet, Abe, you acted as if you were free, knowing full well that the skeins and the cords that are a social unit called a town, a community, had you a prisoner too."

"A hell of a lot of good it did me."

Ed smiled. "You learned the discrepancy between the ideal and the actual, didn't you? That's a big lump to swallow with a small mouth. And I saw a new skin growing on you in that courtroom."

Abe nodded. "I was finding out it isn't fun being a public Jeremiah in a courtroom. It's living people you play with."

"You're warmer to humanity than I ever was. That was my failing, Abe. A cold pride is a vestigial piece of antiquity called Anglo-Saxon law in court. I fought my coldness. And the bottle helped. Mellowed me, you know. But it was a long time before I learned not to misinterpret the nature of my contemporaries. By then it was too late. I was old. And lazy. And always a mite cynical."

"No, Chief, you weren't that cynical."

"The erosion of privacy exposed for judgment makes you sardonic; give me that much. What we see of society at law, with its seams open, isn't always good for our stomachs. I lacked a lot for the full, fat life."

"You're a happily married man."

Ed Hightower smiled. "No sanctuary for the individual but

in the marriage bed, eh? Maybe you're right. Yes, it's been a good, simple marriage. An old-fashioned one maybe. We were both faithful. No mixture of infidelity and bridge in a fashionable suburb. But I didn't come out here to unpack and compare emotions. I came to tell you I wasn't ashamed of you in court. I was proud of you, even when you sometimes disregarded my advice. It was bad advice in some ways. But I just tried to let you down without too much of a bump."

"The last step was the worst. Everything falling apart. You were so right about Maman Celie as a witness."

"Only a guess. She might have been a magnificent witness. Napoleon once said, 'You plan a battle well, and chance, the real general, takes over once the fighting starts.' "

"He said that *after* Waterloo, didn't he, not before?"

"All right, hindsight. The ass view of things maybe is the right view. It isn't pretty and so we don't have false emotions about it."

"I didn't learn much."

"Oh, yes. I sensed it in court, Abe. A lot of growth."

"What?"

"There was a suggestion of prudence, of sagaciousness, son. The maturity will come with the job. And a kind of moral beauty, even if you find out more of men's limitations as men. There is an alienation and an aloneness about all of us who work the law or, rather, are worked by it. Rebellion against society is fine if you're an artist, a maker of new shapes and new words, because society is under the burden of time too and has to hurry along to do its loving, breeding, taxing, killing and lying. The artist in one way is free of this load of time. He's carving out, painting or making marks on paper; these are his escape hatches to the future. But Abe, you and me, we know the dangerous forces that radiate out to tamper with our personal control of our job."

"Henry Adams said, 'Old-fashioned logical drama required unity and sense; the actual drama is a pointless puzzle without even an intrigue.' "

"But think what life would be without that courthouse out

there under the trees and bronze memorials to our biggest mistakes."

Abe shook his head. "It's easy to know all this, Chief, when you've seen as much as you have. But I've just taken a big beating. Not only that. I was only half sure I really had a case at all most of the time."

"Don't give me any answer now. You don't have to announce for office for another thirty days. I've taken up enough of your time."

"Fran will want you to stay for dinner." Abe took out two stogies and handed one to the handsome old man. After they had them burning well, Abe looked up over the soft curling smoke moving like slow motion around them. "Chief, just as a favor and not for publication, did Sarah Rodman and the two Hawley brothers murder George Rodman and Helen Nash?"

Ed Hightower looked at the glowing end of the cigar in his hand. "You'll never be a great D.A. or a good judge until you understand that what goes on in a courtroom is a ritual, where you make proper responses, try to approach an absolute, and don't. But it's this trying to make an absolute in a world where absolutes no longer exist that makes it worthwhile."

Abe stood up. "Let's go up to the house.

"I always felt in the courtroom that I was taking part in some kind of a game."

"I once read someplace about a temple which was raided every year at holiday time by tigers who drank the sacred wine, and after a time these raids became a fixed part of the ritual."

The two men walked slowly toward the farmhouse. Abe asked again, "Did the three of them commit the crime?"

"Abe, Sarah Rodman had been receiving the minister, Doctor Romar, twice a week when she was in the jail. There was a rumor around that she confessed it all to him, and asked prayers to be forgiven. Of course, when I put it square to the Doc, he wouldn't say a word. I'm passing on the rumor to you only because I know you were kind of fascinated by her. Don't ask me how I know that either."

On the porch Abe said, "Mr. Hightower is staying for dinner."

"Hello, Mr. Hightower," Fran called from the kitchen.

"Hello, Fran."

There was a little lilting wind, and Abe lighted a fire of hickory limbs in the outdoor fireplace and they sat on the porch and watched the breeze make little billows on the water. Down below the stream someone was playing a radio, and the muted tones of Respighi's *Pines of Rome* came over the waters. The music seemed to mellow on its journey across and then break into little forms that came together again, Abe felt, before they went into the ear, like an elusive recollection of the original music. A canoe drifted by on the stream, a shape paddling and another shape merging into it. Silently, as if cut from black paper, it passed.

The two men could hear Fran inside humming the lake tune. Abe stood up and trod his stogie to shreds. His hands opened, closed. Ed Hightower watched the canoe disappear into the merging mist on green leaves. Abe's hand shook as he reached for another stogie. He lighted it, his face appearing for a moment hard, expressionless; then he spit out a shred of tobacco.

Wood smoke mingled with the sound of the bees blustering among the zinnias and helianthus and globe amaranth.

Fran came out. "The trout will be ready in a few minutes. We'll eat out here."

She sat beside them. Ahead was the long white tongue of the road. On either side, the opaque outline of hills ran beside them —hills curiously symmetrical, hills bounded by creviced stone walls and smelling of honeysuckle. It grew darker.

Abe took her hand in his. She smiled up at him, came closer. From the dark foliage came the orchestral crescendo of insects. Stars gradually gained their luster.

"Fran?"

"Yes, Abe?" She stirred against him, her bright eyes searching his face. He had a poignant impression of her mouth, her little white teeth showing as she spoke to him.

"Ed wants me to stay in office. Run for election."

"Make up your own mind."

Ed said, "The trout are fat this year."

There was an understanding, or something they accepted as an understanding, among the three of them. They sat together watching the night spaces. If anyone had more to say, no one said it. Abe felt perhaps now it was all lucid to them. This thing, this agitation, this atmosphere. And a clarified mutual understanding among people was not something to drag out and examine too closely. (It needs a pathological clairvoyance, a brutal, direct approach, and then the answers may still be all wrong. So let's cover our doubts. If we have any.)

Fran said, "Let's eat."

Ed said, "Smells good."

They heard the night. Sad, plaintive sounds—the boom of frogs, the mechanical rasping buzz of crickets, the far-off swamp groans, and the high crackle of deer and rabbits.

They ate on the porch, the trout cooked in twists of bacon, the apple pie crisp and brown. They drank the hot, strong coffee.

Fran said, "Nobody move. I'll just pile up the dishes."

Ed rejected a stogie and took out a pipe. It was very still by the stream, a restful stagnation. Even the night insects were not so chipper as usual. There was a dampness in the air, as though a storm were rising. The stream was the dumb blue of glaciers.

Ed puffed the strong burley pipe tobacco. "It's a fine night."

"More rain coming," said Abe.

The sinister *om om* of a mouse-hunting owl could be heard far off, bumping above the trees. They smelled the cool, pungent night. The owl kept on *om-om*ing with his deep, resonant voice. No one paid him any attention. There was a rumble of thunder, like a ghost cannonade. The leaves shook.

Ed said, "Here it comes."

Rain. A veil of crumbled water hit the porch, fell, bespattering, splashed and hissed in agitation. There was in their nostrils the strong musk odor of wet wood, of green, damp growing things.

Lightning gave a ferocious grimace in the sky. The wild sky in electrical rumbles tore the covering sky apart. The thunder grew in painful volleys, and then, with a red burst, shattered in one long rolling syllable across the heavens. The regular rhythms of the rains went on, grew in volume, more incessant; then, in one plaintive moan, stopped.

The landscape lay suspended in action. There was a stillness. And that odor of thyme—cool and startling after rain. A pall of suspended moisture still hung in a wet transparency over the farmhouse. There was the *drip drip* from leaf to ground; then that too stopped. A fatigue held the landscape.

Fran called from inside, "You'll have to stay the night, Mr. Hightower."

The old man knocked his pipe out on the palm of a hand. "No. I'll get rolling before the storm gets going again."

They shook hands. Abe walked Ed Hightower to his car.

"What will happen to the Hawleys now?" Abe asked.

"Mikel will shove off to Africa, most likely, and blow apart a lot of large and dangerous animals. Batty Billie will wander around the gardens and carriage house at the old house over the river and in time mellow into the town's ripe old eccentric, and be pointed out as a kind of celebrity once tried for murder. And Sarah Rodman—"

"What will happen to her?"

Ed Hightower shook his head. "Sarah Rodman? I think she's aware that happiness in many ways is enjoying one's own nature, and can she face *that?* She'll live in Europe, I think, in one of those comfortable hill villas overlooking the fashionable coast line in the south of France. Very plainly, for all her money, but with servants, and a good chef and a little English car."

"She might marry again."

"I doubt it. The concentric passions of the flesh are now the circles of hell to her. I've been talking to my old classmate, the Reverend Romar, and he claims she has really a faith in the power of prayer and the mercy of God. But I'm afraid the Reverend Romar is going to lose her. Sarah will become a convert, and take the wafer, and keep a pet priest, and become handsomely bony, with immaculate skin on a fashionable skeleton."

"Maybe not, Chief. She may let go all the other way now— the clipped poodles, the long jade cigarette holder, the Argentines and the dancing partners. Didn't you once say we begin as friends and end as accomplices?"

(The voice of long ago is fading, but I can just make it out. "I am a princess of my tribe. . . . Don't be such a stick. . . . Kiss me. . . . You do like it, don't you? What is your name?" The Game for me is ended in the river garden. . . .)

Abe watched the car go jolting off, winking its tail lights as it hit the ruts.

Far away to the east the gorged owl was again *om-om*ing.

ABOUT THE AUTHOR

STEPHEN LONGSTREET'S widely diversified career as artist, author and playwright has included writing and drawing for such magazines as *The New Yorker, The Saturday Evening Post* and *Esquire,* and the publication of several novels, including *The Pedlocks, The Promoters* and *The Lion at Morning* and also *The Real Jazz Old and New.*

He has been active on the editorial staff of *Time* and *The Saturday Review,* in the production of plays and motion pictures, and has had a number of one-man shows of his paintings. In 1948 he received the *Billboard* Award for the best play of the year, *High Button Shoes,* and the *Photoplay* Gold Medal Gallup Poll Award for the most popular picture of the year, *The Jolson Story.* He has received, too, many important awards for his paintings.

Mr. Longstreet is an avid world traveler, and he has recorded some of his adventures in a best seller, *The World Revisited.* In 1956 he published the charming account of a transcontinental tour of the United States that he took at the age of twelve, *The Boy in the Model-T,* and he collaborated with Billy Pearson, the famous jockey and art expert, on *Never Look Back.*